VANQUISH

PAM GODWIN

Interior Designer: Jovana Shirley, Unforeseen Editing, www.unforeseenediting.com

Editor: Jacy Mackin

Cover photographer: David Gillispie at www.gillispiephoto.com

Cover models: Matt Rich and Jessica Roland

Visit my website at pamgodwin.com

ISBN-13: 978-150077859

CONTENTS

A NOTE TO THOSE WHO HAVEN'T READ *DELIVER*

VANQUISH is a stand-alone, BUT if you intend to read Book #1, *DELIVER*, DO NOT read *VANQUISH* first. There are numerous references in this book that will spoil the surprises in *DELIVER*.

If you don't plan to read *DELIVER*, carry on.

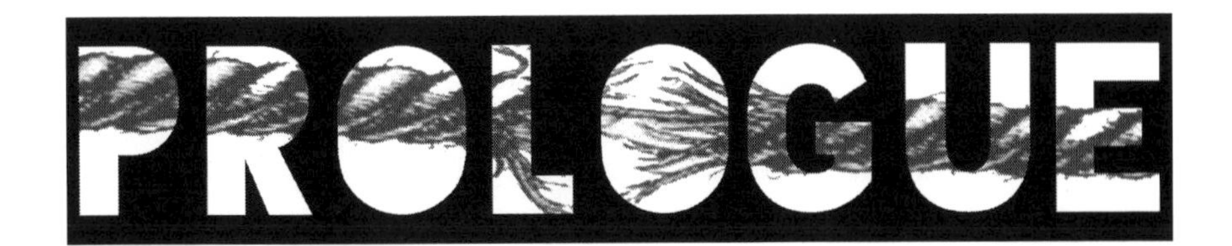

Pain. Dense, maddening bursts of pain splintered through Van Quiso's shoulder and reduced him to a pathetic mouth-breather on the kitchen floor. Heaviness settled over him, pooling down his arm and collapsing his chest. Each slogging beat of his heart drained more blood from his body, chilling his veins, soaking his t-shirt.

He should've known Liv Reed would be the death of him. If he could focus past the throbbing wound, maybe he'd hear a haunting serenade beneath her breath, beckoning him toward the cliff of oblivion with seduction dripping from her lips. He could only hope his descent into hell would be so enthralling.

He dragged his eyes heavenward and met the bleak despair wetting hers. Their gazes clung, motionless, as shock deadened the air between them. She'd shot him. Too damned late to take it back. He wanted to slam his fist into her beautiful face. Even more, he ached to kiss the path of tears streaking her scarred cheek.

The cold linoleum pressed against his back. He'd fucked her on this floor countless times, bent their joined bodies over the wobbly kitchen table, and slammed her against the fridge until her moans drowned out the whine of the old motor.

But their best moments had happened in the attic chamber, where her ass reddened under the fall of his whip as her lithe body hung from the ceiling, the sound-deadening walls absorbing her screams. For seven years, she'd been his to discipline, fuck, mentor, and keep.

Pulsating shadows framed his vision, closing in and threatening to take him from her permanently. Final judgment awaited him in death, but his punishment had already been inflicted. She no longer feared him. She was no longer his. The burn in his shoulder ignited. If he died, what would become of her?

His lungs clenched, not from injury, but from something more debilitating. He suffocated with the need to tangle a fist in her hair and never let go. She knew better than anyone the justice of his death, yet her full lips quivered. Lips that tasted like butter-soft caramel.

She knelt over him, shocks of brown hair tangling around her arms, the curve of her body taunting him. What he wouldn't give to feel her tight, reluctant cunt gripping his cock one more time. But she loved another man.

His ribs squeezed against the swell of rejection. She'd actually pulled the trigger. How could she think he was going to kill her? Didn't she know he'd die without her?

Dots blotted his vision. From the blood loss? Or was it the tremor of ice-cold fear passing through him? Hard to deny that he'd earned her distrust, kidnapping her when she was seventeen, taking her virginity without asking, and blackmailing her into delivering slaves for Mr. E.

Despite all that, every second at her side had nurtured Van's stupid-as-shit hope that she'd grow to love him. A hope that slipped through his grasp the night she abducted Joshua Carter against her will. She'd fallen in love with her newest slave, and that betrayal hurt worse than the lead buried in his shoulder.

But the blow that turned him against Mr. E's operation came six days ago. Van had sent her to meet with a slave buyer. There was a disagreement, and the buyer brutally raped her.

Renewed rage boiled in his gut. If he'd gone with her, he could've protected her. Sweat beaded on his lip. What was he thinking? He couldn't even protect her from himself.

He stared into the gorgeous, watery eyes of his first captive as her fingers caressed his jaw. He'd beaten and fucked her into submission and failed to stop Mr. E from killing her mother. Still she cried for him. His breath hitched. He loved her suffering in a way he couldn't rationally understand.

When he'd gone after her rapist, it hadn't been some chivalrous act of heroism. He'd fucking reveled in the dismemberment of limbs, the flaying of skin, and the gurgled screams of a man as atrocious as he himself. With the stain of his first kill dripping from his hands, he'd put his exit plan in motion. One that would free them from Mr. E's operation and bind them together. A family.

But her pretty boy was a menacing blockade to his plan. Joshua hovered behind her, his ridiculous linebacker brawn flexing to finish the job if the bullet failed. Despite the boy's apparent willingness to sacrifice his life for her, he couldn't protect her from their boss.

Was she still trying to wrap her mind around everything she'd just learned? Her face had blanched a chilling shade of white when he'd told her Mr. E was not only his father but also the police chief of Austin. And he hadn't disclosed the worst of it.

His pulse weakened, and his breathing thrashed. He needed to get the bullet out. If he survived, it would take days to recover. Days he and Liv didn't have.

"Have to kill him." He blinked through fading flashes of light. "He'll avenge me." Now that she knew Mr. E's identity, he was certain she'd hunt down their boss and finish the job, but she needed motivation to do it quickly. “He'll kill Livana.” If Mr. E hadn't killed her already. His throat tightened, choking his breaths.

“Livana?”

The angelic quality of her voice and the shape of her lips forming their daughter's name for the first time produced a wet burn in the corners of his eyes. There was so much he needed to tell her.

The flat line of her mouth wobbled. “Mattie's real name is Livana?”

He lifted his chin, attempting a nod. Beyond the infrequent video footage of their daughter, they'd never been allowed to see her. Liv didn't know where she lived, didn't even know her real name. For six years, she'd heartbreakingly referred to her as Mattie.

A helpless, foreign feeling stabbed his chest from the inside, over and over, pulling him further into darkness. Killing Mr. E meant he could finally meet their daughter. He was so damned close. He *would not* die.

Shivers wracked his body, and Liv's features vanished behind a veil of black.

“Van? Where's Livana?”

“She's...” He forced his eyes open. The outline of her face seemed so far away, yet he could make out her slim brown eyebrows as they formed a sharp *V*. He reached for her cheek, his fingers tingling, numb.

She leaned in to meet his hand, her eyes swimming in tears. “Van.” Her voice rasped, and the tears fell over, splattering his chin. “What's Livana's last name?”

She needed a name to find their daughter, but she wouldn't have to look far. His fingers fumbled over her scar. From her eye to her lips, the seven-year-old laceration mirrored his own. Even now, he didn't regret the actions that had led to their matching punishments. Her pregnancy had given him immeasurable relief, a means to ensure she wouldn't be sold as a slave. She belonged to him, his greatest accomplishment.

The pain in his shoulder jolted deep into his bones as he traced her lips and lingered on her jaw, dreading the answer he'd kept from her for so long. He'd had no say in who raised Livana, but he'd controlled Liv by withholding Livana's name and whereabouts. He didn't carry Mr. E's last name, but his daughter did. Liv might very well shoot him again when she learned Mr. E had been raising Livana since birth.

He opened his mouth and strangled on the words. Pinpricks assaulted his body. His vision blurred. He clung to the edge of consciousness as the muscles in his arm shook and gave up. His hand hit the floor.

“Nooo.” She scrambled atop him, fingers trembling over his face. “No, Van. No, don't go,” she screamed.

Wails bellowed from her throat. Such an outpour of emotion from a woman who always remained guarded behind a stone-cold mask. Her anguish filled him with warmth, pumping his heart. She cared. He tried to open his eyes and failed. His body grew heavy, struggling against the leaden weight of gravity. But that was okay. She thought he was dead and fucking cared.

"Oh, Van. I'm so sorry." She hugged his waist, weeping, nose sniffling.

He melted against the floor, blacking in and out. Time seemed to stop and start, his mind full of cotton, spinning around...something. He'd lost so much blood, but there were things to do. He needed to get up.

The warmth of her body vanished, and a scuffle of rubber soles squeaked on the linoleum. Joshua must've dragged her away. Was she fighting him? *Come back.*

He couldn't lift his arms. Couldn't open his eyes. Her hiccupping sobs teetered off. Or did he teeter off? He strained his ears through the hum of white noise. Somewhere, water dripped. *Plop. Plop.* Too soon, his world faded to nothingness.

He woke to the silence of an empty room and blinked rapidly, catching the low rays of the sun where it had dipped below the kitchen window. Christ, he'd passed out. For twenty, thirty minutes? Long enough for Liv to determine him dead and leave, but it wasn't dusk yet.

Now that the shock of watching her pull the trigger had passed, he needed to find his balls and get the fuck out of there. He wiggled his fingers and toes and tested his strength in his wrists and ankles. Breathing noisily but still coherent, he slowly bent his elbows and knees. With a surge of impatience, he rolled his shoulder and jerked against the sudden stab of pain. "Fuuuuck."

If she failed in her attempt to kill Mr. E, the cops would come. If she succeeded, she might alert the cops anyway. He needed to get his ass up, make a call, and disappear.

Getting shot wasn't part of his plan, and dealing with a lodged bullet magnified his aggravation. A hospital would report the gunshot wound. He could wedge it out with a steak knife. And inflict nerve damage. And gouge a damned artery. Or he could drive to Mexico and pay a seedy doctor to take care of it.

Fucking Mexico. *Ahi vamos.*

He tugged a disposable phone from his pocket and dialed.

"Yeah?" rasped the CTS Decon technician.

"Change of plans." Van had approached the professional cleaner a day earlier and offered a quarter of a million to discreetly and quickly mop up a crime scene. The blood was supposed to have been Mr. E's, the prearrangement to remove Van's DNA from the scene, therefore, eliminating him as a murder suspect. Liv's bullet changed that. Now, she would have to deal with Mr. E on her own while the technician dealt with Van's blood.

He rattled off the address of his location. "Need this done by the end of the hour."

"On my way." The technician disconnected.

Now for the grueling part. He gnashed his teeth and dragged his body up the side of the counter, stars invading his vision. After a few long, ragged breaths, he finished the climb and stumbled to the medical kit beneath the sink.

As he collected bandages, he tried not to think about what Liv was doing, if she had killed his father or if he'd killed her. He pulled his shirt over his head, and the damnable pain staggered him sideways.

He gripped the counter-top and panted through the blades of heat ripping up and down his arm. The pain was real, pushing his pulse and inflaming his skin. He was breathing, hurting. Alive.

With Liv and Livana's uncertain future, he had a helluva incentive to live. And to avoid arrest. He draped his upper body over the sink, splashed water over the dime-sized wound, and taped up his shoulder. He needed a bottle of Tequila Herradura and a long nap in the worst fucking way.

Blood smeared the counter, the cabinets, and the linoleum. He had no choice but to trust the expertise and discretion of the technician to erase all evidence of his existence. Hopefully, it would be enough to deceive detectives if they went hunting for DNA.

He dragged his feet to the kitchen table, each step heavier than the last. Two mannequins sat in the chair where he'd left them. When he reached them, he slid his fingers through their silken mahogany hair. Liv's hair. He'd collected it for years, meticulously weaving it through the mesh caps made for the dolls, one large, one small. His perfected replicas of Liv and Livana. No one could fucking take them away.

Liv didn't understand his need for the dolls. Only someone who'd experienced a lifetime of loneliness could comprehend what they meant to him and why he couldn't let them go.

With his arm hanging limp at his side, he gathered them under the other, careful not to overextend their joints, and carried them to the van in the garage.

Liv thought he was dead. And he was certain she would succeed in killing Mr. E, which meant she would be free for the first time in seven years. Would she leave town and try to disappear or would she stay in Austin, near their daughter? Either way, he'd find her. He'd always find her.

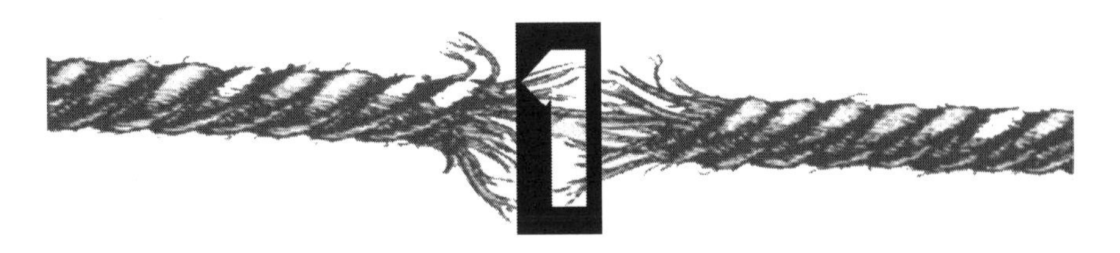

One year later...

Simple, mutually-satisfying sex was an acceptable way to alleviate loneliness, even if it was just twenty minutes in the dark with the delivery guy. At least, that's what Amber Rosenfeld told herself as she flicked off the table lamp in her bedroom, perched on the bed, and waited.

It was silly the way she collected those twenty minutes, treasuring them like souvenirs. Her mementos of normalcy. Proof that fear didn't own *every* minute of her life.

The overhead light flipped on, and her breath caught. She blinked through the unexpected glare, narrowing on Zach's finger where it poised over the wall switch. Oh no. Something was wrong.

She straightened her spine as he regarded her with a heavy slant in his eyebrows. She fidgeted with her hair, arranging the curls to lay in a sensual fall down her chest. Maybe he didn't like blondes. She brushed it behind her shoulders, out of view. Did he desire a prettier girl? If he turned the lights off, he wouldn't have to look at her.

"The lights, Zach." Her tone held steady despite the pleading drum of her heart.

He fingered the collar of his *Saddler's Tool Company* work shirt and freed the buttons down the front, revealing a thin, hairless torso. Brown hair hung in strands around his whiskered jawline, his blue eyes watching her with too much scrutiny. "Let's mix it up today."

A swallow stuck in her throat. The only thing he was mixing up was the neat edge of carpet beneath his boots. He rocked on the molding between the hardwoods and the bedroom, the rubber-soled toes smashing the fibers with each lift of his heels.

Why did he insist on disturbing the carpet? Couldn't he see the uniformity of the vacuum lines, how the threads lifted in one-foot rows of symmetry? Her walk to the bed had followed the outskirt of the small room. She'd hopped the lines easy enough, leaving four tiptoed indentations she would comb after he left.

Fuck, she was doing it again. She pinched the bridge of her nose. The carpet didn't need to be perfect. *She* wasn't perfect.

He shrugged off the shirt and tossed it on the floor, flattening two rows.

Her stomach clenched, but she forced herself to look at the disorder, to accept it. "It's better without lights."

"No, it isn't." He bent to remove his boots, trampling more fibers. "What if I trip in the dark and put an eye out?"

What a joke. The floor had been spotless before he arrived. Besides, "You don't need eyes for this." She shaped her mouth into a smile, lifting a shoulder. Did he notice the hollowness in her movements? What if he gave her an ultimatum about the lights or said something hateful? Did he have a cruel side?

Fat, worthless cunt.

When are you going to do something about your udders and schedule a boob job?

You're a fucking head case. Just like your mother.

She bent her fingers and cracked each knuckle in order. Index, middle, ring, pinkie. Zach wasn't *him.*

As he watched her knuckle-cracking ritual, lines formed in his brow. He should've been used to it by now, but something was off. He had never put this much focus on her quirks.

Finally, he blinked away, pushed his jeans and briefs to his ankles, and stepped from the unfolded mess. Pale skin smoothed over a narrow thirty-something physique. He scratched his flat stomach, eyes on hers, his partial erection hanging long and lean like the rest of him. He was attractive in a nonthreatening, easy-to-please manner. And he seemed to like her in a way that hardened his cock. A tingling awoke between her legs and fanned heat through her body.

But the light remained on. He touched the switch, staring at it as if he were asking it useless questions.

Her palms grew sticky and hot. For six months, he'd delivered her supplies, brought in her mail, taken her to bed, and left with her shipments. If she had trash, he would kindly drop it at the curb. He didn't make demands, express opinions, or try to complicate the routine. However, their unspoken arrangement had already extended twice as long as the previous delivery guys.

She knew what came next, and her gut twisted. "Just say it, Zach."

His attention shifted to the hem of her dress where it covered her thighs, roamed over her chest, and rested on her eyes. "I want to see you. Just once with the lights on and your clothes off."

A cringe jerked her shoulders, and her tongue thickened with all the wrong things to say. He waited for a response, one she knew she'd fuck up. She raised her chin. "I like it dark." For twenty minutes, every Tuesday and Friday.

His jaw stiffened, and he averted his eyes.

An empty feeling gutted the pit of her stomach. *Please, don't leave.* He was her only tether to the outside world, but she needed to nip this desperation for his company. Distancing herself kept her safe in her self-made asylum.

She attacked the middle joints of her fingers, synchronizing her exhales with each flex and pop. It took twenty-four minutes for the gas to redissolve into the joint fluid. If she continued cracking at this rate, she'd run out of knuckles. She really needed a better distraction.

His gaze flitted around the room, never settling on one thing for long...until something behind her gave him pause. What was he looking at? She followed his line of sight to the blacked-out window.

Oh God, no. Stinging heat crawled over her cheeks. If he opened the shade, the absolute terror and despair waiting on the other side would find her. It would liquefy her bones and seal up her throat until she had no control, no power to stop it.

His sigh penetrated the clamor in her head. "All right." He flicked the switch and smothered her storm with blackness.

A gust of relief freed her lungs and loosened her fists. Jesus, she needed to stop spazzing about what-ifs. She didn't want to be this scared little mouse trapped in her cage. What if Dr. Michaels was right? If she let the panic in, would it really show her a way out?

A shiver lifted the hairs on her arms. Yeah, right. Screw the free world.

She clung to the sound of Zach's footfalls and rationalized his tracks on the carpet as a form of therapy. She was supposed to challenge the anxiety, vary the landscape. He helped with that, even if he didn't know it.

The fifth footprint landed an inch away, and her teeth clamped together. Why did he have to take that last step? Four was even. There were four sides to a square. Four seasons to a year. Four fingers on a hand. Four was complete. Exact. Calming.

His palm touched her bicep, distracting and warm. She gripped his fingers and pulled him onto the bed, reclining on her back. Chest-to-chest, the weight of his body strengthened her in a way solitude couldn't. Her nerve-endings pulsed against every point of contact, her only connection with another human being. The tops of his feet around her ankles. His fingertips on her face. His thighs and groin exquisitely aligned over hers.

Soft lips brushed a stimulating path over her jaw, her cheek, her mouth. Slowly, her doubts and fixations gave way to anticipation of his kiss and his cock and the comfort they would bring. Fuck her unhealthy mind. Her carnal nature, her flesh hummed with vitality.

Lifting his body, he slid the dress up her thighs and tugged down the lace panties she wore for his visits. Fingers found her opening, gently circling, spreading her wetness, and coaxing a tremor of excitement. "I bet your pussy looks as beautiful as it feels." He pushed in two fingers, shooting shock waves down her legs. "Will you let me taste you this time?"

Don't ask me to put my mouth down there. Smells like a dead cow.

She cringed at *his* voice in her head. "Not today." Never again, no matter how badly she wanted it.

"Okay." He reached for the condom on the side table. The wrapper crinkled as he knelt above her. "How do you want me?"

"Rough, unrestrained, and perfect." Everything she wasn't.

Chuckling, he fell over her and thrust his hips, entering her in one liberating stroke. His ass flexed beneath her hands as he glided his length. In and out, he rubbed her inner walls into a blaze of sensations. Through the darkness, he found her mouth, his tongue rolling with hers and his fingers tingling over her ribs. Every caress and attentive lick left a trail of vibrations.

Until his palm cupped her breast. She jerked back against the mattress. Even through the dress and bra, he would feel the hard, oversized implants. What must he think of her? Maybe she should explain how much she hated them, how the surgery had dulled the sensations there. No, that would be worse. Only a weak woman would get a boob job she didn't want.

He let her pull his hand away and move it to her throat. His grip tightened as he pounded into her. Ahhh, right there. He didn't squeeze hard enough, but she was in the zone, rocking against him and holding onto the moment with both arms.

The thrust of her hips didn't come from a place in her mind. Fucking was a primal impulse, an urgent action that dulled the noise in her head. The musk of his sweat wrapped her in a cocoon. The hum of her pulse swished through her veins. Almost perfect.

Repeatedly, his cock hit the spot, the right tempo but never enough pressure. Did she feel good to him? Was her pussy tight enough? She clenched her inner muscles with each invasion of his length and moaned. *Come on, Zach. Let out a groan.*

He remained unnervingly quiet as he rotated his pelvis. The scent of sex filled the air, sweet and tangy. What if he didn't like the way she smelled? Was he holding his breath?

His exhales brushed warmly across her mouth, his exertion heating and slicking their bodies. Was it difficult for him to get off with her? Was he imagining fucking a different woman?

She shook off her hateful thoughts and savored the moment, biting at his lips and angling her pelvis. If only he would thrust harder. That brief stretch of solace was in reach. It tingled the flesh that spread around his cock and tiptoed up her spine. She trembled, anticipating the moment when everything inside her would still.

Then it came, the gallop of climax beating along her scalp and booming behind her ears. She moaned as the ripples washed over her, numbing her legs and carrying her to a place where voices and shame didn't dwell.

He followed with an erratic buck of his hips and a breathy groan. She buried her face in his neck, twitching with the aftershocks of tranquility.

Too soon, disappointment invaded her peace. First, came the dissipation of orgasm. Always too weak, too fleeting, it never sustained. Then, the absence of his body as he disposed of the condom. And finally, his tracks across the carpet and the click of the light switch. Her stomach sank.

She shoved the dress over her thighs, despising the chill of loneliness creeping into her skin.

"Your mail and supplies are in the kitchen." He pulled on his clothes, shooting sidelong glances in her direction.

She swiped her thumbs beneath her eyes to clear away mascara and combed fingers through her hair. "A bag of trash and my shipments are ready by the door." She hated her dependency on him as much as she dreaded the post-sex awkwardness. Nevertheless, her merchandise had to be mailed or her bills wouldn't be paid.

She'd tried the door-to-door mail service once, but when her packages were stolen right off her porch, she'd lost a month's income. She couldn't risk that again. Zach was the dependable solution.

A knot tightened beneath her breastbone. How the hell did she become so lonely and helpless? Perhaps those traits had always existed, hidden beneath beauty pageant crowns and fake smiles.

Separation from people hadn't cured her need to please. She longed to lift the hem of isolation, look into eyes full of acceptance, and see in them the reflection of a woman who didn't give a rat's ass.

Neither of them spoke as he laced his boots, each second straining longer than the last. Should she say something? Maybe compliment his performance?

He straightened and lingered in the doorway, deep lines etching his forehead. *Stay* trembled on her lips, but he didn't owe her anything. They didn't have dinner dates or interact beyond their routine. He always arrived at the scheduled time. She always left the front door unlocked and waited in the bedroom. No conversation. No deviation. No questions.

What did she have to offer him besides a scheduled orgasm? If he stayed, he might suggest they go out and do normal things. If he found out she hadn't ventured beyond her front door in two years, he'd never come back.

She cracked her knuckles. She needed to stop the unproductive waffling. Either she continued with him as a detached fuck buddy or she pursued the relationship with a deeper connection. She couldn't have both. The former worked. The latter would end swiftly and painfully.

Squaring her shoulders, she met his eyes. "See you Friday."

A subtle inhale flared his nostrils. He studied her for a long moment, nodded his head, and left.

She curled her fists in the bedding, her muscles straining to run after him.

The slam of the front door knocked the wind from her lungs. *Way to go, Amber.* Might as well add a few dozen cats to the paranoid, anti-social routine and call it what it was.

She hung the dress in the closet, where it would stay until Friday, and put on yoga pants and a t-shirt. She vacuumed, ran four miles on the treadmill, and showered. A few hours later, she finished the filigree carving on a leathercraft order, ate a pancake, and showered again.

As the nightly news ended, she stood before the bathroom mirror and pinched the flab hugging her hips.

If you exercised more, maybe I wouldn't be thinking about your sister all the time.

She shouldn't have eaten that pancake. If she weren't ten years older than Tawny, maybe she would've held *his* attention. Her stomach clenched painfully, and she bent at the waist, gripping her knees.

Was he in bed with Tawny now? Kissing her sister the way he'd once kissed her? Of course, he was. They were married now.

She turned away from the mirror, squatted before the toilet, and gagged with the reflex of a practiced vomiter. Her eyes watered, and her throat contracted and burned. The partially-digested pancake splattered the bowl.

She didn't look in the mirror as she brushed her teeth. Didn't glance at her midsection as she dressed and sat on the couch. She had zero resistance to self-deprecating thoughts, and the white envelope on the coffee table didn’t help.

The notice of default was proof of her worthlessness. She had ninety days to reinstate the mortgage or she'd lose the house, her safe place.

Her head hurt, and her chest felt hollow.

She would have to increase the sales on her leather goods, but it wouldn't be enough. She'd already cut all her expenses. All but one.

She popped her knuckles and dialed Dr. Michaels.

"Good evening, Amber." Dr. Emery Michaels' warm greeting was always unassuming, despite the fact that her calls were sporadic and often panic-stricken. "How are you doing?"

Which problem should she tackle first? She blew out a breath. "He wanted the lights on."

A pause. "The young man who delivers your supplies?"

Zach wasn't that young. Probably older than her thirty-four years. "Yeah."

"Is this the man you want the lights on with?"

His tone wasn't judgmental, but her hackles flared. "He's the man I want to fuck, Dr. Michaels. Lights or no lights, you said my libido was a good thing."

"Yes, as long as sex doesn't become an addiction."

"I can live without it." The thump in her chest disagreed.

"Has your relationship expanded beyond sex? Have you talked with him about your healing path?"

Secrecy and shame were interwoven with her condition, and she excelled at being a psychiatric textbook. "No and no."

"Have you given more thought to attending a self-help group?"

Sweat trickled down her spine, and the muscles in her neck went taut. "I can't—"

"*Agoraphobics Outbound* meets bi-monthly at Austin State Hospital. It's a ten minute cab ride from your house."

She chewed the inside of her cheek and imagined all those people staring at her, examining, criticizing. How would she escape? What if she got lost, stuck in a crowded place, or fainted?

Not only that, her mother was a patient in that hospital. Her breathing quickened. She couldn't bear to be in the same building with a woman who wanted nothing to do with her.

"Amber, you need the solidarity of a support group."

Something she would never receive from her family. She gripped her knuckles. *Crack. Crack. Crack. Crack.* Strangers would be worse. They wouldn't know her, yet they'd weigh her worth as she lost her shit.

"Amber." His soothing timbre steadied her pulse. "Tell me what you're thinking."

"They'll see how undesirable I am."

A sigh whispered over the line. "You are a lovely woman, but you will never hear that until you believe it yourself."

"*He* didn't think so." She winced, hating herself for mentioning him.

"Yet he didn't want to give you up."

She'd once viewed marriage as a sacred covenant, arrogant in her belief that only three A's justified divorce. Adultery. Addiction. Abuse. *He* had committed none of them—never acted on his desire for her sister while they were married, never hit her, never so much as got drunk—yet she'd divorced him. She'd given up, taken the easy way out. "I failed him."

"Eliminating the toxicity in your life is not a failure. It's curative and courageous and never, ever easy."

She blinked against the achy burn in her eyes. Brent hadn't always been toxic. Sixteen years ago, he looked at her like she was so much more than a sparkling accessory on his arm. She deeply missed the man she'd fallen in love with. "Leaving him was the hardest thing I've ever done."

"That's right. So the *Outbound* meeting would be a piece of cake in comparison."

She straightened the envelope on the table, leaving a four-inch, right-angle gap from the table's corner. "I won't be calling you anymore."

"These sessions are necessary in your recovery."

"I know what I need to do to get better." Face her fears. Remember to belly breathe. Ask for help.

"What have you eaten today?"

The purged pancake floating in the toilet. Had she remembered to flush it? Gripping the phone, she ran to the bathroom and relaxed when she saw the clean bowl. "I can't afford to pay you."

"I see." Wariness breathed through his voice, but he didn't offer to counsel her for free.

She wasn't worth his charity. Not that she would've accepted it anyway.

His movements rustled through the phone. "The self-help group is free. That's your next goal. I'll forward links to online support groups and see if I can find a therapist who might be more affordable."

She'd already looked, but maybe he'd have better luck. "Thank you." Jesus, she was going to miss him. "I'll look for your bill in the mail." And hopefully, she'd have the funds to cover it.

"Be patient with yourself, Amber. Sometimes you have to step back to open the door."

Three days later, she glared at the front door, her legs paralyzed with fear. Clutching the cell phone to her ear, she said into the receiver, "I call bullshit."

"Amber, ring my boss if you don't believe me." Zach sniffled through the speaker, his voice leaden with congestion. "He sent me home. I feel like I'm going to die."

"You can't die from a cold." But a heart attack was fatal. She could feel one coiling around her chest, squeezing the life from her body. "What about my mail?" She covered the phone to muffle her panicked gasps.

"Why can't you get it?" He sneezed, followed by a nasty, wet inhale. "Are you on house arrest or something?"

Unbelievable. They'd had this arrangement for six months. He was just now asking why? She released a thready breath. "I just can't. Will you ask someone else at the store to bring my mail to the door? Or maybe you know someone who wouldn't mind swinging by?"

"No. No one lives near you, and I can't just ask people to do that." He coughed. "Listen, I need to go."

The palpitations in her heart wobbled her legs. "I need my mail *today*." She needed it two days ago. The leather dye she'd ordered sat twenty-six steps from the door. She couldn't finish the knife sheaths without it. If she didn't mail out the completed sales by tomorrow, the water would be shut off.

He hacked through the phone. "I'm sorry, Amber."

Guilt formed a hard, jagged lump in her stomach. "Please don't apologize. This isn't your fault." She rubbed her forehead with cold, shaking fingers. Her stomach gurgled with dread. "Get some rest. Hope you feel better."

"Yeah, okay. See you Tuesday."

The phone disconnected, and she slumped to the floor, sucking harshly for air. She hugged her stomach against an onslaught of queasiness and glared at the front door. It stood between her and her paycheck. The damned thing wasn't a terminal disease. It wasn't swinging a chainsaw. It was just a door. A bolted, four-sided shield against certain suffering.

Sometimes you have to step back to open the door.

One step back and twenty-six steps to the mailbox. She could do it in twenty-four, a semi-perfect number. Twenty-four hours in a day. Twenty-four carats in pure gold. Four and twenty blackbirds baked in a pie.

Good God, she was drowning in her own crazy. *Just get it over with.* She swiped a palm over her face, smearing her makeup with sweat. Shit. She darted to the bedroom and changed into a white halter dress and matching heeled sandals. A check in the bathroom confirmed her hair held its curl. Her makeup was still flawless. She returned to the door.

Deep breath in. Out. Twenty-four paces there and back. She used to make that trek before Zach and Kevin and Chet and...oh, fuck it. She could take her phone. If she panicked, she could call Dr. Michaels.

No, she couldn't. She swayed and gripped the doorframe. Okay, not a deal breaker. She wouldn't need him. She had this.

Her heart rate doubled. What if she broke down so spectacularly she couldn't walk? What if she couldn't get back to the house?

She flattened a hand over her sternum, hating this, hating herself. What happened to the brave girl who stood on stage time after time, shaping her mouth into a practiced *O* of surprise as tiaras were placed on her head? Oh yeah. That girl tried too hard to please people, and look where it got her.

She smoothed down the dress and stared at the knob. *Reach out and turn it.* Twenty-four steps. She could walk them to the tune of *kick the fear habit, embrace the new, don't beat yourself up* and all the other psychosmart mantras that sounded invigorating until they were put into action.

How about the shit that kept her up at night? Overdue utilities, no showers, no flushing, no clean dishes?

She flipped the deadbolt four times and yanked open the door.

The sun hit her face in blinding white. She raised an arm to shade her eyes, the blanket of humidity seeping into her pores. A winged insect buzzed past her ear. The smell of fresh-cut grass tickled her nose. The hum of air conditioning units had her spinning in every direction. Were the neighbors home, watching from the shadows of their windows?

A truck motored by, and she jumped, stumbling into her first step.

Don't look at the street. Her gaze caught on the bushes lining her porch. Jesus, they'd doubled in size, blocking the bench she hadn't used in two years. The wood seat was weathered, neglected, forgotten.

Dammit, she couldn't dwell on that, on any of it. A terrible pressure already pushed against her ribs. She bent into the next step, dizzy, fighting for breath.

Ignore it. She ground her molars. Two steps, eight percent of the way there.

Tremors assaulted her body. The landscape spun around her. The mailbox. A passing car. Open windows on houses. A woman walking her dog. Everyone showed up to watch the freak show.

God, she was so fucked up. This should've been a thousand times easier than being crowned Miss Texas. She was wearing her heels. Her curls shimmered around her arms. She could take the third step. Just like on stage.

She raised her leg with the grace that came from years of discipline. Suddenly, as if her foot had landed in the spotlight, she turned on her pageant best. Fingers relaxed and together, shoulders back, chin up, bright eyes, and big smile, she held the pose. The persona strengthened her stance. She was the best. Knowing it meant winning it. She was doing it.

The honk of a slowing car scattered her delusion. She flinched, blinked. Bright green lawns, twittering birds, and the scent of hot asphalt knocked her back to reality.

She glanced down and took in her ridiculous pose. Decked out in heels with one leg bent and a hand on her hip? Her smile slipped, and her ankles teetered.

Stop it. She held her arms at her sides. Tingling numbed her fingers, her sense of control slipping.

Why couldn't she stop these reactions? She wanted this step, needed it. *Move, dammit.*

Spots blackened her vision. The pressure in her chest... It was stifling. She couldn't breathe. Oh God, her body was giving up on her, overheating, growing heavy. The ground tilted.

She squatted to avoid collapsing and fell back on her ass, shaking uncontrollably. "Noooo." She cried out in anguish and curled into a ball. *Make it stop hurting. So scared.*

The open crack of the door wavered through her tears, an arm's length away. She crawled on elbows, stiffened by chest pain and gasping for air. She dragged her body over the threshold and kicked the door. It shut with a thunk, silencing the cars, the windows, the witnesses. She folded herself into the corner of her cage and wept.

Eventually, she peeled her tear-soaked face off the oak floor and leaned against the door. The sun no longer glowed through the cracks, and she was no closer to the mailbox.

She'd have to try again.

As if. She was still strung out and trembling like a mouse. She'd only fail.

Yeah, but she always felt that way.

She could call Zach. He might feel well enough to drive over.

Maybe he would. Or maybe she could do it herself and feel better for it. Nighttime might conceal her from onlookers.

But the predators came out at night.

Fucking ridiculous. Everyone went out after dark. Except her.

Forget it. She'd tried once already and failed.

But she'd stepped outside. Three huge steps. *Not four.* That was the opposite of giving up.

Damn right. The corners of her mouth relaxed. They might've even curved up a little. She rose on quivering legs and walked to the bedroom. She needed to change clothes and fix her makeup. Maybe it would take her all night to walk twenty-four steps, but she'd do it. The alternative was unimaginably worse.

For a while, Van pretended he didn't miss her. Not her fierce looks or her hot, wet pussy or her beautiful agony. The ache she'd left behind should eventually seal up and scab over like the wound in his shoulder.

But it didn't. It inflamed and festered until he had woken weeks later, twisting in sweat-soaked sheets and fucking his fist, unable to think about anything but Liv Reed.

That was a year ago, and still, she possessed his thoughts every second of every day. He imagined the satisfaction she must've felt when Mr. E died. The quiver in her arms as she hugged their daughter. Her thighs spreading for that cumgargling bible-basher, the fuck who had stolen his place in her life. That shit really fucked with him.

Stagnant air coated his skin in a wet sheen as he locked up his 1965 Mustang GT Fastback. To think the humidity in Austin was relatively mild this time of year. In a couple months, the heat of summer would suffocate his nightly walks.

The hood of his sweatshirt sloped over his forehead, his chin tucked discreetly to his chest. The street's only source of light flickered overhead, months overdue for repair. Somewhere in the distance, the trill of a frog warbled through the silence, calling in the darkest hour of night.

If he were a man with uncontrollable urges, he would've grabbed Liv the night she'd killed his father. When he'd followed her from the police station to Joshua's farm, the bullet wound painful but patched up, he could've snatched her from the cocksucker's bed and taken her to Mexico with him. If he were a psychopath, he wouldn't have been able to stop himself.

Instead, he gave her six of the seven million they'd earned in slave trafficking, the gift alerting her he was still alive. When he'd healed from the bullet, he'd looked for her in the one city he knew she'd be.

Surrounded by one-story bungalows, he strode across the suburban Austin street, dangling a grocery bag from one finger. He cut between two houses as if it were a Sunday stroll. As if it weren't past eleven on a Friday night.

His strides fell in harmony with his pulse, steady and confident. He'd cased the neighborhood long before he'd claimed this route. He knew the names, habits, and lack of awareness of every resident for two blocks. Knew the elderly occupants on either side of his shortcut had been tucked in bed for hours.

Past the overgrown side yard, ducking beneath the low-hanging hickory behind the houses, he followed the path he'd taken hundreds of times. If he weren't trying to pass unnoticed, he might've whistled one of Liv's favorite tunes.

She loved their child so selflessly, he knew she'd never take Livana from Mr. E's wife, the only mother Livana had ever known. Though he'd known his daughter's location since the day she was born, he'd only ever seen her through the lens of a camera—Mr. E's video footage her first six years and his own camera the last year.

Christ, he wanted to meet her, to touch her angelic face, to hold her tiny hand, and look into her brown eyes and see them smiling back. But she lived with Mr. E's widow, who hadn't been part of his father's slave ring but was wrapped up in the aftermath of the police chief's death. Authorities didn't know Van existed, and his freedom depended on maintaining that anonymity.

It'd only taken him a couple weeks to find Liv in a modest rental house minutes from where Livana lived. No surprise she hadn't spent the money he'd given her. Perhaps she'd never touch it because of where it came from and the memories that clung to it.

Which was why he'd kept one million. It served as a parachute should his daughter need it. Livana had come into the world same as him—born of a slave and a slave owner. He would do whatever was needed to ensure she didn't end up like him.

But he didn't mistake his intentions as selfless generosity. He didn't want the fucking money. He wanted Liv. He wanted his daughter. Whether he deserved them or not, he would have his goddamned family.

Loose, curling bark snagged his hoodie, and the ground covering was redolent of sweet peppermint as it stirred beneath his sneakers. He broke from the trees, sheltered by the black sky, and crossed the backyard of his destination.

The single-story house faced the street one block over from where he'd parked. Though no one lived there, he approached the back porch with tightening muscles, ready to slip away at the first sign of life.

Three windows and a glass door broke up the monotony of weathered brick. Heavy-duty shades blocked light from escaping. The shades hadn't moved, not once, in the six months he'd been coming to Liv's neighborhood. A lawn service maintained the small lot of grass, but there were no flowerbeds, no lawn furniture, no inhabitants.

His black hoodie and dark jeans blended with the backdrop of the unlit house as he checked the locks on the rear windows and door, looking for a disruption in the pattern, any indication that someone had moved in.

All clear, he approached the south side that would take him to the front porch and the bench that awaited him. As he rounded the corner, he dug his heels into the wet grass, flattening his body against the vacant house.

One of two windows on the house next door cast a warm glow between the foundations. His pulse sped up, and an excited warmth of energy swirled through his stomach. Liv lived next door to the abandoned house.

He crept toward her illuminated window. His crouched position below prevented a good look at the inside, but he knew it was her kitchen.

The dark window beside it drew his attention. Her bedroom. Was she in there now? Removing her clothes? Humming a seductive melody? He closed his eyes briefly as his dick pulsed against the tight confines of his jeans.

When he regained his focus, he edged around the band of light on the grass and removed two wireless microphones from the bag, following his nightly ritual. The high sensitivity mics penetrated glass and transmitted to his phone. A whole lot safer than bugging the inside of her house.

He powered them on and left them on Liv's brick windowsills. Camouflaged by shadows, he ducked across the yard between the houses, retreating from Liv's and slipping onto the front porch of the vacant house. He strode past the bench and reached a finger inside the porch lantern. The bulb he'd removed months ago hadn't been replaced. Good. With a suspended breath, he checked the lock on the door. The knob wobbled but didn't turn, as expected.

On his way back to the bench, he stopped at the wide picture window and leaned his cheek against it. At that angle, he could see a sliver of light along the bottom of the blackout shade. Always closed with the same millimeter glow.

Though the mail was addressed to Amber Rosenfeld, the only person who came and went was Zachary Kaufman. The *Saddler's Tool Company* employee arrived at noon on Tuesdays and Fridays—a simple inquiry at the tool store confirmed the man's identity and his schedule.

After watching him for months, Van was certain the moron was using the house to grow marijuana. Given his stupid smiles and flushed cheeks when he exited the house, he was toking the merchandise during his visits.

Who cared? As long as Zachary Kaufman didn't get busted, Van had an ideal place to squat.

Hidden from the street by overgrown shrubs, he reclined on the shadowed bench of a house where no one lived and looked to the right. The elevation of the porch put him at the perfect height to peer through the two windows on the side of the house next door. The opening in the foliage gave him a sliver of sight into Liv's life.

He connected ear buds to his phone and pressed one into his ear. A few minutes later, he cracked open a beer, lit a cigarette, and watched Liv's windows like the dirty voyeur he was.

The mic picked up indiscernible voices from deep within the house, and his heart skipped. He squashed the cigarette and concentrated on the sounds in the earpiece. Footsteps?

Liv's front door opened and a tall man with dark, shoulder-length hair strode down the driveway. Van leaned his head back, slouching deeper within the hood. It wasn't necessary. Ricky wouldn't have been able to see him through the foliage.

Good ol' Ricky. The second of seven slaves she'd delivered. Seven million dollars had been paid by seven buyers. Yet seven *sold* slaves flitted in and out of her house, carting side dishes for bar-b-que parties, drinking beer, and braiding her friggin' hair as if she hadn't spent ten weeks beating the ever-loving shit out of them.

Van had discovered the depth of her deceit the night she'd shot him and left him. He'd driven to the police station, his shoulder throbbing like a motherfucker, and watched her walk out of the station and make contact with her first slave. Fuck, he'd never in a million fucking years guessed she'd been freeing the slaves after delivering them.

During the months of monitoring her house, he'd gleaned the details from their conversations, how she'd delivered them, secured the financial transaction then killed the buyer by bullet, knife, garrote, or any means possible. The fact she hadn't been caught was beyond impressive. Perhaps, she'd made it look like they were killed by rival gangs or cartel.

She'd outsmarted him, his father, and a network of buyers. Her treachery only made him want her more. She wore his scar on her face. She was the mother of his child. She'd saved him the unsavory task of killing his father. She belonged to him.

The sac of misery in his chest contracted and heaved. As Ricky climbed in the truck and drove away, he wanted to run after him, drag him to the pavement, and pummel his face. Not because the boy was free, but because he was free to see *her*. To make eye contact. To touch.

Lighting another smoke, he stared at her windows, willing her to appear. As he inhaled the last drag, the hum of a heavenly voice trickled through the ear bud. He sagged against the bench as every molecule in his body absorbed the decadent notes.

Through the window, he saw her hourglass figure fill the doorway of the kitchen. Her full lips moved, and her voice rose in a deathless composition of memories, evoking emotions in him that patched his heart and shredded it all over again.

She glanced to the side, a smile stretching her mouth. Her hum tumbled into a laugh as Joshua appeared from the room beyond and enfolded her in his arms.

"You look gorgeous tonight." The bastard's voice was grating. Besides, she was always gorgeous.

She turned in his arms and whispered something, but he didn't miss the last three words. "I love you."

The beefed-up Boy Scout palmed her ass. "Love you, too."

Van's chest clenched. He'd said those words to her often, but it hadn't changed a damned thing. Hadn't prompted her to say them back. Hadn't prevented another man's hands from groping her now.

As those hands caressed her, he remembered her velvety skin, the minty fragrance of her hair, and the biting flavor of her pussy. His dick grew warm and hard, throbbing for her touch.

He unzipped his jeans as Joshua removed his. He stroked his length, anticipating and dreading the scene he'd witnessed so many times. They would fuck on the table, their go-to in the kitchen. As she slid off her panties, he jerked his fist, hating the man she loved and hoping one of these kitchen romps would roll him onto the fatal end of a butcher knife.

She angled Joshua's bulky body against the table edge, pushing him onto his back and pinning his arms above his head. Her skirt hiked up, and the view of her heart-shaped ass rushed more blood to Van's cock. He stroked harder, his breath quickening with the sound of hers.

After a few wriggles of her hips, she seated herself on Joshua Carter and fucked him the way she did every night. Hard and wild, her face slackened with passion. All the ways she'd never fucked Van.

He knew he should stop. He should stop coming here and fucking his hand. Stop fucking up his head with something he'd never have.

But he could have her if he took her.

His fist tightened, and his balls pulled up. He was close. So was she. Her head fell back, and her features morphed in pure bliss as her body bucked. On another man.

He lost the rush to climax, which happened more often than not. The lonely, wretched feeling that took its place made him want to knock on her door and remind her he existed. Then what? Wait for her to invite him in for a beer? What if she turned him away and started closing her blinds? What if she shot him again?

He relaxed his fist, his insides squeezing in a miserable grip despite the needy throb in his engorged dick. She was happy, and her happiness meant more dark porches and unreachable orgasms in his future. He needed to let her go.

Same damned thing he told himself every night.

Had anything changed since that night six months ago when he decided to put mics on her window? The intel he'd gained through spying hadn't brought him any closer to his daughter. As for Liv, he'd tried for seven years to make her want him. It was an impossible pursuit then, and even more so now.

Watching her night after night with Joshua might've killed some of his desperation for her. But for some perverse reason, he couldn't stop. Witnessing her get off gave him more satisfaction than the faceless men and women he fucked when he left her window.

A click sounded from the door behind him, lifting the hairs on his neck. The deadbolt twisted three more times. What the fuck? He turned, yanking the ear bud from his ear, and his blood ran cold.

Five feet away, the front door opened, and a high-heeled foot tapped slowly, inch by inch, over the threshold. The interior light highlighted long, toned legs and a narrow body wrapped in a short skirt and business jacket.

She lingered in the doorway, half-in, half-out, fingers gripping the frame. She stared at the street as if unsure whether she was coming or going. In fact, she clung to the house as if it were supplying her air. A house that no one lived in.

He didn't move, didn't blink. He could slip off the side of the porch, but he was glued to the bench, captivated by shock and curiosity.

Her breaths grew louder and more shallow, and her profile shifted from the concealment of the doorway. A mass of blond curls framed her face, her delicate features twisted in indisputable pain and horror. It wasn't him she feared. Her focus hadn't moved from the end of the driveway, her wide eyes cutting a circle around the mailbox.

The empty street was dimly lit. Not a car or a snake or a bogeyman in sight.

She stumbled forward, releasing her clutch on the doorframe, and choked on a sob. Another step. Her heels wobbled, and her hands flew to her busty chest as she gasped.

Fuck, she was a beautiful sight. Dainty fingers, tiny nose, pink cheeks streaked with tears. His cock twitched in his hand. He was sick and selfish and insanely turned on by her body and the lost look in her wide eyes, the whole damned package. He stroked his arousal, praying she wouldn't turn his way, hoping she would.

She threw herself forward, her heels landing with a clop. She bent over, hands on knees, and whispered, "Four."

The light from inside outlined the cuts of muscle in her calves, thighs, and ass. Muscles that quivered so violently he was surprised she could stand. But the girl was built. Not an ounce of fat. Perhaps too thin, like body-builder dehydrated, but Christ, she worked it with those huge tits and tiny waist.

And she still hadn't noticed the pervert rubbing his dick behind her. She cracked her knuckles and shook out her arms, seemingly lost in her head. Then her shoulders jerked back and her chest heaved. He leaned forward. What was she up to?

She took off. Amazingly fast in heels, she sprinted down the driveway, her ass flexing with her strides. She slammed to a stop in front of the mailbox and yanked out the envelopes. Her free hand covered her mouth, and the muffled sound of her sobs reached the porch.

What was wrong with this girl? The intensity of her fear resonated deep within the depraved part of his being. It was as intoxicating as her beauty, but where did it come from? What was she afraid of? How the hell did she live in this house? That would mean she never left. Watching her stagger up the driveway, it made sense. Kind of.

She was heading back to the door, and however breathlessly and hunched over, she would surely see him. He tucked his semi-hard dick in his pants and shoved his things in the bag. The side windows on Liv's house glowed from within, the rooms empty. He needed to get the fuck out of there.

Wobbling, she squeezed the mail to her chest, eyes fixed on her feet as if willing them to keep moving. Her shoulders curled forward and seemed to be dragging her toward the ground with each step. She didn't look like she'd make it to the porch.

A few steps away, her attention jerked up, fixed on the cracked door. As she inched toward it, her gaze cut right, then left and collided with his. The anticipation in his stomach coiled into a knot, and he stared right back, daring her to look away. Would she scream? Run? Or confront him? Fuck if he couldn't wait to find out.

Color bled from her face, the whites of her eyes rounding with terror. Her muscles spasmed, shaking her arms and loosening packages from her grip. Several dropped around her feet. Was she having a seizure?

She reached back, squatting, as if she knew she was going to fall. Fuck it. He jumped off the porch and closed the distance in three strides.

Sweet God, why was there a man on her porch? Oh fuck, a murky, fast-moving wall of man. He charged toward Amber in a blur of dark clothes and unimaginable purpose. Why was he running toward *her*? She didn't need help. She just wanted to be left alone to return to her house.

The door was so close. Eight feet at most. But convulsions shook her hands so uncontrollably she lost her grip on the remaining envelopes.

Silver eyes stabbed from the depths of his hood, seizing every cell in her body. She couldn't look away, couldn't breathe. Not when her stomach bucked and her chest simmered with bile. And not when his hands shot out and locked around her elbows, preventing her fall.

Saliva rushed over her tongue, and vomit hit the back of her throat, hot and humiliating. What if he was trying to help her? She couldn't puke on him. Please, no. She swallowed past the burn and breathed through her mouth as bursts of black dotted her vision.

The man's fingers clamped her arms, his chest too close to hers. She needed air, tried to jerk back. Her knees buckled. No, she wouldn't let her panic beat her. Not when she was so close. But she couldn't stop it as the assault bore down in crippling dizziness, the path to the door whirling around her feet.

Another surge of nausea ripped chills through her bones and liquefied her joints. She twisted to face away, stumbled, and fell into the darkness.

The steel brace of his arm caught her mid-section, and she hung there, mucus and anxiety spewing from her mouth and stringing over the mail at her feet. Thank God there was nothing in her stomach to eject. The saliva on her lips was embarrassing enough.

He bent over her, his body surrounding her back, hard thighs supporting her butt, his arm hooked beneath her folded waist. "There you go." His low, steady whisper sounded like a shout in the wind, snuffing out her surroundings. "Better?"

Her vision tunneled. Ringing blared in her head. She couldn't focus. "I'm fine. You can let go."

"Do you have meds? Do you need a doctor?"

A paralyzing freeze spread through her veins, sucking heat from her face in tingling waves. No doctor. No medication. None of that fixed a damned thing. She clutched the muscled forearm at her belly, pushing at it, dry heaving.

Who was this man? No way was he just passing by in the middle of the night. Was he going to hurt her? Rape her? Or do something that would disfigure or permanently damage her body? Did he have a gun?

She choked. Why her? The rapid wallop of her heart accelerated. She yanked at the arm, an unmoving restraint, and forced bravado in her voice. "What do you want?"

He leaned in, his chest heavy against her back and his breath feathering her hair. "You live here?"

His gentle tone conflicted with the pressure of his fingers. She rammed her head backward. He dodged her strike, and the cage of his body curled around her, straightening her with his arms around her chest.

Blood thundered in her ears, and her heart hammered to escape, to give up, to shrink and die. She stretched her jaw and wheezed a pathetic shout. "Help." Need air. The door. She angled toward it, throwing her fists behind her and colliding with nothing.

"Easy." The coil of his arms held her upright, his body a brick wall at her back. "If there's no heart condition, no epilepsy, then what's wrong with you?"

She might've laughed if she weren't failing to breathe. This man didn't give a shit about her condition. No one did. With his arms wrapped around her and his exhales on her neck, she'd never felt more helpless. She wanted to drop to the ground and retreat into herself, but she was better than that, dammit. "Let go."

He didn't. She might not be able to overpower him, but she still had her voice. If all he wanted was an answer, she could give him a revolting one. "You want to know what's wrong with me? My genital herpes has flared up. You know, blistering sores, cracked open and itching? My Valtrex prescription is in one of these packages." She scanned the ground, gasping, humiliation screeching through her voice. "To make matters worse, I started my period. I can feel it dripping down my leg." There. That would send any guy running.

He laughed. The motherfucker *laughed.* Either he knew she was lying or he was a sick fuck.

Somehow, her struggling only shifted her closer. A waft of cut hickory and citrus flooded her nose as his lips brushed her cheek. "You are a captivating surprise, Amber Rosenfeld."

Oh my God, he knew her name? Her muscles heated, more desperate than ever to get away from him. She threw an elbow, and it bounced off his rigid stomach. "If you don't let me go, I...I'm—" She sucked in a breath, her voice gravelly and broken. "I'm going to bleed all over you."

He chuckled. "I don't mind a little blood." He tightened his grip. "Besides, you can't even stand on your own."

Ragged sobs swallowed her breaths. She lurched forward, hands slashing at the air, reaching for the door, going nowhere. "How do you know my name?"

He kicked at the scattered envelopes. Her name and address labeled overdue bills, fliers, and catalogs in block print, glowing in the stripe of light that escaped the crack in the door.

Okay, so he knew her name. She just needed to grab the package with the dye and hustle her ass inside. She twisted in his arms and swept a foot, toeing for an envelope with bulk. Her lungs burned with exertion. Fucking shit, where was it?

A renewed bout of panic hiked her pulse and sealed her airway. What the hell was she thinking? Fuck the package. She had to break free. Lock the door. Call the cops. She could reach the door in one or two running leaps.

Her heart raced, nearly exploding, as she thrashed against him. His arms pinned her biceps, so she swung her fists, aiming for his groin and missing. He wrestled her hands to her sides, everything moving too quickly to process. She simply reacted, slamming her head back again and collided with his chest.

The grunt of pain that followed resuscitated her flight response. She thrust all her weight against his arms, her heels scraping the concrete. "Let me go, you psycho."

His exhales grew heavy, curling over her shoulder and pitching her into a breathless frenzy. The more she shoved against him, the tighter his arms constricted, lifting her until her feet kicked air. "What are you fighting? Fear?" His mouth touched her ear, his timbre a silken noose around her neck. "Fear is an imposture, little girl. It doesn't bruise or thrust or bite." His grip tightened. "*Fear* is not your Master."

Oh, holy mother. What was he saying? The terrible dread that occupied her belly bristled with thorns, impaling her with nightmares of public places, crowds, nowhere to hide, loss of motor control. And now her superficial fears embodied a very real, in-the-flesh threat.

He was going to take her, discover all her imperfections, and reject her. Abandon her somewhere away from home. Or kill her.

A furor of tears shot through her eyes and soaked her lashes. She clawed at his arms and stabbed her heels at his shins. If she could refill her lungs, she might be able to muster a scream big enough to wake the neighbors.

But she'd never seen a single person who lived on her street. How judgmental were they? If they came out, would they just stand there and gape? Oh God. "I have nothing you want." She panted, choked. "I'm nothing. Let me...go."

"As you wish." His arms vanished.

The concrete stoop crashed against her knees, and pain ricocheted through her legs. Oh God, maybe he'd only been trying to help her stand? She'd overreacted, made a freak of herself.

She gagged on a sobbing exhale, and her fingers scraped the ground, searching for the package and coming up empty. Another torrent of nausea gripped her body, singeing her insides and spinning the ground beneath her.

She pushed through the disorientation and crawled toward the door as fast as she could. The metal threshold sliced her knees, but she was too numb and dizzy, seconds from fainting. She could feel him behind her, a thick cloud of judgment with eyes scorching her skin, witnessing her shame.

You think they don't know how fucked up you are? Everyone knows. You're a fucking embarrassment.

Oh, if Brent could see her now, dragging her body, snot dripping from her nose. What a fool she was. Maybe the prowler would shoot her and put her out of her misery.

She gripped the doorjamb. Fuck Brent. Fuck all of them. She pulled her legs inside and glanced at the blockhouse of muscle behind her as she swung the door. And froze.

The interior light caught the face within the hood. Her heart constricted, and her hand stopped the door, just a crack.

He hadn't moved from where he'd released her. Hands in his pockets, he regarded her with a lift of one dark eyebrow. His full lips pursed around a toothpick, hollowing his cheeks. A strong jaw and hard gray eyes roughened his model-like prettiness. But the thick scar bisecting his cheek was what stayed her hand, pinning her to the floor and summoning the deepest, most troubled part of her.

The gash curved from the outer crease of his eye to the crook of his mouth. It should've impaired his confident gaze and brutalized the symmetry of his deep-set eyes and chiseled nose. It should've made her look away.

Instead, it demanded tolerance, homage even, and fortified the savagery of his beauty. He was a perfect imperfection.

Her ogling had only lasted a heartbeat. Perhaps, another second drinking in his good looks wouldn't hurt, but as she leaned in, the door swung closed and erased him from view.

The air returned to her lungs. She locked the dead bolt four times and collapsed onto her back.

Who was he? How did he get the scar? What did he want? She replayed the potency of his voice, the strength of his arms, and the flaw in his flawless face. He was fascinating. Though to be fair, she hadn't been outside in two years. A stray dog might've been just as enchanting. Actually, what was more fascinating was that she was thinking about him and not her lost mail.

She sat up, her pulse redoubling. Her mail. Her fucking package. Goddammit, she couldn't go back out there. It was a guaranteed panic attack, one she might not survive. She gripped the middle row of knuckles and exhaled with each crack. If she didn't go back out there, she wouldn't have the dye to finish the leathercraft orders. She wouldn't get paid. Wouldn't be able to stop the water from being shut off.

She released a heavy sigh. She'd made it to the mailbox, albeit ungracefully and shamefully. She could make a few more steps to gather the packages. She rose, exhaustion weighing down her limbs.

God, her silly fears had such incredible power over her. Just a quick sprint right outside, and she'd have what she needed to finish her orders.

With a spike of courage kick-boxing her heart, she placed a trembling hand on the knob—

A fist pounded on the door.

She jumped, rattling her teeth.

"Amber?"

His voice shivered through her, and her breaths burst in and out. Why was he still here? Should she call the cops? Would they force her outside or to the station to make a statement? She faced the door and shouted, "Go away."

More pounding. "Amber, if you want your mail, you're gonna have to open the door."

Van narrowed his eyes at Amber's door as a restless vibration itched behind his ribs. What the hell was this girl's problem? And why was he so hypnotized? Was it her slap-it-hard, fuck-it-harder physique? The breathless waver in her voice? Or the challenge of not knowing what made her freak the fuck out?

Beneath her trembling, however, lay an assload of backbone. And a very, very fine ass. What if every torrid trigger that had ever set him on fire waited behind that door?

He dropped his brow on the weather-beaten frame and tilted his face toward the dark windows next door, his real reason for being there. Liv and the dick monk had moved to the other side of the house and out of hearing range. He should move along, too, return to his cold, empty cabin, and forget all about the fear widening Amber's gorgeous eyes.

And yet, despite the risk of being seen, he gathered the last of her mail and knocked on her door a second time. Christ, he was riding a vicious need to discover her secrets, a craving to break her apart and play with the pieces.

He knocked again and infused his tone with authority. "Amber."

"You should run," she shouted. "I've got a gun aimed at the door."

Sure she did. "What kind of gun?"

"The kind that shoots ball-seeking super-bullets at unwanted visitors."

Cute. Even if she owned a gun, she wouldn't be able to still her fingers long enough to pull the trigger. He released a slow breath, an attempt to expel the impulse to pop the deadbolt. He should leave the poor girl to deal with her demons, but instinct demanded he take control of this...of her.

He was the worst combination of his parents, his very blood blackened with human slavery. Hell, his moral code was fucking fried the moment he was conceived by a ruthless slave owner and a weak, used-up slave. Besides, it was easier to blame his DNA than to examine the decisions he'd made or, rather, the choices that continued to choose him.

A nice guy—like Saint NinnyBalls next door—would stop, but he ripped the edge of one envelope, slid out the document, and activated the light on his phone. "You should see this, Amber. Looks like your electricity is going to be shut off" —he skimmed the red print— "in five days."

A thump jiggled the door. Her fist? "Opening peoples' mail is a federal offense, you sick pig."

He smirked. Couldn't argue with the truth. "Don't insult pigs. It's dirty, and the pig likes it."

"Until they're slaughtered," she yelled, "and served with eggs and coffee."

A smile tickled his cheeks. "You inviting me to stay for breakfast?"

Funny how brave she sounded behind the barrier of a door. A cheap door, in fact, given the hollow rattle and the sorry-ass lock. Didn't she realize one kick would bend it from the casing? He tapped the tarnished kick plate with his sneaker and made it clatter, just to taunt her.

"I'm calling the cops." Her threat pierced through the door, but the waver in her shriek lacked conviction.

She wouldn't be calling anyone. Was it a general fear of people? Or something far more complicated? He leaned a shoulder against the jamb and thumbed through her bills and leathercraft catalogs. "What would keep a beautiful woman locked up in her house?"

His stomach hardened in anticipation of her voice as soundless seconds crawled down his spine. Her silence deterred him more than the door. What was she doing in there? Texting a friend? The friendly neighborhood delivery guy, perhaps? Or was she pressed against the frame, same as him? Was her hand on the knob? He didn't dare twist it. Didn't want her to flee deep within the house where he couldn't talk to her. Instead, he opened the largest package, ripping through the bubble wrap. Four bottles of...leather dye? "I'm waiting, Amber. What's the reason?"

More silence. He rolled the toothpick between his lips. If she didn't respond in three seconds, he'd simply move the mics to her windows. Three, two—

"Why does there have to be a reason?" Her voice reverberated through the wood, soft, close.

He shifted, his mouth hovering over the seal in the door, and matched her tone. "What's the leather dye for?" He turned the bottles in the envelope, revealing directions on how to dye shoes and furniture. "Fixing up a pair of cowgirl boots?" Fuck, those toned legs would radiate sex in a miniskirt and boots.

She growled, loud and guttural, and the door thumped again. "After I flay the skin from your body, I'm going to dye it and sew it into a handbag. Special order from your momma."

A laugh erupted from his throat, and he darted a glance at Liv's windows. "Hate to disappoint you, gorgeous. My dead mother has no use for handbags."

The door held as still as the quiet behind it. If she felt bad about his mother, she shouldn't bother. Isadora Quiso chose the slow death of crack over feeding and protecting her son. She could burn in hell.

"C'mon. Just open the door." He dropped his forehead on the frame. What would he do if she let him in?

Fantasies spilled from the oily, malignant lesion that was his mind. He would take her was what he'd do. Strap down those toned limbs until they strained in agony and bury himself in her so deep she'd never be able to purge the stench of him. He was his father's son, after all.

Except Mr. E had not only enslaved and ruined his mother, he'd left her to rot in an El Paso *colonia* with her unwanted infant.

Van bit down on the toothpick, snapping it in half. He pocketed the pieces, his bitterness cursing at him to embrace his nature. The rancid bits of his life in that ghetto were inside of him. He wanted to pocket those, too.

Yet here he was, growing hard at the thought of ruining another life.

She'd grown too quiet on her side of the door. Had she decided to end the conversation and retreat to another room? He tightened his hands into fists. "Amber?"

The door jostled with her movements.

He sighed in relief. "Just give me one reason why you're holed up." Give him something vulnerable he could break off and sharpen into teeth.

"I'll give you several." Her tone was clipped, angry. "I'm allergic to pollen. I'm hiding a dead body. And I don't like you."

There it was. She *did* like him. He hadn't missed her gape of appreciation when she'd shut the door. What she seemed to be oblivious to, however, was her enjoyment in their verbal scrimmage. But where was the terrified girl who could barely utter a sentence outside? She really put a lot of faith in that door. He grinned. "Maybe I'm the reason."

"Mighty full of yourself." Her volume rose. "Let me clear it up for you. Fuck. Off."

He'd rather fuck *her*. And he would. The brick walls of her bungalow might've suspended her earlier panic, but it was a deception he could shatter with little effort. He could wait till she fell asleep and pry open the rear sliding door. A precaution he should've taken six months ago rather than assuming the house was vacant. He'd been careless, and now his favorite bench—and its view—was compromised.

Though, since the moment Amber had stumbled out, something had happened to his focus. "Are we done talking through the door?"

"What are you doing on my porch in the middle of the night?" She sounded tired, defeated.

"I was looking for some old friends and got the wrong house. You're not exactly rolling out the welcome mat, but I kind of like here. It beats going back to an empty home." It was more truth than he'd planned to share.

"You don't have—"

He pressed his ear against the wood, desperate to hear the rest of it. *Let it out, Amber.*

"You don't have anyone...at home?"

His pulse hopped through his veins. His honesty had opened a precious doorway into hers. "No one, Amber. There's not a soul that cares if I live or would miss me if I died." Maybe he'd laid it on too thick, but the truth was always denser and darker than shit.

The flooring creaked beneath her footsteps. Was she pacing? Considering another swine-related retort?

Finally, the creaking stilled, and her voice drifted over him, sealing her fate. "I'd like to make you an offer."

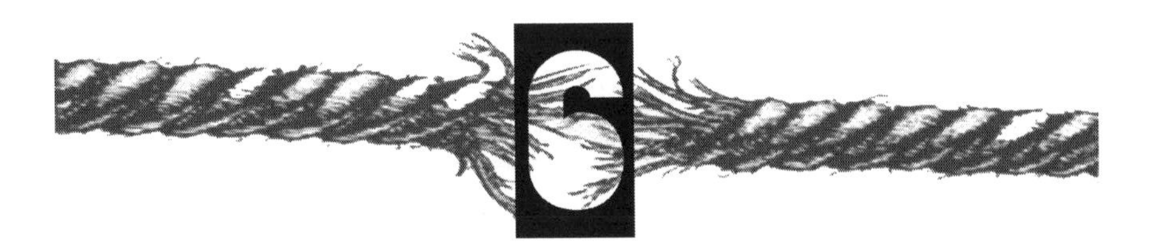

Whatever sanity Amber had left evaporated in her desperate state of do-or-die. The decision roiled through her stomach. She needed the dye to complete the projects, and even more troublesome was how she would transport the finished orders from the door to the mailbox before the Saturday mail carrier motored by.

Was enlisting the help from this man the smart thing to do? It felt right, like a nuzzling, belly warming, union-of-lonely-souls kind of right. She knew, too well, how forceful loneliness was, how it could make a person desperate enough to grasp at strangers.

She rubbed her temples and released a frustrated breath. She was making an emotional decision, as Dr. Michaels liked to say, anchored in empathy and illogic. And Brent had always said she was too stupid to think for herself.

Her hands dropped to her sides. There had been a time in her life when she'd ignored Brent's commentary, when her self-image was as true and sturdy as her pageant pose. Perhaps too sturdy. The more she'd let his disgust roll off her shoulders, the crueler the words had become. For years, he'd tried to penetrate her pride, to elicit a reaction. One she'd refused to give. Until, eventually, he'd cut too deep.

Maybe she'd hardened herself so much she'd become an undesirable person, a detached wife he could no longer love. For that, she only had herself to blame.

You're excusing his behavior.

Dr. Michaels was right. Besides, she was anything but hardened now, and Brent wasn't around to savor it. She squeezed her over-popped fingers, and the silent bend of joints pushed her pulse to her throat.

"What's the offer, sweetheart?"

Interest wove through his timbre, and the endearment had no business shivering over her skin. Nothing was more comforting, or more narcissistic, than feeling desired.

She leaned toward the door and placed her palm on the cool surface. Even if he did desire her, it had no weight in her decision. His intention did, and she didn't know what that was. She didn't know him.

But she hadn't known any of her previous lovers. Hell, her *I'd like to make you an offer* was the first thing she'd uttered to Zach through the door.

Zach. The recent change in their interactions was the beginning of the end. Perhaps, she'd made such a fool of herself he didn't plan to come back at all. Sometimes, they didn't.

Lack of options was all she had left. "What's your name?"

His pause was brief but unnerving. "Van."

"Van." Her voice rasped past a sandpaper throat. "I'll invite you in for four hours while I dye a project and wait for it to dry. In exchange, you will take my finished packages to the mailbox." She held her breath.

"Does the dyeing and drying involve my skin?"

Her lips twitched, and it felt...safe. "If you misbehave."

"Are you going to give me herpes?"

She laughed at his teasing tone and covered her mouth, startled by the sound. She lowered her hands, but the smile persisted. "If you ask nicely." Her face inflamed. Jesus, she was flirting. Oh, fuckever. Wasn't that what she was offering? The same thing she'd offered the last six delivery guys? Sex in exchange for her deliveries?

But Van's name wasn't stitched on his shirt. He wasn't on his lunch break, for twenty minutes on Tuesday or Friday. He'd opened her mail, for Godssake. He asked questions. *He* pursued *her.*

"It's a deal." His voice was firm, final.

Ohshitohshitohshit. It was one thing to flirt and joke through the safety of the door, but letting him inside after she'd run off her mouth and made an ass of herself? What was she thinking?

Her pulse jumped from zero to a hundred and forty, her legs weakened, and the chest pain barreled in. No, please, not an attack. Not going to happen.

She breathed deeply, flexing and holding her abs on each inhale, four times. She would slap on a fresh face and pull herself together, dammit. The four clocks lined on the far wall read 12:40 AM. "I need twenty-four minutes."

Without waiting for a response, she ran to the bedroom and continued her belly breathing while she changed from her sweat-soaked suit to a clean black minidress. That done, she finger-combed the carpet lines and freshened her makeup in the bathroom.

Blond curls falling perfectly around her heaving chest, she stood by the front door and waited for six minutes.

At 1:04 AM, she spoke. "Still there, Van?"

"Even more impatient than I was twenty-four minutes ago."

His voice matched his words, but she didn't let it stop her from unlocking the deadbolt four times. What if he tracked in dirt or poked around in her things? Would his personal questions continue? Should she maintain a far distance? What if her *Aw, he has a lonely soul* warped into *Sweet God, he has a knife?*

She opened the door, enough to leave a sliver without feeling the malevolent force of the open air. Then she sprinted down the hall, fighting for oxygen and towing a thousand-pound string of reservations behind her.

The deadbolt slid free, not once but four times in rapid succession. Huh. Was this some kind of neurotic indecisiveness? Or was the crazy woman taunting him? Amber was probably the kind of girl who would leave bite marks all over his dick.

Van grinned.

When the knob twisted and a soft glow illuminated the slivered opening, his pulse electrified. There it was, her free will dangling in the open door. He could take it, violently and recklessly, the moment he walked in. He flexed his fingers, anticipating fistfuls of her hair.

His cock pulsed as the thrill of possibilities heated his blood. It would be so damned exhilarating to throw her against the wall, mar her pretty skin, and fuck her before the stunned effect of terror released its first breath.

He stood taller, lighter, no longer bound by slave-buyer virginity requirements or his father's bullshit tyranny. He could be greedy, merciless, unrestrained. He could beat her just for letting him in. He could fuck her any way he wanted. Then he could take her home, chain her in *his* room, and keep her until *he* was done.

He hadn't taken anyone against their will since Joshua Carter, limiting his sexual encounters to quick fucks with men and women to take the edge off. Had it really been a year since he'd felt this rush? Why the hell was he giving into it now?

Because this fearful, sassy, crazy woman had awoken something inside him.

He slid on his leather gloves, unconcerned with how she might react to them. When he nudged open the door, the sound of her heels speed-clicked around the corner and faded into another room. He hadn't expected a red carpet welcome, but seriously? She didn't know his intentions, yet she'd opened the door and run? That was fucked up from the tits up.

As he crossed the threshold, the aroma of bleach and springtime fumigated his nose, a peculiar concoction of citrus, girly gardenias, and enough disinfectant to saturate a morgue. Maybe she *was* hiding a body. He locked the deadbolt and followed the aseptic wisp through the small sitting room.

Up ahead, a doorway opened into the kitchen. The hallway branched off to the left, leading to three rooms. Shadows gathered around the entrances of two. A soft band of light gleamed from the third, presumably where she'd run off to. She could wait. If she was stupid enough to let him roam alone, that was her problem.

Dated but well-kept furniture formed perfect right-angles, enclosed by gray walls, wood floors, black fabrics, and the sheer absence of color. What halted his steps, however, were the four round wall clocks, hanging side-by-side, identical in style, and synced down to the motherfucking second hand.

The oddity propelled him to examine the room closer as he listened for her footsteps. Four candles lined the glossy coffee table, four black pillows sat at rigid attention on the gray couch, and four bookshelves filled one wall. No TV. No knick-knacks. No picture frames. And definitely no trace of the pungency that would come with harvesting marijuana. Not that he still entertained that assumption.

Which raised new questions about her twice-a-week visitor. Zachary Kaufman was an unknown who would need to be dealt with.

With the envelopes tucked under one arm, he brushed a gloved finger over the dust-free surfaces, turning in a circle and searching for a deviation in the patterned decor. Everything was in symmetrical groups of four. The row of leather coasters, the books on the shelves, and the five-light chandelier...yep, missing the fifth bulb. Even the damned orchid on the sofa table had four white blooms with four petals each, as if she'd plucked the poor thing to fit an obscene idea of perfect proportion.

While the impersonal space offered little insight into who she was, one thing was certain. She was a straight-up freak of orderly foursomes.

"Come here, Van." Her voice skipped down the hall, strong and confident.

He stiffened, and his head tilted. *She* was beckoning *him*? Oh, how he wanted to answer with a cruel laugh just to expose her misunderstanding. Little did she know, he'd moved the mics during the twenty-four minute wait and had listened to her frantic footsteps running in and out of the back rooms. And why had she made him wait exactly twenty-four minutes? Was it an even-numbered thing or something more practical, like setting up a plan to trap him? If it were the latter, the pistol tucked in his ass crack would let her know she'd surrendered the instant she invited him inside.

He slid his tongue over his lips, seeking the toothpick he'd forgotten to replace. The worst part about being a sick bastard was the internal view of his perversions. He'd watch, like a helpless witness, as his body instilled fear in the eyes of his captives, his memories molding them into a weaker version of himself. In those moments, when his hands became manacles and his strikes connected with flesh, he beat the living shit out of the pathetic boy he once was. Nothing was more therapeutic. Or fucked up.

A jolt of heat pulsated his groin. Christ, he couldn't wait to introduce her to the realm of his imagination.

He leaned over the coffee table and stacked three coasters in a lopsided pile. As he passed the couch, he rotated one square pillow to sit on its cornered edge. His grin stretched so big his mouth hurt. Sometimes, it was the little things that teased sadistic pleasures.

Circling back to the front door, he toed off his sneakers and left them there. His silent gait carried him to the kitchen where he unlocked the sliding door. Would she check the locks? He dropped the thick drape back in place to cover the glass, adjusting the pleats to their former order so she wouldn't notice he'd touched them.

A couple of minutes had passed since she'd let him in. Was she clutching a butter knife, waiting to pounce? Counting to four over and over? He smiled at the thought of keeping her waiting.

With easy breaths and slow strides, he entered the short hallway, embracing the pursuit, stalking the innocent, preying exclusively on trust.

She'd willingly opened her door for the last time. Her naiveté would be the first thing vanquished by the hard, heavy weight between his legs.

Filling his lungs, he swallowed his enthusiasm and paused at the first of the three doors in the hall, an empty bathroom. As much as he craved an impulsive fuck-fight, he would take her the way he'd captured all the others, with planning and patience.

He dug a toothpick from his pocket and gripped it between his teeth, buying a few seconds to relax his dick. To speed things along, he shifted his thoughts to the one pure thing in his life. His daughter's vibrant smile, her lively mannerisms, and the crescendo of her precious voice spiraled breathless warmth through his chest and eased the strain against his zipper.

God, he wanted a place in her life, but she lived with Mr. E's widow. Revealing his identity to Livana was a long-term plan-in-progress.

It'd been easy for Liv to slip into Livana's life. The authorities knew she was Livana's biological mother. Legally, she was entitled to claim custody. She had a steady job, plus the six million he'd given her. But he didn't think she'd ever take their daughter from her stable home. Liv was a recovering slave after all, with her own aftermath of healing and maturing to work through.

Unfortunately, his ability to claim custody was nonexistent because *he* didn't exist. Not to the authorities and not to Mr. E's widow. Exposing his identity would link him to Mr. E's trafficking operation and land him life in prison. So his safest avenue to Livana was through Liv.

He gnashed his teeth. Before he could approach Liv, he needed to understand how she'd freed eight slaves and made the buyers *disappear*. Cartel? Hired hit man? Last thing he wanted was to become one of her disposed bodies.

With a swift adjustment of his finally-flaccid cock, he strode toward the only illuminated doorway in the hall and stopped at the entrance, his thumb on his hip, fingers near the concealed gun at his back.

She perched on a stool at the center of a bed-less bedroom, facing him, her back rigidly straight and her gaze on his gloved hand.

Four leather knife sheaths lay on the workbench behind her. His eyebrows crept up his forehead. Definitely a far cry from cowgirl boots. Would she ever cease to surprise him?

Rubber utility mats lined the floor. One wall held a treadmill, a Smith machine, and a metal rack stacked with free weights, arranged by size. No wonder her ass was a wicked bounce of muscle. He imagined her bent over and the inviting space her firm cheeks would create between her thighs.

Heat pierced through his body, contracting his muscles and leaving little room for patience. Fuck, the wait felt like a hundred searing needles, but he relished it, wanting her beneath his skin.

His bulk filled the doorway, legs spread wide, arms loose at his sides, confident he could draw the gun before she could wedge a hidden weapon from that tight dress. While he waited for her to look up, he drank in her features. The regal curves of her face. The tiny slope of her nose. The way her lips naturally tipped upward despite the tension around her mouth. But why the hell had she changed her clothes?

The overhead light reflected off the blond curtain of her hair. The color seemed...wrong, too pale for her honey-light skin. It fell over her face as she stared at the floor, a paradox of insecure beauty.

He tilted his head. Of course, he knew very little about her, but he was missing something crucial, a fragile facet beneath the pristine makeup and trained physique.

He rolled the toothpick with his tongue. "Why do you bleach your hair?"

Golden-brown eyes connected with his, blinking furiously, so deliciously nervous. "It's..." She huffed. "None of your business."

Slowly, cautiously, he slid back the hood of his sleeveless sweatshirt. Her breathing quickened as her gaze skimmed his exposed biceps, his face, and lingered on the scar that divided his cheek. She looked away, her shoulders curling around her ears.

He knew the effect he had on women. Whether it was their fascination with big, scary men with scars or their complete dismissal of danger, he only needed to flash a smile to lure them in. Amber was no different, despite the self-berating that was likely occurring in her flustered mind.

Short breaths rattled her lips. Her knees squeezed together, and her fingers entwined beneath her perky tits, pressing against the knuckles of the opposite hand.

Watching her battle her distress felt a little like foreplay. For every tremble across her skin, his mouth moistened, his pulse purred, and the nerve-endings in his fingers stirred and tingled. His body fed from the energy clashing between them, rushing blood below his waist and hardening him for a fight between her uptight thighs.

She glanced down, and her breath caught.

He followed her gaze, past the discomfort straining his jeans, to his socked feet. He flexed his toes. "What?"

"Where are your shoes?"

Her disregard for his arousal was a shocker. No matter. He'd prepared for this line of questioning. "By the front door."

Her nose scrunched in a naively erotic way. "Why are you wearing gloves?"

"Same reason my shoes are by the door." He lifted a shoulder, deliberately vague, letting her squirm.

Her lips pressed together, and her chest heaved. "I don't understand."

"Your house is obscenely clean." Which had fuck-all to do with covering his fingerprints and softening his footsteps. He caught her eyes and winked. "So I put on my driving gloves and left my shoes."

"Driving gloves haven't been fashionable since the sixties."

"My '65 Mustang might be dated, too, but it's bad-ass.

He savored the little nuances of her floundering expression. The skin tightening over arches of her cheekbones. The vertical lines between her eyebrows. The bounce in her gaze, ping-ponging everywhere but in his direction. And finally, her wavering sigh.

Got her. Earlier, when his arms were locked around her, she might've sensed his cruelty. But now that she'd let him in, she would be fighting that intuition, convincing herself he wouldn't bother with conversation if he intended to harm her. Lucky for him, she didn't know how he operated.

He held up his gloved fingers, wiggling them. "You should thank me. You don't know where my hands have been."

Her nose twitched again, her eyes fixed on the packages beneath his arm. "Um...thanks?" She squared her shoulders and dragged her gaze to his, the display of courage ten times more forced than her voice. "My mail?"

As he crossed the room, she rose like an animated mannequin, a vision of posed glamour, an artist's illusion. He stopped a few feet away, mesmerized by the unnatural yet graceful way she held herself, until she raised a stiff arm and gestured for the packages.

He handed them over and nodded at the sheaths behind her. "Should I worry about where the knives are?"

"Probably." She turned toward the bench and removed the bottles of dye, arranging them in a neat little line with the labels facing her.

"Your vagueness isn't very friendly."

She sighed. "I don't forge blades. I make things from leather and sell them online."

Her only source of income? That would explain her financial problems and her urgency to ship this project.

She unscrewed the first bottle, and the plasticky smell of chemicals singed the air. "You can sit on the stool while I finish and tell me the real reason you were on my porch."

Perceptive little thing. Bossy, too. He let it go and sat, facing her backside as she worked. "When was the last time you left the house?"

Her shoulders bunched. "Thirty minutes ago."

"Before that."

"None—"

"Of my business?" He stretched his legs out in front of him and angled his head to watch the glorious flex of her ass. "Do you know your neighbors?"

Her hands paused; then she blotted a rag with brown stain. "No, so I won't be able to answer questions about your *old friends*."

The six months he'd spent watching her house, he hadn't seen a twitch in the shades. "Gonna go out on a limb here and say you've never even seen your neighbors."

Her hip cocked out as if she'd lost her balance, but her hands continued to work the dye into the carved designs.

The flourish of knotted swirls in the leather appeared impressively intricate, even if the details weren't clear from where he sat. "You always work in a dress and heels?"

"You always chatter like a fourth grade girl?"

He snapped his molars together. Fuck, she was frustrating. "If you'd answer my questions—"

"You didn't answer mine." She bent over to inspect her work, and sweet Jesus, the short dress rose a good two inches up her thighs. Much more of that and those hard cheeks would be gripping his dick.

He swiped a gloved hand over his face. What was her question? Oh. "Why was I on your porch?" He smirked at her back. "Your bench has a great view of your kinky neighbors. Did you know they fuck on their kitchen table?"

She spun, her wide bright eyes colliding with his.

His smile stretched, giving her a good show of teeth.

She studied him, nibbling the corner of her lip, and her face relaxed. "You're fucking with me."

He hadn't even begun. "If that's what you think."

Her eyebrows pulled together as she returned to her dye. "I'm almost done," she mumbled. "Then it'll need a few hours to dry."

And he needed to poke around, unsupervised. "Got anything to drink?"

"Juice and beer in the fridge. Tequila under the sink."

He moved toward the door. "Want anything?"

She glanced over her shoulder, eyes on his gloved hands. "No, thanks."

Smart girl, but not smart enough.

In the kitchen, he opened every cabinet and drawer and found the same diabolical order as the rest of the house. Condiments and plastic containers grouped in fours, organized by size, labels facing out. Same thing in the fridge.

He poured two fingers of gold tequila. Cheap stuff, but even a watered-down mixto pretending to be tequila was better than domestic beer.

Drink in hand, he slipped into the sitting room and made a beeline to the books. When he'd sought out his victims as a human trafficker, he'd been bound by the contract of the slave buyers. Gender, hair color, body type, temperament, everything had a requirement. Now, he was free to choose whom he wanted for *his* pleasure, and tracking, watching, and studying a quarry was the most exhilarating part of a capture.

He had no reason to enslave another person again, but he couldn't fight his nature forever. Would Amber be an adaptable slave? Would she be missed? Did she have any nasty secrets he wouldn't be able to work with? Who *was* Amber Rosenfeld?

His investigation began with the top shelves of her bookcases, which held hundreds of hardbacks. Stacked in a repeating pattern of vertical and horizontal groups of four, the covers featured moonlit mansions, bloody handprints, shadowed doorways, and demonic eyes. While the horror collection was unexpected, the alphabetized order wasn't. His fingers twitched, and his smile built.

It took him less than a minute to fuck up her program, swapping out books and rotating some upside down. As he switched the final books, one of the flaps opened, revealing a signature and a personalized message. *For Paul, with best wishes.*

Something pinched in his chest. Who the fuck was Paul?

He opened another. *To Teresa.* He released a breath. The next five he checked were also autographed and personalized to random somebodies.

He gnawed on the toothpick, his mind racing. Did she steal from people's autographed collections? Why would she do that?

Crouching, he inspected the spines on the lower shelf, which was hidden behind a leather ottoman. He shoved it aside, and the font on the spines told him these texts didn't contain stories of ax murderers and ghosts. He leaned in closer to read the titles, and oh baby, there she was, all laid out in a dozen manuals.

Break Out Guide for Shut-ins. Face Your Phobia. Imperfect OCD. Living With Agoraphobia.

OCD was a term he knew, and one that had been scraping at the back of his mind since he'd walked in. But what the fuck was agoraphobia? He cracked open the text *Out Without Fear* and flipped to the first page.

Agoraphobia is an anxiety disorder in which a person has a fear of being in open places where it is hard to escape. The individual might feel embarrassed, helpless, or trapped, and the intense fear can manifest into a panic attack. Agoraphobics avoid attacks by restricting or completely eliminating activities outside the home.

No shit? That solved the mystery behind her meltdown outside, and maybe why she'd run from the door when she unlocked it. He skimmed a few chapters as a weird mix of emotions clumped in his stomach. Part of him felt bad for the girl, a quaint feeling to be sure. If he were a fucking pansy, maybe he'd explore that. Instead, he focused on the sharper, more familiar sentiment that clung to his gut.

He wanted her vulnerability. To use her body. To bleed off the pent-up shit inside of him. To fill the emptiness. To get his fucking mind off Liv Reed.

Amber was the one he'd been waiting for, and considering the irony that she lived right next door to Liv, maybe Amber had been waiting for him.

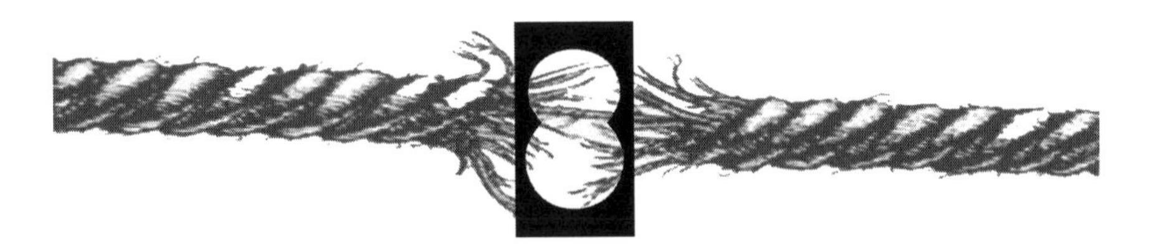

Van knew the risks in kidnapping all too well, but taking an agoraphobic outside her door? Christ, that was a new one. Were there medical considerations? Would Amber keel the fuck over and die from an aneurysm?

Wait, why did he care if she had seizures and shit? *Because he didn't want to kill her.* If he managed to successfully move her, she probably wouldn't even try to escape. His muscles swelled with heat just thinking about her locked in his house. *Locks optional?*

The swoosh of the bathroom faucet interrupted his romantic thoughts, followed by the approaching click of her heels.

"What are you doing?" Her horrified whisper sent a quiver of pleasure down his spine.

Just to rile her a bit more, he didn't stand, didn't turn to acknowledge her. Instead, he pocketed the toothpick, lifted the glass of mixto tequila from the shelf, and drained half. He took his time, drawing out the tension that wafted from her, savoring it. Unlike the piss burning his throat. Lighter fluid would've gone down smoother.

Eventually, he returned the book, out of order, and rose with his back to her. "How long have you been shut in, Amber?"

"You need to leave." Her voice was so strangled it sounded like she'd lost the ability to breathe.

He shifted to face her, his expression relaxed, his tone more so. "Are you medicated?" An inventory of her medicine cabinet was on his list of to-dos. He needed a better understanding of the disorders.

"Leave right this minute, and I won't call the cops." She clutched her knuckles and raised her chin, the sinews in her neck pressing against delicate skin.

Was she telling him to leave because he'd discovered her phobia? A smile crooked one corner of his mouth. "Go ahead. Call in the pigs." He waved a hand at the door. "If you don't mind them tracking the outside world all over your nice floors." The self-help text had said, *The individual might feel embarrassed.* "Maybe they won't jump to conclusions about someone with a mental disorder going ape-shit on her house-guest."

A noise squeaked in her throat, and her eyes darted from him, to the front door, and back again. Then they lowered, as did her chin. "What do you want from me?"

Ah, fuck, he was screwed. The only thing missing from her response was *Master.* He drew a deep breath through his nose and tried to calm the *fuck-her-take-her-break-her* rap against his ribs.

"I'm going to finish my drink" —he raised the glass, his voice soft and casual— "while we wait for your projects to dry. Then I'll drop them in the mailbox when I leave. Isn't that why you invited me in?"

She shifted her weight from one foot to the other, her hands twitching at her sides. So damned beautiful, all dolled up with nowhere to go. "Yes." She swallowed. "Of course."

He leaned against the bookshelf and hooked a thumb in his pocket. "A shallow bastard might've bolted after discovering your disorder, blabbering some excuse as he ran far, far away." He watched her sharp inhale and suppressed the satisfaction tugging at his lips. "So you have issues. Don't we all?" Fucking understatement.

"I don't want to talk about this." Even as she said it, her eyes fell on the coffee table, and a tremor overtook her body. She charged toward the source of her horror, sucking air as she realigned the coasters with trembling fingers.

He hid his grin behind the lip of his raised glass.

A gasp followed, and she tackled the pillow on the couch, straightening and fluffing with asthmatic breaths. Then she stood, brushed down the hem of her dress, and leveled a hard stare in his direction. "Stop fucking with my things."

He stared right back, but what he really wanted to do was yank up that dress and sink his teeth into her twisted panties. With the casual swipe of a hand, he shifted the swollen head of his cock.

She didn't seem to notice, her eyes too busy shooting fire at his face. "And no more personal questions."

For a little thing, she sure had a big voice when she was angry. It was really quite cute, and he suddenly wanted to know if she was ticklish. What a fucked up thought, and probably not the time to explore it. She appeared to be seconds from self-destructing.

Her heels echoed through the room as she paced, seething through her teeth and wiping fingers beneath her dry eyes. Then she stopped and glanced at the clocks, at the door, back to the clocks. Was she weighing her options? *Go to the mailbox herself? Or let him stay to do it for her?*

When her eyes landed on him, they had cooled by several degrees. "No more snooping. Don't touch my stuff. Don't even look at it."

Terrible choice, little girl. He tipped her a crooked smile, made of sugar and shit. "Right on."

She nodded, her bottom lip caught between polished white teeth. "Then the offer to stay four hours stands. Follow me." With that, she turned and clickety-clacked down the hall.

He watched her ass until it disappeared within her unlit bedroom. For all his smugness in manipulating her, he knew better than to pursue this. She had some serious dysfunction—perhaps worse than his—and he'd only scratched the surface. He glanced at the front door. He should be the shallow bastard and leave, but the challenge invigorated him. God help him, but he wanted to lose his mind with this crazy woman.

He threw back the remainder of the mixto and set it on the coffee table. Flicking a coaster to the floor, he strolled down the hall, a hand in his pocket and dark dreams in his head.

At the doorway of her bedroom, he took in her most personal space. A dim lamp now glowing on the nightstand, a single blacked-out window, a small TV that should've been thrown out two decades ago. And a stunning woman sitting on the edge of the bed.

She watched him from beneath her lashes, her slender legs dangling off the side, the toes of her shoes flexed above the carpet. Not a single footprint indented the threads between her and the door. Had she hurdled the ten-foot distance? Impossible. How did she erase her tracks so fast?

Her silence pushed against him, scattering into the hallway and pulsing with the faint rasp of her inhales. She sat motionless, eyes lowering, as if held by an innate need to please. As if waiting for her Master to speak.

A warm current ran the length of his body, prickling his skin. Subservient Amber did *not* help his obsessive thoughts. His cock ached, but the greedy bastard didn't run things. He wouldn't take her impulsively. Not without planning. Maybe not ever.

He pushed off the doorframe and crossed the room, subtly scuffing his heels to smudge the vacuumed stripes in his path.

She glared at his tracks, and her jaw clenched. Yeah, her OCD harbored some affection for clean lines.

He paused before her, brushing his knees against hers and coaxing an exhale from her sweet lips. A discreet scan of the room revealed the same rigid order as the rest of the house. But what the fuck was the bizarre display in the corner?

A glass aquarium sat on a stand, brimming with twisted bits of filigree metalwork, broken bronze statues, and beveled gems—some attached to strips of metal, others loose and chipped.

He narrowed his eyes at her. "Are those—?"

"*Those* are nothing," she snapped, meeting his gaze.

Either she designed metal art, or she'd unleashed a pissed-off hammer on a trophy collection. Her locked jaw suggested the latter. Strange she hadn't covered it the way she'd concealed the self-help books, but he let it go for now.

"Why are we here?" He nodded at the bed.

"Why not?"

Because phobic girls didn't invite strangers where they slept. He gave her a human smile. "It wasn't a personal question." But he hoped it would incite a personal answer.

"Right." She looked at the bed and smoothed the white quilt beside her hip. "This is part of the offer."

His head jerked back. What the—

"Sex in exchange for dropping off my shipments." Her tone was unshakably and incautiously determined. She'd done this before.

The cold splash of realization doused his brain. And his libido. Christ, why hadn't he seen this coming? Of course, her mental condition would force her to depend on people. People with hard dicks weeping to accept her non-cash payments. People like Zachary Fucking Kaufman.

Goddammit, her offer stung. He wasn't some delivery bitch boy, earning pussy for a walk to the mailbox. He was there for his own purpose, not hers, and he'd damned well fuck her on his terms. "No."

Her face fell. "Oh. I thought—"

"I was so hard-up I had to run errands to get my dick wet?" His tone was harsh, though his anger had nothing to do with being hard-up.

Hell, eight years ago, *he* had been the whore, exchanging blowjobs for crack. No doubt, he would've been bent under some rutting drug-dealer at that very moment if Mr. E hadn't returned for him. Twenty-five years late, and still, he'd been overjoyed to meet long lost Dad.

A vein pulsed, hot and angry, on his forehead. Well, didn't that memory darken his mood? He should thank the good people of Austin for promoting Mr. E to police chief. The new position had come with too much scrutiny for a figurehead who trafficked slaves on the side. Mr. E had needed a front man to run the operation and remembered he had a twenty-five-year-old bastard son. A son, as it turned out, who had no qualms about profiting from sexual services.

Unless those services involved Amber and dipshit deliverymen. A beautiful woman should never sell herself so cheaply. She deserved better than Zachary Kaufman, and she definitely deserved better than what *he* had planned for her.

Fuck it. This irrational jealousy, or whatever it was, pissed him the hell off. He wanted to wash his hands of her. More than that, he wanted to brand her with a hundred possessive welts.

She fussed with her hair, hands shaking, and eyelids heavy with shame. "Can we just forget I said...that?"

Seriously? He squeezed his fingers into a fist, fighting the impulse to swing and knock her on her ass. He didn't want to scare her too badly. Not yet. Nor did he want to let this Zachary shit go. "Do you fuck all your house-guests?"

"That's a personal question." Her stubborn chin and hard eyes only fueled his need to punch her.

He leaned over her, hands on the bed beside her hips, and pushed his face into hers. "Your offer to fuck bowled straight through personal and landed smack between your legs. Might as well spread 'em and air it all out."

"Oh my God." Her chest rose, brushing his, but she didn't lean away, didn't look away. "Can you please step back?"

His lips were so close to hers he could taste the toothpaste on her breath. "Answer the question."

"No. I mean, yes." Her voice was angry and rushed, her dilated pupils resolutely locked on his. "I like sex, okay? I thought the attraction was mutual."

A burst of lust ignited through his cock. He grabbed her hand and pressed it against his erection, grinding his hips. Nothing said *I'm attracted to you* like a thrusting boner.

But the tentative squeeze of her fingers sent his head spinning. With her mouth so close and wet from her breaths, he took her lips. It wasn't a gentle touch-and-tease kiss, either. He went for it, dominating her mouth, spreading it open with his jaw, and angling her head with a fist in her hair. His tongue chased hers, lashing and taking.

She didn't fight back, so he unsheathed his teeth, catching and slicing her lips. His pulse raced, and his lungs pumped. Jesus, he couldn't reach any deeper, and she met him stroke for stroke, bite for bloody bite.

Her taste was insufferably sweet, much like the fingers stroking his cock. Which reminded him of his position on her offer.

He released her, and the room stumbled to a dizzying standstill. They shared a suspended look, panting in unison. He stepped back and wiped his mouth with the back of his hand. "The answer is still 'No'."

She slapped a palm over her mouth, eyes closed and forehead pinched. Then she shot from the bed and ran out of the room, leaving a trail of messy footprints in her wake.

He scratched his jaw. Huh. Apparently, OCD-ness came second to Oh-God-he-rejected-me-ness.

Perhaps he should've assured her of her attractiveness with words.

Maybe he should wear a tutu and over-pluck his eyebrows while he was at it.

He crossed the room to the aquarium and dug out a cracked statue of a bronze woman missing her head. The marred scratches across the base were vicious, but the engraving was still legible.

Fitness Model World Championship
1st Place
Amber Rosenfeld

His mouth fell open, though he shouldn't have been surprised. Her body rocked some killer biceps, thighs, and calves, and God knew what lay beneath that dress. It was a rare thing to find a woman with a ten body paired with a ten face, but this fitness model was a hundred from head to toe. So when he pulled out a wad of sashes printed with *Miss Tri County, Miss Heart of the USA, and Miss Texas*, it wasn't shock that caught his breath. It was a very strong feeling of wonder, reverence, and something akin to fear.

There must've been fifty demolished tiaras and trophies in that tank. Why would she destroy something she'd worked so hard to earn? Or had someone else hurt them? Hurt her? The notion sent blood roaring through his ears, leaving him shaken, edgy, and, worst of all, heartsick.

The sudden urge to flee shuffled him back a step. He needed to shed these feelings, this room, *her*. The last time he involved his emotions, he got a blade across his face and a bullet in his shoulder. Hard to forget those lessons.

He dropped the sashes in the aquarium and strode toward the hall, not stopping until he heard muffled sniffles through the bathroom door. He braced an arm on the wall beside it.

Could he be the kind of guy who apologized? How about the guy who walked her mail down the driveway?

He pulled a toothpick from its holder in his pocket and stared at the white cotton of his socked feet. The heavy thump of his heart felt way too foreboding.

Thump noted and rejected. He slid the pick between his lips. Her sniveling didn't affect him. Nope. He backed away from the bathroom door, pretending he didn't feel the thump growing harder and faster with each step.

He wasn't her guy, and he sure as fuck didn't need more scars.

At the front door, he slipped on his sneakers and shifted the hood over his head.

He most definitely wasn't Zachary Kaufman, and the fuckwad would be back in three days to honor his Tuesday/Friday tradition.

Could her shipments wait until then? Would she attempt to walk them out that night? What if she had a seizure on the way?

He pressed his gloved fingers against his eyes. Not his goddamned problem. He opened the door and gripped it, fighting not to close it and return to her. Instead, he stepped beneath the somberness of a sleepy sky and slammed the door behind him with enough rattle to reach the bathroom.

The slam of the front door lurched Amber's stomach into a fit of cramps. Van was gone. *Gone.*

She dropped before the toilet and hung her head. Her mouth swelled with a burst of saliva, and she dry-heaved until her throat was raw. But the pain was nothing compared to the hot stabs of self-loathing perforating her insides.

What did she expect? She'd strutted her crazy all over the house and thought he'd hang around and maybe have sex with her? No shit, she'd overestimated her worth. Though, to be fair, he'd been the first man to reject her offer.

This was her fault. She hadn't even tried to seduce him. She should've said something sexy, maybe flashed a nipple. A man like Van could have any woman he wanted. He wouldn't have just shoved her on the bed and fucked her because she wore a skimpy dress.

A strand of hair fell in her face, and she shoved it away. She used to turn heads once without even trying, but that was *then.* She'd lost her edge. Beauty faded, and certainly being shut in and crazy for two years had sped that along.

And now she faced an impossible trip to the mailbox. *Thumbs up, Amber. Job well done.*

Her chin quivered. *Pathetic crybaby.* She locked her jaw, pushed away from the toilet, and sat on her heels. Beside her, the shower plinked a steady drip, a reminder that it would be several more months before she could afford to repair it.

It took four attempts to stand, and when she finished brushing her teeth, her heart rate rallied, ready to panic all over again.

Fuck that. She breathed deeply, engaging her abs, and forced her feet to move to the front door. Her head swam with dizziness, and by the time she locked the deadbolt four times, the heave of her lungs had elevated into hyperventilation.

Stop it. She could peek out the window and make sure he wasn't on the porch.

She sucked in, sharply. No, she couldn't. Looking outside was a surefire way to make this night worse. Besides, there was no way he stuck around.

She stomped to the kitchen, slamming her heels four times on the wood floor to drown out her gasping breaths. That man had been intrusive, rude, dangerous...sexy as fuck. His departure was a blessing. She grabbed a beer from the fridge. The first sip burned the cuts his teeth had left on her lips.

Oh God, that kiss. Her taste buds tingled, not from the hops but from the remembered pleasure of his skillful tongue, the bite of tequila on his breath, and the spicy flavor that seemed to be inherently him. A taste she would never experience again.

Good riddance. She tipped back the bitter ale, hellbent on creating a new night through alcoholic osmosis. In a few days, she would be contemplating her life while sitting in the dark without water or electricity. Because she wouldn't be going to the mailbox. Not tonight. Not ever again.

Might as well drink the beer while it was still cold. She dropped the empty bottle in the trash and grabbed another. "Fucking sucks." She sucked. Shallow bastards with silver eyes sucked. She slumped onto the kitchen stool, hung her head over the counter, and cursed her sucky self and the sucky bastard who had just ran far, far away.

A six-pack later, she'd vacuumed out the footprints in the bedroom carpet, packaged up the sheaths, printed the postage labels, and barfed as much of the caloric beer as her stomach was willing to release. Then she spent the next hour engaged in a standoff with the front door.

"This is all your fault." She struck the wood panel, and her palm landed like a sloppy slap. "If you weren't in my way, I'd be out there right now shipping my shit."

It was a lie, but the door didn't know that. It just stood there like an unfeeling asshole.

"Ever heard of a sledgehammer?" she yelled then burped and laughed hysterically. "That's right, motherfucker. All I have to do is smash your hinges, and you won't even be able to stand." Momentarily distracted by the jumping sensation of her hiccup, she touched her chest and swayed not-so beauty-pageant–*hic*—ably in her heels.

Now what was she doing? Oh right. She lunged for the door, determined to open it, just drunk enough to not give a damn. She wobbled as her hand touched the knob and jumped back, dizzy and confused.

"You're nothing. You hear me?" She thrust out a finger at the deadbolt to punctuate her point.

What was her point again? Jesus, her brain felt heavy as she watched the slow, mesmerizing movements of her arms. She tossed them in the air and stumbled. Whoa, the floor was rocking. Earthquake in Texas? Nah, it was just a blowout of pent-up funk along her psychotic fault lines and stuff. She laughed, bent-over, snorting, though she couldn't recall what was so damned funny.

Probably a good time to call it a night. With a middle finger aimed at the door, she grabbed the bottle of tequila from the kitchen and climbed into bed. Tequila made the tongue taste delicious, especially when it belonged to sinful lips and sharp teeth. She unscrewed the lid and drank. And drank. Until she couldn't remember why she didn't do this every night.

The next morning, she woke with a second heartbeat pulsating behind her eyes and the hot burn of tequila-laced vapors in her throat. At some point during the night, her mouth had forgotten how to produce saliva, and her tongue had withered into a suffocating gag of sandpaper.

Then she remembered the prick who had the nerve to be offended by her proposal. And the fact that she deserved it. Death sounded like a great plan for the day. His. Hers. Definitely his.

She tried to raise her head, and a starburst of pain stole her vision. Not happening. She rolled to her side and her cheek landed in a puddle of drool on the pillow. Not just slobber but the vomit-scented variety that sent her stomach contracting to the tune of *curl up and die.*

What a miserable thing she'd become. A victim of her own destruction. But self-indulgent pity did little more than exaggerate excuses. True comfort came from order and routine. She glanced at the clock.

Oh, no, no, no. She was late. The pounding in her head exploded, and her hands started shaking. Hangover be damned, she needed to get her ass up.

She pushed with weak arms to a sitting position and waited for the queasiness to pass. The bedside lamp was still on, its light intensifying the headache. She swung her legs over the side of the mattress and stopped breathing. Footprints indented the carpet from the bed to the door. Man-sized tracks. But she'd vacuumed sometime between the sixth beer and the tequila chaser. Or were the fumes in her head making up memories?

A terrifying thought hurdled her stomach to her throat. She stumbled from the bed and ran to the front door, clutching her churning belly.

She wiggled the door handle, and the deadbolt held as it should have. She knew she'd locked it before she'd destroyed all her brain cells. Glancing around, nothing seemed out of order, until her attention narrowed on the books.

Oh God, the titles were rotated and no longer alphabetized by author. The lines weren't there, the spines zig-zagging along the shelves. Her hands clenched and unclenched, and her skin swelled so hot, she was surprised it didn't catch fire. The meddling dick!

She scrambled to the shelves, breathing from her diaphragm. Terrible, unimaginable chaos invaded her head when the lines weren't straight and things weren't grouped as they should be. Sweet mother, she'd slept all night while the spines lay in a shuffled, incongruent mess.

Her hands flew through the books, fixing and straightening. Why had she let him anywhere in the house alone? She hadn't even looked at the shelves when he'd left. How could she have been so sidetracked?

Halfway through reordering the novels, her mind wandered back to the footprints in the carpet. When did those happen? Surely, he hadn't messed with any of the other locks while he'd been there and come back after she'd passed out? Her fingers turned cold, and an ache ballooned in the back of her throat.

Heart racing, she sprinted through the house and checked the windows and the rear sliding door. With a trembling hand behind each and every drape, she confirmed they were all locked. She buckled over the kitchen counter, her skin clammy. Jesus, that little freak-out had not helped her nausea.

She gulped down a large glass of water. Then she returned to the shelves, sagged onto her knees, and straightened the self-help books. He knew she was fucked up. Of course, he wouldn't return to mess up her carpet. She wasn't worth the trouble. She must've left the footprints in a drunken sleepwalk.

Never again. No more drinking. No more muscled men with alluring scars and invasive questions. And no more acts of desperation.

The clocks on the wall read 9:54 AM. Her daily routine was one hour and fifty minutes behind schedule. She'd just have to start in ten minutes and skip the two hours of baseboard scrubbing and furniture polishing to reset the clock. Her pulse elevated at the notion, but she would survive this. She had to. Soon, she would be back on schedule and realigning her world.

10:04 AM: She vacuumed, mopped the floors, and washed the bedding.

12:04 PM: She ran four miles on the treadmill, sweating tequila and hops from her pores.

1:04 PM: She ate lunch—a baloney sandwich and four pickle slices. Just like every Sunday. Twenty minutes later, her stomach felt grossly distended. She purged the sandwich.

1:34 PM: She lifted weights—back and biceps on Sunday and Wednesday.

2:04 PM: She worked on her remaining leathercraft orders.

Eight hours later, she finished the carvings on two belts, three wallets, and tied off the last stitch on a sweet throw pillow made from the recycled leather of men's worn loafers.

At 10:04 PM, she slumped onto the couch with her laptop, fresh from a shower and dressed in a tank top and boy shorts. The straight lines and symmetrical flawlessness of the sitting room soothed her heart rate, even as she probed every detail for an imperfect tilt or wrinkle. She exhaled a heavy sigh and relaxed against the cushions. Her world felt pretty damned realigned.

She hadn't thought of him or her overdue bills once in twelve hours. So she didn't feel too obsessive when she logged into an online agoraphobics group and searched the discussions on *I told him to leave when he found out about my disorder.* Zero results returned.

Not surprised, she tried, *He won't sleep with me.* Zero results returned.

Her face heated. "Bullshit." She bit her lip and typed, *He thinks I'm nuts.* Thirty-three pages of results, but none of the discussions applied to her situation.

Had she overreacted when she found him reading her self-help books? She sniffed and rolled her shoulders. Didn't matter. He left anyway. She closed the laptop and leaned back. It was for the best.

Except she couldn't distract her mind from the prior night, reliving the strength of his arms around her, the spicy scent of his breath, the pressure of his mouth against her lips, and the way he owned her with a flick of his tongue.

She tried not to listen to the silent slither of loneliness as it snaked its way around her. Tried not to analyze why she felt colder and more hollow tonight than any other night. Tried not think about how much she missed the intoxicating warmth of a man sleeping beside her, skin on skin, even if that memory had been created and destroyed by Brent.

None of that solved her financial problems. If she could ship her completed sales by Tuesday, maybe she'd only be without water and electricity for a few days.

She grabbed her cell phone and opened a text to contact Zach. They never communicated this way, and she waffled with how to start the conversation. She went with courtesy. *Are you feeling better?*

Thirty seconds later, he replied,*yes will b there tues.*

Her heart soared then plummeted. Would he still want sex or had she scared him away from that? She imagined his lips on hers, and the remembered sensation suddenly seemed...uncertain. Maybe, he'd kissed her weakly because he didn't want to kiss her at all. A swallow lodged in her throat. She was flawed, after all.

After Van's repulsion to her offer for sex, she felt used and unclean. She cracked her knuckles not really feeling them. Her insides twisted in knots. Sleeping with Zach had lost its appeal, but she had nothing else to offer him.

She wouldn't be so dependent if she'd gone to the mailbox while soaring on liquid courage. But no amount of tequila would help her conquer the fear. She didn't want to conquer it, because she needed it, the adrenaline rush and the lung-squeezing pain. Like an addiction, the fear fed her, made her feel alive, and gave her something to focus on. She was so messed up.

The phone dinged with a new text. *will u keep the lights on this time?*

An onslaught of trembling tightened her muscles. If she said *Yes*, it would be a new low in her desperation. If she said *No*, she would lose the one person she had to depend on.

Is this the man you want the lights on with?

Unbidden, Dr. Michael's words filled her mind with another man, one with a seductive smile and a perfect scar.

With visions of a sleeping Amber teasing the surface of his mind, Van pushed the key into the deadbolt on her front door. The key he'd swiped from her kitchen drawer the prior night *after* he'd sneaked back in.

He'd tried to stay away, but it was a compulsion. Coming to this neighborhood. Watching Liv. And now, he had an even more compelling motive to *stop by.*

Strange how Amber hadn't moved the drape on the door and checked the lock before her alcohol-induced haze. He knew this because he'd used that unlocked door to slip back in after she'd passed out. Apparently, the agoraphobia thing had a stronger hold on her than the OCD. If not the agoraphobia, then it had to have been *him* knocking the little compulsive-order-checker off her game.

Whatever the reason, it worked in his favor. He'd crept back in after she'd passed out, locked it behind him, and quickly located a house key.

His pulse thrummed a calming tempo as he closed the front door soundlessly behind him. Just like the night before, he'd listened through her windows with the mics and ear buds, tracking her movements and waiting for her breathing to fall into an even rhythm of sleep.

A grin stretched his lips as he recalled her slurred monologues. She'd been wildly entertaining. Even more satisfying was knowing *he* had driven her to drink. Because let's be honest, she was entirely too uptight to drink for no good reason. So when he'd found her snoring with a bottle of mixto tucked beneath her arm, he'd left tracks in the carpet just to mess with her little hungover mind.

Tonight, she'd fallen asleep sober. Tonight, he would be more cautious. Besides, he was only there to run reconnaissance and return the key—now that he had his own copy.

He wore his quiet-soled sneakers, which dampened his footfalls as he crept through the house. In the kitchen, he placed the key in the kitchen drawer, rotating it to lie exactly how he'd found it.

He entered the hall, his path illuminated by the lamp in her bedroom. There was a chance she might've woken in the short time that had passed since he left her window, but it was worth the risk. He needed to see her, to attach her tangible body to the fantasies he'd been envisioning all day.

A sudden realization halted him midway down the hall. He'd taken the same backyard stroll that night he'd taken every night for the past six months, yet he hadn't even considered setting up the mics on Liv's windows. He pushed a gloved hand through his hair and stared at the light from her bedroom, watching for a flicker of movement.

Amber was a conundrum of distraction. In one night, she'd managed to divert his obsession from Liv. For the first time in eight years, he'd woken without the burning need to beat and fuck his former slave. But Liv was a crucial component in obtaining his daughter. Monitoring her conversations with the slaves she'd released would eventually reveal if Liv had any cartel or FBI connections and if she could use them to stop him in his pursuit of his daughter.

Heavy pressure pushed against his chest. He fumbled through the pocket of his hoodie and pulled out a toothpick, certain he should walk away from Amber and utterly perplexed by the fact he wouldn't.

He'd spent the past ten hours investigating the fascinating beauty queen on the Internet. He was already in too deep, his focus unwaveringly set on the outcome. Especially when he reached her bedroom and took in the view.

Long, blond hair spread out in waves around her head. She lay on her side, facing the door, her tiny hands curled beneath her chin. A thin sheet draped the curves of her thigh and hip, stopping just below her bare shoulder. Christ almighty, was that firm ass accessibly bare beneath the sheet? Would her cunt feel as tight as the rest of her?

His mouth dried, and he licked his lips around the toothpick. There were more important things to investigate before he could even think about taking her, namely Zachary Kaufman.

He couldn't, he shouldn't, but he approached her anyway. Despite the blood rushing to his dick, he lengthened his gait, patiently and carefully, as to not disturb too many carpet fibers.

Three long strides brought him to her side. His arm moved before his brain could argue, his finger hooking the edge of the sheet between her tits and moving it down, down, slowly, until her pinkish-brown nipples appeared.

He snapped his gaping jaw shut and inhaled quietly through his nose. Fucking breathtaking. She certainly hadn't struck him as the kind of woman to sleep naked. Amber was a little hidden world of seductive surprises.

Her eyes shifted behind her lids but remained closed, her dark lashes fanning over her delicate cheekbones. Jesus, she was a heavy sleeper. He glanced at the bedside table and spotted a bottle of sleeping pills.

He squatted, chin level with the mattress, and lowered the sheet to the flat expanse of her belly. Little dips and cut edges defined her feminine abs, framed by the soft curves of her hip, waist, and tits. He leaned in, his knees loose and growing weak. Just a few more seconds of looking, then he'd finish what he came to do.

Her breasts were huge, round, and definitely not real. The faded scars beneath her nipples confirmed his suspicion. Maybe implants had given her an edge in her modeling career, but she wouldn't have needed them. Her natural attributes were enough to make him come in his pants, her raw beauty superior to every woman he'd ever laid eyes on.

Schooling his breaths, he slipped the sheet past her shaved mound and clamped his teeth on the toothpick. His heart swooshed in his ears, and his body heated.

Her thighs were pressed together, giving him a tiny peek of her cleft. He angled his head, his face and fingers hovering over her shadowed pussy. The sweet scent of oranges and flowers bathed his nose. Fuck, he wanted to shove his fingers inside as much as he wanted to roll her over and bury his cock in her soul.

With a great amount of willpower, he returned the sheet and stood. *Soon, Amber Rosenfeld.*

Stepping back on the tracks he'd left on the way in, he balanced awkwardly and brushed up the smashed carpet with curled fingers as he crept backward toward the door.

Two more days. Until Zachary Kaufman's scheduled visit. Until she was all his.

On his way to the kitchen, he stopped in the bathroom and checked the medicine cabinet, the drawers, and under the sink. The sight of the condoms made his blood boil.

The toiletries were grouped in fours, labels aligned. Not a pill bottle in sight.

His research on agoraphobia had come up with a plethora of anti-depressants to numb the disorder, but the recommendation for treatment was consistent. She needed exposure.

He breathed deeply, letting loose a smile. Yeah, he'd expose her, all right.

The prior night, he'd verified she didn't have a landline phone. Now, he found her cell on the charger in the kitchen, and worked the stylus from the case with a gloved finger. A couple taps showed there had been no calls or texts since he'd checked the night before. In fact, the log's six-month history only showed two contacts. One was a Dr. Emery Michaels, whom she hadn't spoken with in five days.

The other was Zachary. His last text—*will u keep the lights on this time?*—induced the same bloodthirsty, muscle-tightening reaction he'd had the first time he saw it. His vision blurred and the phone case groaned in his clenched fist. He set it down and strode to the front door with determined steps.

By this time tomorrow, he would be quite intimate with the fuck digger.

The next night, Van drummed his fingers on the steering wheel in the *Saddler's Tool Company* parking lot, listening to "Stay Wide Awake" by *Eminem* and waiting for Zachary McToolLess to leave work.

His jaw ached from clenching, and his muscles were stiff from his shoulders to his ass. Where the fuck was his target? The store had closed a fucking hour ago.

He squinted through the dark empty lot and reached for the camera on the seat beside him. Flipping through the photos, he paused on the shots he'd snapped at the schoolyard that morning. Long brown hair, angelic face, and a glowing smile, Livana looked so much like Liv it made his chest hurt. But as he studied a close-up of her features, he recognized his own thick eyelashes fringing her brown eyes and the exact shape of his lips outlining her grin. He closed his eyes and tipped his head back.

Now seven-years-old, she was safe and cared for by Mr. E's widow, the woman who had raised her. But nothing compared to a father's love and protection. He'd never had that, and he'd be damned if his daughter grew up without it. She needed him as much as he needed her, but she was ferociously guarded by Liv and her circle of freed slaves. He knew Liv would never allow him even a brief encounter. Unless he could convince her.

Ten minutes later, a pickup appeared from behind the building and took off in the opposite direction. It was the same truck he'd seen parked in Amber's driveway while scoping Liv's house.

His heart rate elevated. He threw the Mustang in drive and followed at an unassuming distance. Fifteen miles brought them into the heart of Austin's entertainment district, surrounded by historic buildings, old-fashioned neon signs, and live music.

Was her fucktoy headed for a bar? If so, he'd soon have a new drinking buddy.

Monday night traffic was predictably sparse. Zachary parked beside a little bar off Sixth Street called *Cyanide* and went inside with a prissy little hop in his step.

Okay, maybe he'd imagined the hop, but fuck if he couldn't see how Amber let that skinny rodent put his dick in her. He pressed a fist against the burning sensation in his chest and parked in a nearby lot. When his blood pressure cooled to normal, he locked up and strolled to the bar.

The sky was dark, but the interior of *Cyanide* was darker. Soft electronic beats and a thin crowd set a casual ambiance. He wove around the high-tops and winked at a gaggle of college girls who openly stared at him with *we're-dumb-and-in-heat* googley eyes.

Van's white button-down shirt opened at the collar, and his crisp, dark jeans rode low on his hips. Not his usual attire, but he was dressed to kill.

He found his target straddling a stool at the bar and chugging a domestic beer—*alone*. He approached, thumped the counter, and nodded at the silver-haired bartender. "Three shots of tequila. Neat, not chilled."

When the old geezer reached for *Jose Cuervo*, he growled. "No, man. I said *tequila*." Fucking Americans. "If it doesn't say one-hundred percent agave, it's not tequila." He scanned the top shelf and pointed at the bottle of *Real Gusto*. "That one."

As the bartender poured the shots, Van grabbed a stool two down from Zachary without acknowledging him. A few minutes later, he splashed the first shot down his gullet, relishing the smooth, complex flavor. Then he leaned back and waited.

It didn't take five minutes before the first bitch approached Van.

"Hey, there." She cocked a round hip against his knee. "The girls and I voted." She flicked her claws at a table of giddy women in the corner. "You are by and far the sexiest man in three counties." Her gaze landed on the scar on his cheek and skittered away.

When her eyes returned—they always did—he made a show of checking her out, from the fake-baked tits to the sparkled heels, and moved his leg away from her hip. "Not interested, honey."

She huffed. "You're no fun."

He held his mouth in a flat line of no-fun and didn't blink.

She picked at a plastic fingernail, lingering two seconds too long, and strode away.

Five women and five rejections later, the cock stuffer beside him finally spoke. "You...uh...gay or something?"

Van threw back the second shot to smother the raging words burning up his throat. Fucking twat. Yeah, he fucked men. For his one-night delights, all he required was a submissive body and a clean hole. So what? He also made dolls with the same hands he fingered assholes with. If any of that made him gay, then he'd take it up the ass all the way to hell.

No, that wasn't true. He hadn't endured it that way since he left the ghetto. Now that he was free of his mother's drug-dealing bottom-feeders, he was the one who did the fucking.

Tilting his head, he looked directly at Zachary for the first time. Those twinkling, beady blue eyes made him want to gouge them out and pop them between his curled fingers. "Just want the right girl, man." The girl Zachary Kaufman would never fuck again.

The beady eyes blinked. "Damn, dude. All those women you turned down seemed pretty fucking *right* to me."

He lifted a shoulder. "I want a gorgeous girl with spirit, know what I mean? Quick wit, blond hair, brown eyes, big tits, and lots of personality." He rubbed a finger on the counter, delivering the spiel with a monotone, down-on-his-luck kind of vibe. "You know, someone...unusual. Special. With crazy little quirks and stuff."

A laugh choked in Zachary's throat, and he shook his head. "Boy, do I have a *special* girl with quirks."

Bastard didn't have shit. He covered his scowl with the third shot, slammed it down, and tempered his tone. "Oh yeah?"

"Yeah. She's got my damned head reeling nonstop. It's messed up, but I keep going back for more."

Motherfuck, he didn't want to hear this, but he needed to know the depth of Zachary's attachment. Killing him would be gratifying. And messy. But that wasn't his style. Manipulating him was the smart play.

Van bounced his eyebrows, and his insides twisted with nausea. "She hot?"

A smile took hold of Zachary's face, toothy and weasel-like. "Tits out to here." He cupped the air in front of him as if juggling watermelons like a goddamned retard. "Pretty face. Tight little pussy."

Van's vision clouded in red, the blood in his veins boiling to burst. Zachary was a dead man. He slapped a hand on the counter. "Another shot, and hurry the fuck up, old man."

The tool on the stool must have mistaken his rage for excitement. He let out an ear-splitting cackle. "Thing is, dude, she's got serious issues. Talk about quirks. I don't think she leaves the house much. She won't let me fuck her with the lights on. Been doing her for six months. Always at her place. I still haven't seen her naked."

Six months and the ass didn't know she was agoraphobic. The shot slid in front of Van, and he tossed it back, swallowing down images of Zachary *doing* her. His stomach hardened, and his breaths pushed out so fast and coarse. No way would he be able to speak without roaring.

Goddammit, he could handle this conversation. This was his fucking forte. Control and coercion without physical force. Hell, he'd spent weeks drinking with the drug-dealing slime who'd lived with Kate, the last girl he'd taken for Mr. E. Her brothers might've protected her virginity, but their drunken, wagging tongues had lost her in the end. He liked to think he'd saved that girl, seeing how he'd freed her from her brothers' crack-house and Liv had freed her from Mr. E's trafficking.

Zachary nursed his beer, all quiet and thoughtful, as he pushed his hair away from his puckered eyebrows. When he opened his mouth, he seemed to be talking to himself. "I have to go to her house at a set time on the same days. Thirty seconds early or late, and she freaks the fuck out." He swiped at his hair. "But there I am, syncing my clocks to hers and showing up *right on time*."

This wasn't like the other captures. Amber wasn't going to a slave buyer. She was...unique and fascinatingly crazy. And she was *his*. Hell, he'd take her even if the sole purpose was to make sure she wasn't Zachary's—which it wasn't. But the moron didn't deserve her. Of course, neither did he.

He set the empty shot glass down and plucked a toothpick from a container on the bar. He'd only killed two people in his life. Shooting the wife of Liv's rapist had just been a means to torture the monster before killing him, too.

Zachary wasn't a rapist. He was just a ball-less queef in the fucking way.

He shifted to face the queef. "She the only pussy you're banging?

"Yeah, why?"

He thrust his chin at a flock of ladies who had just walked in. "Want to stick your dick in a real woman? With the lights on?"

Zachary's dark eyebrows rose beneath the falling strands of his hair. "Seriously?"

What a cunt. "Follow my lead." He pivoted on the stool toward the women and let his thighs fall subtly apart, knowing the stretch in his jeans cupped his junk just right. He leaned his elbows on the bar top behind him and gnawed on the toothpick.

Four pairs of eyes looked his way. He blanked his expression in a portrait of indifference, his eyes roaming the group as a whole with little commitment.

Like a pack of hungry Chihuahuas, they scampered as one in his direction. A stagger of *Hi's* came next, followed by flushed cheeks, cleared throats, and smoldering stares.

Time to put them out of their misery. "I'm gay."

A chorus of whiny *Oooooh's* blubbered out.

He chuckled. "I know the feeling. This guy here" —he squeezed Zachary's neck, probably with more force than was necessary— "turned me down. I saw his cock in the men's room. Un-fucking-real, ladies. Have fun with it." He dropped a wad of cash on the counter, patted Zachary on the back, and gamboled to the door.

He moved the Mustang a few parking spots down from Zachary's truck and set up his camera. Forty-five minutes later, the two-timing prick strolled out of the bar with one of the girls under his arm and his tongue down her throat. Took the fucker long enough to snag a girl.

Camera raised, Van clicked away from his shadowed position in the Mustang. Zachary pressed her against the passenger door of the truck, one hand fumbling for his keys, the other shoved up her skirt.

Click. Click. Click.

Van's lungs expanded to their fullest with each deep, satisfied breath. Damn straight, he was smug. Not only did he restrain himself from gutting the guy, but also he did Amber a favor. She might not have cared who Zachary was fucking—especially given her willingness to fuck *him* a couple days ago—but he'd read agoraphobics didn't just cling to their homes. They attached themselves to people, too. At the moment, there was only one person she could've been attached to.

Zachary pushed the girl onto her back across the truck's seat. Without bothering to close the door, he proceeded to eat her face then her cunt beneath the glow of the streetlight.

After a few more clicks, Van set the camera down and lit a cigarette. Tomorrow, Amber wouldn't have a choice when she cut ties with Zachary Kaufman. But he needed her to be convincing when she did it.

Ordering groceries online was a Tuesday morning task, an item to check off a list. But as Amber squinted at her online bank account balance, she knew her routine was about to change. A tic twitched in her eyelid. Everything her sanity depended on required electricity or water. The vacuum, treadmill, shower, laundry, online groups...

She tucked her hands beneath her armpits and hugged herself, burrowing into the couch as the weight of her situation pushed air from her chest.

This fear was different from what she was used to. When she'd stepped outside, the paralysis, suffocation, and loss of body control was a physical, heart-rate-in-the-red-zone kind of fear. But the horror of losing her connectedness—to her house, her schedule, her courier and lover—made her feel breathless, empty, and lost, like a non-person.

Who would she be without order and routine? If not a beauty contestant or a neat freak, then what? A hollow husk in a padded room like her mother?

But the most tangible threat was losing her house. Foreclosure meant she would have to leave. She'd have to go *outside*. She'd rather die.

She closed the laptop. She didn't need groceries anyway. There would be no cooking and no refrigeration when the electricity shut off. The city had already turned off her water service that morning.

The clocks on the wall told her she had fifteen minutes before Zach's arrival. He would ship all her packages and, in a few days, she'd receive her payments and get the utilities back on. Until next month.

She stared at nothing for a long moment, searching inside herself for an answer, a reaction, something, but all she found was the absence of value and meaning.

She set her phone and laptop on the coffee table, lining them up in right-angles, and trudged toward the hall to prepare for Zach. As she reached the bedroom doorway, the hairs on her nape lifted. She paused. Something felt...off.

A click echoed from the front room, followed by a creak in the floor. A shriek crawled up her throat, and she snapped her mouth shut, listening without breathing, heart thundering. Was someone in the house? How was that possible?

A few silent seconds passed as she trembled in a gridlock of clenched muscles and stifled breaths. She should've heard a crash if someone had broken in. She gripped the doorframe to her room, her legs shaking to run, her brain telling her not to make a sound.

The stillness of the house gathered around her, squeezing her chest and slowly, maddeningly, dispersing with her exhale. Was she paranoid now? Fabricating new horrors in her head?

Then she heard it. The soft rasp of socked feet on hardwood, approaching, gaining speed. Time seemed to slam to a halt as her body moved to escape and her eyes swung over her shoulder.

A man stood in the mouth of the hall, with broad shoulders, a baseball cap, a scar on his cheek, and a gun in his hand.

Why was Van in her house, pointing a gun? The shock of it rendered her speechless.

"You won't run." His voice was soft and casual, exactly the way she remembered it. But his outstretched arm aimed the gun at her head, a gloved finger beside the trigger. A tablet dangled in his other gloved hand, and her phone was wedged beneath the buckle of his jeans.

She stood half-in, half-out of the bedroom, her blood pressure rising with every second that passed. Ten feet separated them. How good was his aim? If she ducked into the room, she could escape through the window. *Outside.* OhGodohGodohGod. She couldn't swallow, couldn't breathe.

"I'll shoot through your door before you make it to the window." His lips slid into a terrifying smile. "And we both know you'll have a panic attack the moment you lift the shade."

Hard to argue, but the fact that he knew what crippled her surged anger through her veins, heating her skin and garbling her words. "What do you want?"

"We'll get to that. Stand in the center of the hall with your arms at your sides."

The audacious command made her skin crawl. Worse, she hadn't finished dressing because she didn't want to wrinkle her dress for Zach. The only clothing she wore were white lacy panties and a midriff cami. "Let me grab a robe." And something sharp to stab him with.

"I won't repeat myself." The eerie calm in his voice crept through the narrow space, stealing the strength from her knees. Not a hint of humor surfaced in the rigid lines of his face. He wasn't fucking around.

Maybe he wouldn't shoot her, but he knew about the agoraphobia. If she angered him, would he force her outside?

She shifted into the hall, fighting to keep her hands at her sides as the intensity of his gaze raked her legs, her panties, and lingered on her nipples pressing against the cotton.

He met her eyes. "You have three seconds to tell me how you greet Zachary Kaufman at the door."

The blood drained from her cheeks, and a shiver raced over her spine. "What are you—?"

"Two seconds."

"I don't—"

"One second."

"I unlock the door and wait in the bedroom," she said in a rushed breath. "Please, don't hurt him." Even if she wasn't emotionally attached to Zach, she didn't want to see him harmed.

He prowled toward her with the gun leveled at her chest. Her pulse hammered in her ears, and her neck strained with tension, but she kept her chin up and eyes full of *fuck you.*

A foot away, he stopped and pressed the barrel of the gun against her breastbone, his eyes fixed on her breasts. The cold metal slid down the center of her chest, taking the thin cotton with it, until the neckline reached her nipples. He leaned in, his timbre low and authoritative. "Walk into your room and sit on the bed."

Her body quivered against that voice, itching to obey. But the glow of his silver eyes rooted her to the floor, chilling her with the ferocity that hardened their depths.

She looked away, clenching her hands at her sides and popping the finger joints with her thumbs.

"Now!" he shouted.

She jumped, gasping for air and stumbling toward the room. He followed her in, and when she sat on the bed, he shoved the tablet under her nose.

She didn't look at it, couldn't drag her eyes from the man who towered over her. Thick, dark energy hummed around him, and he oozed malicious, predatory power from his pores. Not wild or manic, not throwing fists or flinging spit. It was calculating, in control, warning her.

With her arms wrapped around her chest and hips, she glared into his eyes, shivering against their sharp animalistic beauty. Maybe if she said his name, it would remind him he was human. "Van, are you going to make me go outside?"

The only thing that moved was his lips. "Look at the screen and swipe through the photos."

Maybe he'd lied about his name. She glanced down, and her brow furrowed as she took in the image. It showed Zach in a parking lot with his hand beneath a brunette's skirt. She blinked rapidly, startled, confused, and shook her head. "How did you—"

"Flip to the next one."

Her mind raced as she swiped the screen with a numb finger. The girl was on her back in the truck with Zach's shaggy head between her spread thighs.

Nausea twisted her stomach as she swiped again. Same scene, same girl, Zach's hips now wedged between her legs, his pants stretched beneath his bare ass. Amber's body temperature skyrocketed, and her chest tightened. What did this mean to Van? Why would he show her this? "How do you know him?"

"I met this guy in a bar on Sixth Street last night. He told me he was fucking a whack job named Amber on Tuesdays and Fridays, and he wanted to stick his dick in a real woman."

Her hands locked into fists. He could've been making that up.

He tucked the tablet beneath his arm. "With the lights on."

Her stomach dropped, and an ache swelled, angry and painful, around her heart. "So you thought you'd...what? Enlighten me? While waving a fucking gun?" It was too much, too many surprises coming at her too damned fast. "Well, guess what? I *am* a whack job, and he can fuck whom he wants. Why do *you* care?"

His pupils flared, swallowing the silver rims of his eyes. "He's due at noon? Yes or no."

Son of a bitch. "No. Twelve-o-*four*."

He glanced at the side table, and she followed his gaze. 11:58 glowed on the clock.

No way did he just happen upon Zach at a bar after he *just happened* upon her porch. She gritted her teeth. "How long have you been watching my house?" And how the hell did he get in? "Oh my God. You stole my key? You arrogant, thieving dickhead!"

"Be careful, Amber." His icy glare raised bumps over her skin. "Cover yourself up." He waved a hand at the closet. "You have thirty seconds."

Of all the women in Austin, why her? If he knew her schedule, maybe he'd figured out Zach was the only person who would notice if she disappeared. Hell, he had her phone. If he'd looked at the log, he'd know she talked to no one, had no one.

She strode to the closet, trying like hell to keep her shaking arms over her thinly-covered boobs. "What are you going to do to him?"

"If you ask another question, I'll kill him, slow and messy, all over your carpet."

Her mind played out that scenario in Technicolor, and her thoughts degraded to a sick, selfish place where her disorder bred and thrived. The damage to her carpet would be permanent, a constant reminder, and she couldn't afford to replace it.

"If you convincingly chase him away, I'll let him live." He glared at her, his lips pressed in a line. "And I do mean convincingly. The fucker better walk out of here without a doubt in his mind he'll never see you again. I just gave you the ammo to do it. Use it. Fifteen seconds."

She dressed in a hurried daze, fumbling on jeans and tugging a t-shirt over the cami. This wasn't happening. If she chased Zach away, how long would it be before someone found her body? Or worse, found her house empty?

Would he try to kidnap her? Her skin grew clammy, and a tremor shook her legs. "I can't go outside. You'll have to shoot me first." Either way, she wouldn't survive.

"I'll be right in here." He stalked to the closet and gripped the door, with the gun trained on her. "If you fuck this up, if Zachary shows a hint of suspicion, I'll shoot him. Sit on the bed."

How had she not seen this coming when she met him? She'd let this man into her house, for fucksake. Such a stupid, stupid girl. She deserved this. She wiped at the copious sweat clinging to her face and arms, her ramping heart rate thrashing pinpricks through her head.

Breathing deeply, over and over, she sat on the bed and prepared to drive away the only person she had in her life.

Van faded within the shadow of the closet, leaving the door open a sliver, with a line of sight directly on her.

Six huge breaths later, the rumble of Zach's truck sounded in the driveway. Her heart hammered so painfully, she wanted to double over from the agony of it. She could do this. Her odds of surviving sucked, but she could save Zach.

The front door opened and rattled shut. Van must've left it unlocked, already knowing her routine. Knowing too much. She didn't dare look at the closet door for fear she'd unravel into a worthless blob of panic.

Footsteps pounded down the hall, and Zach's tall, thin frame appeared in the doorway. Images of him with that girl girded her spine, even as a lump clogged her throat. It wasn't jealousy. It was the strangling reminder that she hadn't been good enough.

He smiled. "Jeans today? Didn't know you owned a pair."

This was going to hurt. She swallowed. *Just do it quick.* "We're done, Zach. No more deliveries. No more sex." Her voice wobbled, dammit.

He narrowed his eyes and pushed a hand through his chin-length hair, gripping it at the back of his head. "What...what do you mean?"

She drew a deep breath and sat taller. "I saw you last night."

He flinched, and his arm flopped to his side. Then he squared his shoulders and started toward her.

"No. Stay where you are." *Get him out of there. Get him safe.* She hardened her eyes and her voice. "I said we're done."

"How—" His eyes widened. "You left the house?"

Dammit, of course not. But he wasn't as perceptive as the prick in the closet. "I saw you with a girl at a bar on Sixth Street. I want you gone. Don't call. Don't come by. I'm taking my business elsewhere."

"Hey, no. Just wait a second." His eyes pleaded, and he swiped a hand over his face. "I can explain."

When he started forward again, she held up a palm. "Don't come any closer." Sweet God, the tension in the room made it impossible to breathe. "If you try to contact me, I'll file a restraining order." *I'm saving your life.* "Now, leave."

"Jesus, a restraining order? On what grounds?" His voice was thready, and his shoulders slumped. "Amber, she meant nothing. It was a mistake."

"I'll tell them you raped me." She cringed inwardly, her insides threatening to heave. "I still have your semen on my sheets. They'll believe me." If Zach knew her at all, he'd call her out on her cleanliness. But he'd never paid attention to her neurosis, which was what she'd liked most about him. She rose and thrust a finger in the vicinity of the front door. "Get. The fuck. Out."

His jaw clenched, and his blue eyes turned to glass, losing focus. He nodded a few times, staring at the floor. Then he smacked a hand against the door, knocking it into the wall. "Crazy bitch." He turned and stomped down the hall. A moment later, the front door slammed.

The truck rumbled through the walls then faded into the distance. Gone. She was officially on her own. And her packages weren't mailed. She released a ragged breath, her eyes burning with tears she refused to shed. She sniffed and looked at the closet door. God help her. It would open any second now.

When he emerged, she met his eyes and spat out her words. "Convincing enough for you?"

"Watch your fucking tone." He strode past her to the doorway and glared down the hall. "I should've killed him for calling you a bitch."

Sudden warmth hit at the core of her. The sentiment touched a needy, vulnerable piece of her psyche she refused to examine. He confused her, and maybe that was part of his game. "So you can break into houses and threaten people's lives, but name calling is a crime?"

"Yes." His pale gray eyes, so contemplative and unnervingly focused on her, made her feel more exposed than a dozen pageant walks before a hundred judges. He de-cocked the gun and tucked it in the waistband at his back. "You can run, but there's nowhere to go but *outside.* If you don't follow my orders, I'll restrain you...*outside.*"

She shook her head in denial and clutched her throat. What he suggested was the worst possible outcome, unless... "Are you going to cut me up in little pieces?"

A cold smile tipped his lips as he chuckled. Then his expression sobered. "Walk to the kitchen."

Fucking psychopath. He stood right in the doorway, taking up the whole damned hall. At over six feet tall with a muscled body cut from stone, he could squash her without breaking a sweat. She didn't want to go near him. He was terrifying. But being forced outside was worse. She straightened her back and headed toward him.

As she slid by, his arm caught her waist and yanked her back against his chest. She slapped at his hand, bucking against him, and his arm clenched tighter. His erection jabbed against her backside, his breath hot at her ear. "Fighting and squirming only turns me on. Don't stop."

She immediately stilled. God, he wasn't lying. His dick was undeniably more pronounced against her back. Feeling him like that, so close, so huge and hard, rushed heat between her legs and prickles over her skin. Why, oh why was she responding this way? She hated and wanted it, and mother of all fucks, she couldn't have been more completely and totally out of her mind.

She drew a ragged breath. *Think, think, think.* But his intention blatantly rubbed against her, scattering her thoughts. "You're going to rape me, aren't you?"

His torso moved up and down with his breath. "I thought you wanted to be fuck buddies. Don't make it weird."

"What? Oh no. Nonononononono. I'm not offering now!" Her voice shrilled, and her elbows rammed into his ribs. "This is me saying 'No'."

Restraining her with an arm around her chest, he pulled off a glove with his teeth and shoved his hand down the front of her jeans, beneath her panties. She gasped and tried to reach for the gun at his back. The glove dropped to the floor as he kept his back twisted away and the brace of his massive arm effectively immobilizing her movements.

The fingers in her jeans descended with strength and determination. They slid over her mound, between her lips, reaching, curling, and oh God, fucking her. He pressed his palm over her pussy, his fingers hooking inside her. The grip yanked her back, grinding her ass against his erection.

Her inner muscles pulsated around the invasion, clenching and shameless. She wanted to cry, knowing how wet she was, humiliated that he was swirling through the depraved evidence of her frail mind and touching her in a place she never wanted anyone to see.

"Please." She squeezed her thighs together, tried to angle her hips away from his fingers. "Please, I don't want this."

He thrust harder and twisted his fingers inside her. "Your cunt disagrees." Without warning, he yanked his hand from her pants and shoved his fingers in her mouth, pressing down on her tongue and jaw. The tang of her arousal mixed with her saliva as he angled her jaw with his hand, forcing her cheek against his chest and shoving his face into hers.

Every human being had a cruel side, but as she looked into the blackness behind his eyes, she didn't see a facet of varying traits. She saw the entire man. He *was* cruelty incarnate.

He released her, and she stumbled. He reached out to catch her arm, but she jerked away, refusing to be dragged. He grabbed his glove from the floor, slid it on, and gestured toward the kitchen. "After you."

His soft gait followed closely behind her. She tried to focus on a plan, a useful weapon, anything but the way her wanton body was reacting to the feel of him behind her, around her, dominating her space.

He stopped beside the kitchen sink and set the tablet on the counter. "Get me a glass of water."

Apparently, breaking-and-entering, fucking with women, and being an all-round asshole made him thirsty. "The water is shut off." She couldn't stop the flush of humiliation that crept up her neck.

The look of detachment on his face irritated her as much as it frightened her. "I bet you prepared for that. Open the fridge."

Her molars crashed together as she stormed to the fridge and yanked out one of the four pitchers of water. When she finished pouring a glass, he tugged a baggie from his pocket and dumped the powdered contents into the water, stirring it with a gloved finger. "Drink."

"No way." She backed away from him with rasping breaths. "What is it?"

In the next heartbeat, he was on her, chest-to-chest, arms around her back, hauling her to the sliding door. He yanked the shades aside, and the blinding light of the backyard set her skin on fire and her heart into overdrive.

Her legs gave out, and she swung her head away from the horror of the open, inescapable space. If she went out there, it would be her ruination. She wouldn't be coherent, wouldn't be able to talk or scream without breath.

She clawed at his hands, to break his hold, to escape the door. Black bursts spotted her vision, and her heart slammed against her ribs. She panted for air and couldn't fill her lungs. Her eyes smeared with hot tears, blinding her. She fought harder, but his arms were everywhere, too tight, constricting and suffocating. Consciousness teased at the back of her mind as a blanket of warmth and aftershave swept in.

The slide of the drapes sounded, and the sunlight receded. Too late, she realized she was on the floor, curled in his lap, with her face buried in the crook of his arm.

She pushed against the hand cupping the back of her head as the rim of the glass touched her lips.

"We can do this all day." He rolled the glass over her chin, sloshing cool water against her mouth. "Or you can drink and fall asleep gently."

So he wanted to knock her out? Well, he could eat a dick. She sealed her lips together and turned her head. "Then what?"

"Then...we go for a ride."

Van knelt on the bed beside Amber and drew a deep, calming breath. After three more stubborn confrontations with the sliding glass door, she'd worked herself into a sniveling, spasmodic conniption. And promptly fainted.

Shaking his head at the irony, he tied her limp arms to the headboard with the belts from her closet. Then he grabbed the drugged water from the side table.

Fainting wouldn't keep her under long enough for the thirty-minute drive, but the Roofy in the water would. Wrestling with her in front of the open door had been a gamble, but he knew the neighbors on either side were at work and the trees out back blocked the view from the other houses.

Still, it had been a risk that could've been avoided by simply pinning her down and forcing her to drink. But watching her struggle with the choice, seeing how far she'd take it, had revealed a lot about how her mind worked.

She'd convinced herself the biggest threat was out there, beyond her doors and windows, and the least amount of pain was in her house, with him. He was certain she would welcome a bullet before drinking the water, knowing the tranquilizer would result in her removal from the house. It was absolutely fascinating.

In his online research of Amber Rosenfeld, he'd validated she'd won countless first place prizes in prestigious contests in fitness modeling and beauty pageantry. Then, after a fourteen-year career, nothing. For two years, no news articles, nothing in the search results except a profile on an online crafts store selling leathercrafts. Why?

Only a year older than his thirty-three years, her firm figure and youthful face would've provided her a comfortable income from modeling. Yet, here she was, carving leather and drowning in debt. What the fuck had happened to her?

She had no social media profiles, and no friends or family mentioned in the public search results. She'd simply vanished from the spotlight with a disqualification from what might've been her fourth win in an international beauty pageant. The significance of the number four hadn't been lost on him.

He straddled her hips, anxious to dig into her complex mind and savoring the feel of her tight little body against his balls. Christ, all her struggling had wreaked havoc on his control. But he wanted to fuck her in his house, on his bed, where the surrounding acreage's dense timber would swallow her screams.

He stabbed the water with the drinking straw he'd found in the kitchen, sealed it with a finger, and trickled it down her throat.

She coughed, swallowing, and gasped awake. He had another strawfull waiting before she opened her eyes. She blinked, lips parting, and he emptied it in her mouth.

Her throat convulsed, her arms yanked uselessly at the restraints, and she angled her neck to look at her hands. Her eyes rounded, her fists clenched, and she roared, "You dirty, conniving" —she bucked her hips— "heavy-ass dick, let me go!"

He slapped a hand over her mouth and nose and howled with laughter. "I'm going to show you how dirty, conniving, and heavy my dick is. First, you need to take a long nap."

Christ, she was cute, but it really wasn't funny. If the neighbors were outside, they might've heard her. He cocked his head and watched her struggle for air beneath the clamp of his hand. Time to get ugly.

Releasing her face, he reared back and slammed a fist into her stomach. Not enough to damage organs, but plenty of *oomph* to knock the wind out of her and get her attention.

She gulped silently, her body straining beneath him. Her lower lip rolled inward, trembling, as she bit down on it. Her eyelids fluttered, brimming but not quite shedding tears. When the pain faded from her eyes, she narrowed them at him.

He held out the glass and raised his brow.

Her lips formed a white stubborn line.

Slowly, he trailed a finger over the cotton covering her stomach, circling the hurt and taunting her until her pupils dilated with fear. She shivered, and sweat beaded along her honey skin. Earlier, it hadn't just been fear that prickled and dampened her flesh. She'd been aroused, too, by his fingers in her pussy, or maybe just from the feel of his erection at her back, from having a man attracted to her. But she'd fought it, fought him, and that had turned him on far more than the juices slicking her cunt.

His finger followed the line of her sternum, traced her collarbone, and roamed over her chin and cheek.

"What are you going to do to me?" The quiver in her voice teased the darkest pleasure centers inside him.

He leaned forward, and his touch caressed a path over her full lips, the bridge of her nose, and her slim eyebrows, drawing out her anxiety. When he reached her nose, he pinched tightly, blocking the airway. Her gaze flew to his, white-eyed and red-rimmed.

Holding her face immobile, he angled the glass beside her chin, using the mattress to balance it. As her lips opened to inhale, he poked the end of the straw between her teeth.

With his fingers clamping her nose, he used the heel of his hand to hold her head down and her jaw shut around the straw. "I'll let you breathe after you drink through the straw. If you pass out, I'll wake you up, and we'll do it again."

Those huge brown eyes glared at him until the pressure of her lungs overpowered her stubbornness. Her throat began to work, swallowing the drug. Gorgeous, watery pools of desperation engulfed her lashes and trickled down her temples.

"Shhh." He bent over her, without releasing her jaw and nose, and kissed the paths of her tears.

When air coughed through the straw, he set the glass on the table and lowered his face to hers. She drew heavy, greedy inhales, tucking her chin to escape him. He chased her lips, catching them with his own and sucking, teasing, enjoying the heave of her chest and her useless struggles to get away. Then he sat back.

She pulled on the restraints and gave up quickly, evidently exhausted. Her eyes slid over the room as if memorizing every detail and locked on the aquarium of mutilated awards. "I can't go outside. I can't." Her voice crept over him, somber and resigned.

"Why did you quit?" He nodded at the aquarium.

She looked at him, her gaze wet and glazed, not really *looking*. "You'll see."

He narrowed his eyes, wanting to press, but he only had twenty minutes before the Roofy took effect. So he offered the same obtuseness. "I'm going to fix you; then *you'll* see."

Tuning out her objection, he strode to the closet. He yanked three duffel bags from the top shelf and stuffed them with the bulk of her wardrobe.

When she figured out what he was doing, she wailed more nonsense about not going outside until he gagged her with a balled up sock from the dresser.

He added her toiletries from the bathroom to the last duffel, followed by the empty water glass with the Roofy evidence, her powered-off phone, laptop, and his tablet.

Twenty minutes later, he found her sleeping heavily, made sure the airway in her nose was clear, and left the gag in place. Then he slid on sunglasses and entered the garage.

Empty. Not even a car. Guess that made sense since she didn't go anywhere. Snatching the garage opener from a bare shelf, he closed the doors behind him. Because it was daylight, he strolled down the street and around the block.

He returned five minutes later in a minivan, parked it in the garage, and shut the door. The van was a purchase he'd made the prior day. A dated model with tinted windows. He'd even gone as far as swiping someone's *County Maids* advertisement, the huge magnet now clinging to the passenger sliding door.

A hired house cleaner wasn't the best explanation for the sudden activity at a seemingly vacant home. Liv certainly wouldn't have bought it, but she was at the airport, instructing skydiving lessons, and Joshua was tied up in his coaching shit at the high school. While a nighttime capture was preferred, taking Amber during the day avoided the most suspicious neighbors.

He shouldn't have been taking her at all, but after he'd researched the disorders, an idea had formed in the back of his mind. Amber might have many uses, one being an unknowing tool in solidifying a relationship with his daughter. First, he had to redirect her attachments until all she needed was him.

As he strode down the hall and into her bedroom; his insides vibrated with excitement. When he freed her arms, removed the gag, and lifted her listless, vulnerable body against his chest, something strange shifted through him and settled around his heart. It felt warm and gentle and...uncontaminated.

Impossible. Besides, his daughter was the only person he would allow himself to nurture a soft spot for. Anyone else would jump on his weakness and twist it into something they could use against him.

He shook off the unnerving feeling and quickened his pace to the garage. He was a cold-hearted fuck with an appetite for blood, come, and tears. And he had the perfect girl to feed it.

A dreamlike blur of sensations sloshed over Amber. Thick darkness. The sluggish thump of her heart. A draft on her skin. The familiar scent of aftershave.

She blinked, tried to clear the haze, and her eyes met a veil of black. Why was her lamp off? She slept with it on. The mattress felt too firm against her back and head. And no pillow? That wasn't right.

Cool air whispered over her body. Her very naked body. Blood rushed past her ears as she tried to sit up, going nowhere.

Nude, dark, cold, she had to be stuck in a dream, tangled in the sheets. She always slept without clothes when no one was looking. No one would be there. Not in her room at night, in her safe place of flawless lines. If only she could see the order to ground herself in her symmetrical world. *Wake up.*

She lifted her head and tried to get her bearings. Fabric rubbed her forehead, cheeks, and the bridge of her nose. Pinpricks bit at her hands. She couldn't move them, so she scrunched her face, wiggling the obstruction, and her eyelashes dragged against whatever held tightly over her eyes. *A blindfold.*

She jerked, and nausea surged through her gut. Her arms and legs wouldn't bend. She yanked and kicked, caught in a web of restraints that dug into her wrists and ankles, pinning her in a spread-eagle position on her back.

A tremor awoke in her chest and exploded outward, shaking every muscle in her body until her limbs numbed and her jaw ached from clenching. Her mind spun through fuzz. She couldn't remember falling asleep, couldn't remember the last thing she did. The nausea, the disorientation, the pounding headache... Had she drank too much again?

Memories swirled in a mist of dizzy fragments. The fading rumble of Zach's truck. A water glass. The drape wrenched from the back door. A fist slamming into her stomach.

Van.

Her heart rate spiked, and pain pounded behind her eyes. Oh shit, oh shit, oh shit. She let out an ear-piercing shriek that echoed around her, and she immediately regretted the outburst. She did *not* want to draw attention, couldn't bear for anyone to see her naked.

Her pulse redoubled. Where was Van? Was he watching her with sick amusement? She stifled her breath and listened. No reassuring hum of the

A/C unit outside her window. No dripping from the leaking shower down the hall. Oh wait, her water had been shut off. But the mattress... It was too hard, too bare.

She wasn't in her bed. Her heart stuttered and stopped. OhmyGodOhmyGod. She wasn't in her house!

"No, no, no." She jerked her head side to side, writhed against the restraints, and choked through panting breaths. "Where am I?"

The mattress shifted between her legs, and a tickle of wiry hair brushed her inner thighs. Then the press of hard muscle. Someone's legs. "You're home."

She froze. His voice, oh God, it came from above her. He was kneeling between her thighs, where he could look at her stretched, godawful shame. She tried to close her legs and failed. The mattress was indented on either side of her shoulders, and she knew his hands were propped there. How long had he been bent over her, watching her, waiting? Or doing whatever he wanted to her while she was unconscious?

Her lungs slammed together, starving for air. Were the lights on? Jesus, fuck, they couldn't be on. He wouldn't want to look between her legs.

Something hard and slick nudged her opening, and his heavy body flattened her against the bed. Her mouth dried. No, this couldn't be happening. She thrashed, pinned by his weight, unable to escape as objections gathered in her constricted throat.

In the next heartbeat, he shoved himself inside her, his girth stretching her hideous flesh with the brutality of the dry thrust. She bit down her tongue, tasting blood, as the invasion tore her open, plowing ruthlessly and igniting a scorching friction along her inner walls.

Her eyes watered behind the blindfold, the agony and humiliation of what he was doing seizing her heart. Her screech escaped without sound, and her body locked in paralyzing shock. Numb, breathless, her fear was stunned into silence, cringing in the corner of her mind.

"Scream," he breathed, his thick exhale searing her ear.

A wail built in her throat, but he slammed into her, giving her no time to free it. No pause to catch her breath. No gentle coaxing to prepare her for his size. He fucked her harder, forcing her body to accommodate him, taking her beyond the point of pain and hurtling her into muscle-locking terror.

The straps chewed into her skin, grinding her bones. His fingers pinched and pulled her nipples, and the spread of her hips extended painfully beneath the unrelenting strength of his driving thrusts.

This was happening. He'd taken her from her house. Bared her before his eyes. He was raping her.

Her heart panted, a helpless terrified thing trapped in her chest. She wanted to ignore it, to be stronger, but as his powerful jabs shredded and battered her insides, death seemed to be a better option.

His teeth scraped across her shoulder, his grunts lashed her skin with wet exhales, and his arms squeezed around her ribs. Could he see all her flaws in the light? Who else had laid eyes on her, judged her? If she wasn't home... Oh no, oh God, he'd taken her *outside.*

Her pulse went wild, tearing through her body. She bucked in his embrace, but there was no escape. He was too heavy, too strong, plunging in and out of her abused flesh.

The horrifying image of her body spread out beneath him collided with the shackles chafing her raw skin and the cramping pain of her cervix or whatever it was inside her he hammered against so mercilessly.

She closed her eyes behind the blindfold and tried to calm her heart by counting the slam of his hips. One...two...three...four. One...two...three...four. Over and over, she counted until her mind tumbled so far away her body grew numb and limp.

His hand gripped her throat and squeezed. "What are you doing?"

Bright hot reality burned through her, sensitizing every cell in her body. She'd always wanted it harder, rougher, with a firmer hand around her neck, strangling her thoughts. But not like this, with no choice, no safe word. And not with the lights on. "Are the lights...?" Her voice quivered, tiny and reedlike. She swallowed around the clamp of his fingers. "Are they on?"

He tsked and slowed his thrusts. "You don't really know someone until you see them in the dark." His timbre rumbled through her as he rolled his hips and tightened his hand around her throat. "I'll show you the dark, my beautiful slave."

Slave. The blackness burst in a constellation of stars as his fingers bit into her tender throat. He flexed his hips, surging forward, pumping faster than the heaving of her chest. Her lungs caught fire, unable to draw air, as her life burned away beneath the vise of his hand.

A prick of light flickered in the dark void, beckoning. She floated toward it, couldn't stop it from taking her. The moment she gave in, the second she stopped fighting, her body felt lighter, her mind quieter. The pain of his thrusts and the clench of his fist receded as wave after wave of serenity sifted in. It nibbled away at her fear and splintered her thoughts until nothing was left but a hundred vibrating tongues licking along her inner walls, swelling wet heat through her pussy, and soaking his entry.

"Aw, God." He loosened his grip, grunting a sound full of lust and satisfaction, and sped up his pace. "There's my girl, dripping all over me."

Her bruised throat sealed up as his words spilled fiery shame through her veins. She'd fantasized about being punished, to be fucked raw and savagely, and maybe she was depraved. But now? Oh God, she didn't want it. Something was missing, something crucial. He took without permission. Every nerve in her body thrummed for more, but he'd stolen her power to stop it.

His balls slapped against her ass, his cock growing thicker inside her. "You love to be dominated." He ground his pelvis against her clit and bit her earlobe. "Even as your conscience tells you to hate it. I dare you to fight it."

Somewhere in the recesses of her fucked-up head, a rational voice screamed in horror, lamenting his truths, hating him. But her pussy swelled with desire, throbbing and gripping him harder. The gluttonous flesh grew slicker with every thrust, welcoming him, urging him on.

After two years of fucking in the dark, she was spread open under the lights. It would've been a huge step for her, but she hadn't chosen it. As she lay there, absorbing the brute force of his cock pounding inside her, she discarded whatever self-worth she had left and replaced it with something she could endure. She let the pleasure in.

His fingers scraped through her hair, ripping the strands and tingling her scalp as he yanked her head back and licked her mouth. "I want your release." His mouth imprisoned hers, sucking the air from her lungs as he drove his tongue in maddening swirls. "Give it to me. Now."

The orgasm exploded from an unbound place inside her, thundering through her body, every muscle rippling with electric tingles. His hips jerked against hers, and he kissed her with a ferocity that buckled her spine. She didn't have the faculties to bite off his tongue, her release so powerful all she could do was ride it as he dragged a piercing cry from her throat. She dug her feet into the mattress, and the ecstasy carried her into oblivion where she drifted in utter peace.

Without warning, he yanked off the blindfold. The quietude evaporated, replaced with the horrifying intrusion of natural light. An A-frame ceiling soared above the bed, its exposed rafters reaching beyond the railing that lined the long, narrow loft where she was held.

She didn't want to look at him, but he was as much a threat as the windows towering above him. She lifted her eyes, and his terribly beautiful face filled her vision. Still deep and hard inside her, he leaned back, his gaze smoldering with blatant lust. Sweat beaded over his forehead, gathering in the furrows and threatening to drip. Oh God, why couldn't he just wipe that away? She couldn't bear for it to fall on her and averted her eyes.

In the corner, a staircase spiraled into a two-story room. The only way to escape was down. Was the room below walled with glass, exposed to the outdoors? She didn't know. All she could see was the source of the light, the glow of twilight bleeding through the triangular windows that crested the two-story wall beyond the railing. The pinkish clouds against the purple sky might've been picturesque if the view of outside wasn't shuddering through her, chattering her teeth and shortening her breaths.

Jesus, stop. The windows were too high to see in. It was just the sky looking back. None of this could hurt her. Breathing deeply, she could feel the heat of his eyes watching her from his kneeling position between her legs, his cock still buried inside her. She refused to look at him again, and her gaze stumbled over her body. The shame of her nudity, all laid out in the light, was sharp and swift as it clenched her insides in a blinding chokehold.

Her arms trembled wildly, her hair sticking to the sweat on her face. The evidence of her arousal smeared her inner thighs. But the worst of the view was her oversized breasts bouncing lewdly as he began to thrust anew with hard-hitting strokes.

"Please cover the windows." She knew he couldn't. They were two-stories up, with no attached curtains or blinds.

He put his face in hers, the pink scar on his cheek bunching with his smile. "You realize, what exists in the light doesn't go away in the dark."

Fuck his condescending smirk. Shadows hung like drapes on the three windowless walls surrounding them, hovering just out of reach, but soon they would close in with the setting sun. The approaching darkness in this unknown place both comforted and scared the shit out of her.

His eyes wandered down her body to lock on where they were connected. All that distended flesh was likely wrapped around his cock, folding up and down his length, so fucking grotesque it made her eyes burn.

"Stop looking." It was a tear-choked plea, one he acknowledged with a furrowed brow then rejected as he sat up, gripped her ass, and angled his head, watching himself slide in and out.

She thrashed and jerked, but her efforts didn't distract him from staring at her pussy.

A twitch tugged the lower lid of her eye, jumping manically, angry and relentless. She squeezed her eyes shut and breathed slow and deep. Numbness settled over her arms, and a throb awoke in her chest, like an over-pressurized artery pulsing above the muscle. If only it was a heart attack.

Instead, it was the smothering pain of panic crashing over her. She tried to calm it by focusing on something other than the sight of her body. She studied his heavy-lidded eyes, strong nose, and full mouth, all arranged in perfect symmetry. The angles of his face followed lines of natural geometry. Uniformed cuts of muscle sculpted his pecs and abs.

He was a kidnapper, a rapist, and she ached to be repulsed by him, just to prove she was sane, but she couldn't. And she wasn't. His scarred beauty radiated seduction and danger, a deadly combination.

She'd told him he would see why she'd given up modeling, yet he continued to fuck her as if he hadn't seen every inch of her terrible nudity. His arms braced beside her waist, his biceps flexing as his cock pistoned in and out of her, scrambling her thoughts, overwhelming her.

The dime-sized scar in his shoulder was the last thing she saw as tremors attacked her nervous system, seizing her body and arching her back. Blackness invaded, the clouds faded from the windows, and she fell into nothingness.

A hand slammed into her jaw, shooting a stinging fire through her nose. She blinked, gasping for air, and his scowl bleared into focus.

"Stay with me, goddammit." Silver flames lit his eyes, sparking above her in blurry, iridescent flashes.

He pulled out, ripped off the condom, and pumped his hand along his length, hard and fast. Bending over her, he propped himself up, his arm straight, biceps straining as his fist stroked. His eyes locked with hers, and his mouth opened with a guttural shout as come squirted over her mound, belly, and chest.

She stared at the globs streaking her body, dazed. Why had he come on her and not in her?

He answered her unspoken question when he swirled his fingers through the ejaculate, spreading it over her skin as if rubbing it into her pores, marking his territory.

"Beautiful." His voice was thick with lust. He leaned down and lapped at it, collecting a white puddle on his tongue.

Before she could analyze the come licking, he crawled up her body and captured her mouth. His salty kiss swirled past her lips, aggressive and consuming. She tried to fight it, but she was too weak, too lost to the drugging glide of his lips, the salacious pressure of his teeth, and the undivided focus of his desire.

He'd seen every shameful flaw, and still he kissed her as if he believed she was beautiful? She closed her eyes and could almost taste a man beneath the cruel lash of his tongue. The flavor bore a hint of cleanliness. Earthy. Carnal. Human. It gave her hope that a modicum of kindness might've been buried in there, too. No doubt it was a hope fabricated from desperation.

He broke the kiss, and his tongue darted out, trailing the seam of her mouth. "If turning off the lights is the only way you can get off, you need to replace it with something else." His lips whispered over her cheek. "With trust."

"Are you shitting me?" She twisted in the restraints, kicking and heaving against his heavy body. "You fucking raped me!"

A dark cloud rolled over his face, and his eyes grew unfocused, his voice eerily quiet. "To call that rape insults the brutality inflicted by the worst kind of man." He blinked, and his eyes cleared. He rubbed his forehead, dropped his hand, and his mouth tilted in a crooked grin. "You liked it too much."

Fire spread over her body, lighting up her nerves and burning her throat. "I'm tied down, dammit. I didn't have a choice." She didn't have a choice to like it? Okay, not a whip-smart response. "Untie me." She glared at him through blurry eyes. "Or do you plan on raping me again?"

"Maybe." He winked. "If you beg."

The fuck she would. "Is your name really Van?"

His fingers caressed a path around the outer swell of her breast, over her ribs and hip, and slipped between the raw skin of her lower lips. "My mother named me Van Quiso." He shoved two fingers in her opening and curled them, coaxing her muscles to clench. "You'll refer to me as Master." His timbre was a velvet sheath swaddling an obnoxious order.

He shifted down her body, hovering like a dark mountain of dread, and wedged his massive shoulders between her thighs.

Her heart rammed against her ribs in a violent protest. Oh God, she never wanted anyone down there. Not after Brent. It was her biggest shame, her eternal regret. "Please, don't. You don't understand."

He bared his teeth, grinning, and bit down on her clit. White-hot pain pierced through her pussy in concentrated heat. She cried out as his teeth continued to pierce and yank the sensitive nub, his tongue flicking back and forth as swiftly as his thrusting fingers.

She screamed thick, sobbing shrills of agony. Hot tears rolled down her face, her cries garbled and raw. He released her, kissing the sore flesh. The tenderness only made her cry harder.

She was on display, naked and hurting, weak and defenseless. And her future would only get worse. What would happen to her without her routine, trapped in some unknown location, at the center of a madman's attention?

For two years, she'd hidden herself in the darkness of her self-pity. She wasn't living. She was barely surviving. The idea of returning to her house was as grim as staying here, with him. Was this the beginning of a new misery, where her days were consumed by a rapist who made her come? The thought trembled through her. That was a whole different kind of sick.

As the edge of pain dimmed, the pinch of something else took hold, a realization as spiteful and psychotic as the monster before her. It hardened her spine and sharpened her focus.

He might've had the upper hand, but he couldn't control the mess in her mind. If he planned to keep her around, he'd damned well better be prepared. She was going to make his life a living hell.

He reached for the buckles around her ankles. "You ready?"

She was ready, for what she had no idea. She'd been beaten, drugged, taken from her house, and raped. She was already fucked in the head, her dignity long gone, and now she was backed into a corner she couldn't escape. She had nothing to lose.

She raised her chin and met his eyes. "Yes."

The shackles around Amber's ankles fell away. She yanked her legs together, knocking her knees, and the sudden movement sent stabbing pain through her hips. But it was anger—the sudden violence of helpless fury—that sharpened every nerve-ending in her body.

Van watched her from beneath hooded eyes and reached for her wrists. "You're an unforgettable fuck, Amber."

She ground her molars, her voice low and harsh. "And you're a fucking rapist."

His eyebrows pinched together. "You're pissed, but you went over the edge and exploded around my dick." He freed one arm and murmured, "You needed that."

The conversation was surreal, as if they weren't discussing an event she would relive and mourn every day for the rest of her life, however short that might be.

The final shackle dropped, and blood tingled through her hands. She scrambled toward the edge of the bed, but he grabbed her ankles, and dragged her back, wrestling her to sit sideways in his lap.

She fought him, slapping and snarling, teeth bared, her muscles screaming with venom. But amidst her struggles slithered the chill of helplessness. If she managed to overpower him, to outsmart him, *to escape*, where would she run? Outside?

Was she seriously trying to convince herself that a naked cuddle with a rapist was less scary than whatever waited beyond the front door?

He took advantage of her hesitation, his nudity slipping around her and his hands controlling her legs until she straddled his lap, sitting chest to chest, his arms locked around her back. Hot skin pressed against hers, slick and hard and entirely too close. She shoved against the twitching muscles on his chest, but his embrace was implacable, a steel cage of limbs.

His lips brushed the sensitive spot beneath her ear, and he breathed deeply, smelling her.

She shivered. She needed clothes, a shower, her routine, and...courage. Her fingernails dug into his back as she scanned the clutter strewn throughout the room. There, her robe, tossed over her duffel bags on the floor in the corner. The rest of the room... Oh my God.

A beer bottle sat on the dresser. Dirty socks piled beside the bed as if he'd just kicked them off and left them there. Two hangers hung on the closet doorknob. The nightstand... Wait. What?

Her aquarium sat against the far wall, filled with the broken fragments of her life. What did he intend to do with it? Would he torture her by destroying them beyond recognition? Would he be so cruel? She sat taller on his lap, her breasts dragging unnervingly against his chest, her voice cracking. "Why is that here?"

The gentle tiptoe of his fingertips along her arms aroused unnerving sensations over her skin. He nuzzled her neck. "It means something to you."

A lump swelled in her throat. It was just a career, but it signified the beginning and end of a normal life. She stared through blurry eyes at the one possession she would've lamented leaving behind.

As heartless and forceful as he was, nothing cruel lingered in his expression now. He studied her with daunting tenderness and an innocent sort of curiosity, and she felt knocked off balance. And naked, which had nothing to do with her lack of clothing. What if he threw the keepsakes away? Or used them against her? "It's just some broken memorabilia."

He held her in place as he massaged the soreness from her wrist. "It was the only sentimental belonging in your house, and you had it displayed." His touch moved over her wrists, gentle and attentive. "You liked to look at it, which tells me someone else destroyed it. Who?"

An angry pulse throbbed behind her eyes. Brent had taken a sledgehammer to everything that mattered to her. Except her career. That was on her. But she wasn't about to tell Van any of that. He didn't know about her ex-husband, and she couldn't afford to expose any more of herself beneath his perceptive eyes. So she decided on stubborn silence.

His hands moved to her calves and ankles, kneading the muscles, coaxing circulation, and easing her stiffness. She didn't trust his tenderness for a second, and her vulnerability escalated with each soothing caress.

He seemed to be distracted with his hands busy on her legs. She could slip off his lap and run.

And run where? The closet? Or she could endure his touch and try to figure him out. "What are you doing?"

"I got carried away. I never checked the cuffs, and they were too tight." His eyes were fixed on his fingers, but she sensed his attention was singularly focused on her. On her shallow breaths, the prickles bumping up her flesh. On what she might say next.

His profile was so painfully striking as he bowed his head, lips parted, face soft with affection. Any woman would've fallen into his bed at the crook of his finger. Hell, she'd offered the night she'd met him, and didn't that just dig under her skin? "You turned me down; then you returned and took me by force. Are you a serial rapist? A stalker? A murderer?" She trembled to put the space of the room between them but forced her eyes to his and whispered, "What are you?"

Something slipped over his expression, a menacing shield that turned his jaw to stone. He gripped her waist and set her on her feet, pushing her away. His elbows dropped to his knees as he watched her from beneath sharp brows, eyes creased in searing slits, voice quiet. "I'm the heir of torment, Amber."

She stepped back, hands shielding her groin and breasts.

He rose and held out his arms, unabashedly nude. "I'm the slippery footprints in your carpet. The creaking floor that steals air from your lungs. The hand that holds the gun." He paced through the room, snagging a pair of jeans from the floor, and met her eyes. "I'm the inescapable curse that caught you when you opened your door."

A shiver rippled through her and settled into her bones. Not a hint of arrogance in his words. Just the steady monotone of unresisting acceptance. As if he'd rehearsed that creepy speech or had at least given it a lot of thought.

She darted for her robe, shrugged it on, and turned to face him with a semblance of courage now that she was covered. "You don't have to be those things." She pushed back her shoulders and gave him a practiced response of her own. "You could be the nemesis of torment."

He pulled on the jeans, regarding her with an unreadable expression. "Is that what Dr. Michaels told you? Some cockamamie horseshit about confronting fear with its adversary, courage?"

How did he know who— Of course. Her call log. Yeah, that was exactly what Dr. Michaels had said. She refused to tell him so, and while seeing him clothed from the waist down should've mollified her somewhat, she couldn't relax. He was too unpredictable. He probably let her put the robe on just so he could tear it off and rape her again.

She glanced around the room, stepping backward and tripping over scattered clothes and shoes. Without thinking, she gathered up shirts, pants, and dirty socks and walked them to the hamper in the closet. "Am I your first?" First stalking? Kidnapping? Rape?

"No." The single word pierced through her back and stabbed her heart. "Your next door neighbor was my first. Her lover was my last. There were seven in between."

Nine slaves. What happened to them if he was still free to keep taking people? Her neighbors were still alive, obviously, but how?

His footsteps creaked the wood floors behind her, thankfully shifting farther away. She needed room to breathe, to focus. Squatting, she tackled the clothes on the floor. The scent of aftershave and the musk of man billowed around her as she stuffed the hamper, hung the belts, and searched for some order in which to place the pile of boots, sneakers, and sandals. But it wasn't enough to soothe her blooming panic. Her neighbors had survived him? They were alive and free right next door to her house? Had he let them go?

"Stop that." His strides neared, pausing right behind her. "Don't ever pick up my shit."

The harshness of his tone jerked her to her feet, and she spun to face him, chin raised. What she really wanted to do was cringe in the corner and hide from the seething brick wall, now wearing a t-shirt, jeans, and an icy glare.

She swallowed hard and found her voice. "My neighbors are your *old friends*? The reason you were on my porch?" Had there been any truth to his comment about watching them fuck on their table? She didn't know them, had never met them. "But they're free?"

"Liv and Joshua got away." His eyelids dipped halfway, shuttering his eyes, but his face softened, almost peaceful-like, as did his voice. "They all got away."

Why was he telling her this? To make sure she understood she was just one in a long line of violated bodies? She felt sick and inconsequential. Put in her place with a smart smack of reality. She was nothing to him but an easy fuck no one would miss.

But the others had escaped? Hope swelled through her insides, bright and full, lifting her nausea. He would grow tired of her neurotic quirks, if he hadn't already. Maybe he'd return her to her house before the mortgage defaulted. Maybe he'd kill her.

"Whatever you're thinking, *don't*. The circumstances with the others were different." He reached out and grabbed her chin, forcing her to look at him. "I ran a sex trafficking operation, Amber. Liv was the deliverer with too much damned power. *She* freed them. Not me."

"Oh my God." Her knees buckled, and she stumbled back into a clump of hanging clothes, clattering the hangers. *Sex trafficking. Slave.* Her lungs squeezed, and her blood drained to her feet. "I can't— Oh God, Van. Please, you can't do this."

"Goddammit," he snarled. "I don't do that shit anymore." He wrenched her out of the closet by her arms and shoved her toward the stairs. "You're not going anywhere. You're *mine*."

"What do you mean?" She tried to turn, to see his face, but he kept pushing her. "What do you want?"

His arm snagged her waist, pulling her back to his chest, and he half-carried her down the spiraling staircase. "You said you were ready. We're starting in the bathroom."

Ready for what? Would he rape her in the shower? Drown her in the bathtub? She twisted, her toes skidding over the steps as he descended. "What starts in the—"

A blast of sunlight hit her face. Floor to ceiling, the two-story wall of glass towered over her. Trees of every size and shade of green spread out as far as she could see. Trails wound through clutches of thick trunks. Any random person could've been out there, gawking at her through the windows.

She flinched away from the exposure and curled against his chest. She wasn't dressed properly. Her hair hung in strands around her face. Full-body tremors arrested her lungs and strangled the shriek in her throat. He hooked an arm beneath her knees, another at her back, and carried her through the room of windows.

She screamed then, clutching his shoulders and hiding her ugly tears in his neck. "The windows...the windows. Please..." She sobbed, desperate, miserable, her skin rippling with terror. "You have to close them." She clawed at his back, choking.

His arms dropped her, yanking her hands from their grip on his shoulders as she fell. Her back hit cushions on a couch with a full frontal view of the windows.

She scrambled backwards, fighting for air and losing her robe in her hellfire hurry to get away. He watched her, his brows sharpening into a *V* over narrowed eyes. Fuck him. She kept going, backing up and over the arm of the couch. Her ass crashed into a small table and sent it sprawling to the floor with her. The hard tiles bit into her tailbone, and tears burned her cheeks. *Escape. Hide.* Where?

The great room extended into an open kitchen and more windows. The stairs went to the loft and no escape. A door below the railing opened to...the bathroom?

Gasping, she jumped to her feet, staggered, and righted herself in a clumsy spin of naked limbs and jiggling tits. She was so fucking humiliated. Her chest contracted painfully, and her shoulders ached with tension.

The path to the door stretched out in an eternal walk through windowy hell. Eight running steps. Two sets of four. *Focus on that.* Her knees wobbled as she lurched forward, her body growing heavier with each step. Goddammit, she could do this.

His arm caught her waist and dragged her to the couch, flipping her to her back. She kicked and spit as he landed atop her, pinning her arms above her head and kneeling on her thrashing legs.

"Jesus." His Adam's apple bobbed, and his beautiful face contorted into a blur. "Calm the fuck down."

She roared and bucked beneath his crushing weight. "Let me go!"

"Are you possessed?" He leaned in, nose-to-nose, stealing her oxygen. "Are you going to start spitting Latin and tell me to lick you?"

His amused tone heightened her embarrassment and fueled the panic. The windows closed in, compressing her chest. She grabbed at the cushions and dug deep, for air, for strength, determined to have the last word. In one rage-filled burst of breath, she shouted, "Shove it up your ass, you cunting dick!"

He jerked back, and faster than the hammer of her heart, his fist slammed into her face. Fire burst through her cheek. Then the sun burned out.

A fuckstorm of conflicting emotions pounded in Van's chest. He sat back on the couch and stared at the gorgeous, complicated woman beneath him. All it had taken was a swift punch to the cluster of nerves below her ear, and the panic attack went *poof.* Lights out. But every time he hit her, it cut open a squishy, remorseful spot inside him, one he didn't know existed.

This wasn't discipline training. It wasn't kinksual pain play. He wasn't experiencing any of the violent, fist-swinging rage Liv used to bring out in him. This was Amber, and hurting her when she was scared felt so goddamned unforgivable.

He rubbed a hand through his hair and jerked at the strands. Fuck, he needed to tread more delicately. Just like the others, the abduction and the sex had pissed her off, but the windows? He shifted to take in the peaceful landscape of wilderness, a view that soothed him on his worst days but terrified the fucking sense out of her.

If she were just dealing with the trauma of captivity, he wouldn't have been second-guessing himself. But the agoraphobic and OCD triggers added layers of complexity. Once upon a time, it might've been an interesting experiment to play with—tormenting her with sex and pain then forcing her outside—just to see which would break her first. But the appeal wasn't there. In its place coiled something else. He wanted her whole.

He climbed off the couch and yanked the drapes shut, buttoning up all the windows on the first story. He glanced at the top row of glass and sighed. Nothing he could do about those.

The open-plan cabin included a kitchen, sitting room, bathroom, and loft. The bathroom was the only windowless space. Except the garage... No, he wasn't ready for her to see his little hobby.

He returned to the couch where she lay exquisitely nude and lost in her dreams. The point of her stubborn chin softened in sleep. Her lips parted seductively, sloping into a small, slender nose. Collarbones pressed against delicate skin, and the fullness of her tits rose and fell with even breaths.

Her ribs were too sharply visible, but he'd fix that with a heartier diet. Despite being underweight, her sleek curves would've filled any man's spank bank. And other than her implants, there were no scars, no abnormalities, which made her poor self-image completely unfathomable. Time to reconcile that.

He gathered her in his arms and carried her to the bathroom. With her limp body perched on the counter, he slapped her face. "Wake up, sweetheart."

Her eyes fluttered, and a scowl bent her lips.

God, how he ached for her to smile at him with those captivating eyes all lit up and dimples denting her pretty cheeks. But why?

His chest tightened. He knew why, and it surfaced a childhood pang, the old starving need to see his mother gaze upon him with the same kind of smile, just once. Just a hint that she might've loved him. But all that memory offered was a boy's squashed hope and a dead mother.

He grunted deep in his chest just to hear the masculine sound of his very adult voice. He wasn't that needy boy anymore. He didn't have to depend on his mother or look to Liv for happiness. He could take what he needed from whomever he wanted.

He shook her, and her head rolled on her shoulders.

"Stop fucking hitting me." Her voice growled with grogginess, her hostile look lost through heavy blinks.

He supported her neck with a hand and softly traced her frowning lips. "When was the last time you smiled, Amber? A real smile?" Liv used to smile at him. When she was plotting his death.

Sitting on the counter, she glanced around the bathroom, orienting herself, as the tension in her body awakened beneath his fingers. When her startled gaze locked on the covered windows beyond the door, her shoulders relaxed, but her hands jumped to cover her tits and lap—and the dried come that coated her skin beautifully. Did she really think she could hide from him?

Gripping her wrists, he pinned them to the counter behind her and wedged his denim-clad hips between her thighs.

Strands of blond hair stuck to the tracks of dried tears on her face. Her brown eyes were so light beneath the glare of the vertical sconces they burned a golden hue. Even tinged pink from exhaustion, they radiated a blinding energy. Absolutely stunning.

Her brows pulled together as she regarded him. "My last smile?"

He nodded, and because her lips were so fucking tempting, he leaned in and kissed them. Just a tease of warm, gliding flesh.

She didn't kiss back but didn't pull away either as she spoke against his mouth. "You were on my porch and asked me if I was going to give you herpes."

The race of his heart drummed in his ears. She'd smiled at that? *He* had made her smile?

She cleared her throat and put an inch between them. "I should thank you for wearing a condom, but I'm not feeling very thankful at the moment."

Shifting her wrists to one hand and pressing them against her back, he opened the drawers beneath the vanity. "I'm clean of STDs, checked regularly. I'll show you the bloodwork later." He leaned back and gave her a few moments to scan the contents of the drawers.

One held six shades of brown hair dye and multiple boxes of each. Her eyebrows and lashes were dark, but since her cunt was shaved and her roots didn't show, he wasn't sure which was closest to her natural color. A home STD test kit waited in the other drawer.

Fascinating how her eyes dismissed the test and instead studied the boxes of dye like they held all the mysteries of the world.

He bent his knees so their faces were level. "I'm going to release your arms. You are *not* to cover yourself."

Her jerky nod didn't tear her eyes from the drawer. When he let go, her hands flew to her hair, her fingers dragging and catching on the tangled length. "You want to change the color." Her combing fingers sped up, shaking and restless. "You don't like it blond?"

Jesus. Her question was unexpected, but he should've seen it coming. It was her nature to please. To please him. And fuck no, he didn't like the bleached-out look against her warm skin. He wanted it the same dark brown as Liv's. And his mother's. Which was way too fucked up to admit out loud, even for him. "*You* don't like it."

Her eyes flashed to his, and her mouth formed a beautiful, gasping *O*. "I don't..." Her brows furrowed. Then her nostrils flared on an inhale, and her gaze hardened. "Why would you assume that?"

"You fuss with your hair like it's the bane of your existence." He shifted forward, sharing her breaths. "What you really want is to be accepted the way you are."

He'd pulled that last part out of his ass, but given the sharp jerk of her shoulders, he hadn't been off the mark.

"Which one is your natural color, Amber?" He tapped on the boxes.

"It'll take at least two boxes." She pointed to the deep brown black. "That one."

His mother's color.

He pretended his stomach didn't just drop to the floor as he gathered the packages. He didn't let her wear a towel as she bent over the sink. Didn't fluster her with questions as she silently rubbed the dye into her hair. But he couldn't stop his fingers from tracing the bumps along her arched spine and watching her skin prickle beneath his touch.

While the dye set on her hair, she peed on the test stick and let him take her blood and swab her mouth and pussy. When he told her to turn around so he could swab her rectum, she backed into the wall, her eyes round and fearful. "No. Please. That's...that's...just no."

He stepped into her space, using his bulk to crowd her. "Ever had a dick in your ass?"

"No!" Her tone was furious and her eyes blazed, but her chin shifted subtly up then down.

He rested a forearm on the wall beside her head. "Did you know body language betrays a lie? For example, the liar might nod while denying she enjoys getting her ass stretched by a cock."

A swallow bobbed in her throat as she stared up at him with glassy eyes. She licked her lips. "It's been two years. I'm clean...there."

"Let's let the lab decide that. Turn around."

"I'll do it myself." A ragged whisper.

He glowered down at her, giving her an eternity of strained silence to contemplate the consequences if she continued to push him. With black dye smearing her forehead and her hair in a lump of wet mess on her head, she looked deliciously vulnerable. Her chin quivered for a breathless moment; then finally, she released her lungs and faced the wall.

Squatting behind her with the swab in hand, he pried her firm cheeks apart. She was so damned tense, and he refused to fight her. "Tell me about your autographed books."

The muscles in her ass twitched and relaxed. "They're just signatures."

"Personalized to other people. Widen your stance."

After a stubborn moment, her feet shifted apart.

He caressed the crease between her thigh and cheek, thrilling in the responsive quiver. "How did you get them?"

"I bought them on Ebay. I like the stories. And the sentimental signatures. The little notes for other people. Normal people."

Ah. "But you don't know them. They may very well be more fucked up than you and me combined." He slid two fingers between her now slightly less tense cheeks, exposed the sweet little pucker of her anus, and swabbed.

Enough time had lapsed between preparing the test swabs, reading the instructions, and collecting the cultures. The color should be set. He patted her hip and stood. "Jump in the shower and rinse your hair while I package up the samples."

Still pressed against the wall, she looked over her shoulder at him with a strange expression on her face. Dark shadows bruised her eyes, her posture slumping. No doubt she was exhausted, hungry, and still working through her shock of the last couple hours.

He turned toward the vanity and listened to her footsteps shuffle to the shower.

Thirty minutes later, he stood behind her as she stared into the mirror. He'd used the hairdryer on her hair and let her keep the towel tied around her chest. Rich deep brown fell like a waterfall around her shoulders and curled damned near to her waist over the white terrycloth. The color highlighted the dark lashes fringing her eyes and illuminated the glow of her honey skin tone.

She was even more beautiful than his mother. Mesmerized, he couldn't look away. "What do you think?"

She glanced at his eyes reflected in the mirror, her fists clenched around the top edge of the towel. "What do you—?"

"No." He gripped the counter's edge beside her hips and pressed his chest against her back, glaring at her. "I asked what *you* thought of it."

A noise squeaked in her throat, and she took a long moment to study her reflection. "It's...me."

His chest pinched. "And *you* outshine any ideal you try to cover yourself with." Her jaw tightened but he didn't miss the catch in her breath. He placed a kiss on her shoulder. "Let's go eat."

"Where's my robe?" Her hands flew between her legs, covering the gap in the towel with a fan of trembling fingers. "Dammit, Van. Eyes up here." She bent forward, trying to further hide her cunt.

He scrubbed a hand over his face. This was such bullshit. Obviously, he wasn't getting through to her. Fine. He would just force her to show him what the problem was. He dug beneath the sink, removed a large handheld mirror and set it on the wide space of counter beside the sink. Then he patted the oval of reflective glass. "Hop up. Legs spread. Knees that way." He pointed at the mirrored wall behind the vanity.

Her head instantly started shaking side to side.

He grabbed her jaw, cupping her cheeks and stilling her. "If you don't hop when I say hop, we're going for a walk." He jerked his head toward the door and the windows beyond. "Out there."

When he released her, she climbed onto the vanity, her limbs shaking and the cords taut in her neck. With her ass on the handheld mirror and her legs spread, her bent knees pressed against the wall mirror. It was an awkward position, but she'd just have to deal with it. He yanked away the towel and tossed it behind him.

Her hands started to move to her pussy, but she caught herself and clutched her knees instead. Good girl.

Leaning against her back, he trailed his fingers around her ribs, beneath her tits, crossed his arms around her waist, and hugged her to him. "How long have you been a shut in?"

"Two years, three months, and five days." She peeked at him from beneath her lashes.

He scraped his stubble against her cheek. "What happened?"

Her finger tapped restlessly on her knee. "I got scared."

"More scared than you are now?"

She nodded, swiftly and passionately.

Damn. He was no psychiatrist. But he knew how to manipulate to get what he wanted. "Does this" —he cupped her pussy— "have something to do with it?"

Her breaths quickened, and her face contorted in pain. Fuck, if she had a meltdown, he'd get nowhere. He moved his hand, placing it over her breastbone, and touched his lips to her ear. "I won't touch your pussy, but I want you to look at it and tell me what you see."

"Why?" Her eyes roamed his face in the mirror, pleading. "What are we doing?"

He was digging too deep, too fast, but he wasn't a patient man. "Let's call it an exorcism. I'm not officially trained, but I'm well-versed in demons."

She watched him, maybe hoping he'd change his mind. Or stalling. But she was a smart girl. She'd make the right choice.

Slowly, her eyes shifted, wandering the room. Then breath by breath, they lowered. Down, down, a little hitch in her chest brought them up before they lowered all the way.

He didn't prompt her, didn't move. He simply took in the splendor of the view between her legs.

Swollen, juicy lips formed a deep crevice of dark flesh, hiding the opening that had felt so fucking tight around his cock. Heat rushed to his groin, hardening him against his jeans and tightening his balls. The hood of her clit was still a beautiful shade of red from his teeth. He wanted to keep it that way.

Her voice shattered his reflective thoughts. "It's grotesque."

What the fuck? He bit down on his tongue to keep his roar from escaping. After a few deep inhales, he asked softly, "Who told you that?"

Her lips pressed together, and her body turned to shivering stone in his arms. After another battle of glares in the mirror, she looked at her hands where they were fisted on her knees. "Lots of people."

"I want names." Blood rushed outward from his core, heated and violent, hardening his muscles around her. "Start with the first fucker who fed you that bullshit."

"What are you going to do?"

"Whatever I want. Give me the name here or outside." He was one second from hauling her naked body through the woods. Thank Christ, his closest neighbor was two-hundred treed acres away. He trusted the waist-high trip wires he'd set up around the perimeter. One touch and the alarm in the cabin would blare. "Choose."

"Brent." Her voice was so soft he would've missed it if he weren't reading her lips.

"Who the fuck is Brent?"

She closed her eyes, opened them, and found his in the mirror. "My ex-husband."

He held his expression blank as his stomach bucked and burned. Not once in his research had he stumbled on an ex-husband. His first instinct was to blame the cocksucker for her disorders then find him and kill him. But he needed the story so he could show her how very wrong it was.

"Eyes on your pussy while you tell me exactly what he said. All of it, from start to finish."

She shifted her ass on the handheld mirror, which gave them both another angle of her beautiful cunt. When her gaze lowered to it, she clenched her teeth. "I've never talked about this."

He dropped his mouth to her shoulder and murmured, "I swear, Amber, I'll burn off my dick if I ever use this to hurt you." He meant it with a startling passion.

She kept her eyes on her pussy, but her gaze shifted inward as she leaned her back against his chest, her shoulders curling forward. "We were at an after-party for the semi-finalists in an international beauty pageant. I might've won the competition, but I let my stupid insecurities destroy my chances, my career, my marriage. My life."

Memories of that night two years ago built behind Amber's eyes as she stared at the flabby flesh between her legs. She wanted to hide it, to hide *from* it, but she couldn't look away. Exposing her shame and *talking about it* was fitting, right here, right now. When her fractured life couldn't sink any lower. With a man she should be repelling rather than attracting.

"It was the eve of the final competition." Her voice wavered. "All the icons of the pageant industry were there." The Master of Ceremony, former pageant winners, handpicked members of the media, and a host of celebrity models and photographers. "It was a night to impress and network with the who's who among the business."

Van's chest pressed against her back, centering her, his attentive silence an unexpected support. Despite being physically abusive, not once had he degraded her verbally. Wrong or right, it was enough to propel her. "Tawny was there."

"Tawny?"

She tensed. Oh fuck, why had she mentioned her sister? Would he go after her next?

His palm caressed her belly, a vulnerable place to touch her. *He'd punched her there.* So why did the intimacy of his hand feel so good?

He kissed the juncture of her neck and shoulder. "If she means something to you, I won't hurt her. I'm only interested in what happened."

"She means a great deal to me."

"A best friend? Or a sister?" Understanding warmed his voice. He had no reason to fake that. He could've simply forced her to answer.

"My only sibling. She's a mid-level fashion model, dabbled in pageantry, but didn't have the same success. She was always at my side." Clinging to Amber's circle of friends, looking for the big break in her own career.

He pushed her hair over one shoulder, and his lips brushed the back of her neck, raising hundreds of tiny bumps across her skin.

She cringed, but didn't lean away. "Brent was entertaining a crowded table with his usual charm when he asked me to grab him a beer. That was his thing. Work the crowd while I...I was an introvert." Her stomach turned, and bile simmered through her chest. "When I returned, more people had gathered around him, and he was...fla— flapping his arms in the air. Men and women, dressed in tuxes and evening gowns, were doubled over, howling with laughter and wiping tears from their eyes."

Van's chest hardened behind her as she contemplated the ugly dark folds of skin around her vulva. "I knew it had something to do with me, something awful." It usually did. Her voice strained. "He was a crowd pleaser. Everybody loved him." Which was why she fell so hard for him, so fast, at the naive age of eighteen. Her head bent forward, her entire body aching, as visible tremors coursed through her. "Always the center of attention. Even when it was at my expense."

"Why?" His sharp tone cut through her. "What did he gain from that?"

Her spread legs shook beneath her hands, and her heart twisted painfully. She searched for the right answer, the one Dr. Michaels had helped her come to terms with. "We met in high school and married at eighteen, right about the time I entered the world of pageantry. Things were good. Better than good." A flutter brushed against the ache in her heart and faded just as quick. "Time and the stress of my career changed him."

By age thirty, Brent's physique had softened with extra weight. He never looked less handsome to her, but it bothered him, especially as her body continued to firm and tighten with her pursuit of fitness modeling. "He grew angry and unhappy, and I was the target for his bitterness, a way to redirect his insecurities from himself. That realization didn't come until later. At the time, I felt like a constant disappointment."

Her legs squeezed closed, protectively, but Van caught her thigh and gave her a warning pinch on the tender skin inside her knee.

When his hand returned to her belly, she let her legs fall open and swallowed around the surging emotion. "He nitpicked and scrutinized *everything*, convinced me to...uh...well, to get this awful boob job, bleach my hair, and bake in a tanning bed. I wanted to please him, to absorb his sadness, so I guess I let him slowly transform me. But his insults grew crueler, more public."

It was when Brent stopped looking her in the eye, when he stopped looking at her at all, that hurt the most. To think she'd kept the light *on* back then, hoping he would *see* her, so driven to please him. She was so goddamned tragic.

Van's thumb shifted upward, along her sternum, and traced circles in the hollow of her throat. "He's fucking weak."

"Says the man who hits women." She braced herself for a strangling squeeze of his fist.

The thumb stilled, and his teeth lowered to her nape, scratching gently, his breath shooting sparks of heat down her spine. "I'm far worse than your sissy bitch of an ex. Don't ever forget that."

Her spine tingled anew, itching to put space between them. At the same time, it'd been years since she felt this at ease with her body. Not that she was relaxed. Far from it. Hell, she was sitting on a mirror with her legs open. *With the lights on.* Her muscles ached and trembled, and her hips burned. But the pain was a startling distraction. Her vision wasn't consumed by black snow. Her heart wasn't flat-lining. The absence of a looming breakdown made her head spin.

He kissed her neck and placed his palms on her inner thighs, widening her legs. "Continue."

Cool air drifted over her labium, bringing with it the chill of memory. "Right." She cleared her throat. "Well, I approached the table, and dozens of eyes flew in my direction, leering, crinkling with laughter. Lowering to my groin." Which had suddenly felt obscenely pronounced in the tight satin of her gown.

Truth was, she'd grown insecure about the way her lips had stretched over the years, enough to stupidly mention it to Brent while he was fucking her the night before. A desperate attempt to seek his approval. His only response had been a series of grunts.

Tears rose up, then and now. She exhaled through it. "Brent was too busy flopping his bent arms like a chicken and squawking hysterically to notice my return. 'Flapping wings,' he said. God, it was...so loud. So fucking mean." When he'd finally made eye contact with her, he leaned over to Tawny. *I feel bad for her. You should see how the skin hangs. It's grotesque.*

Sharp pain seared through her sinuses, stabbing needles behind her eyes. "Then he played the role of concerned husband, asking if anyone could recommend a...a g-good labial plastic surgeon to help me with my...*problem*." She whispered the last word as if that would make it less real.

It had been a defining moment. The accumulation of all his hurtful words, the years of insecurities that came with posing before judges, and her lifelong battle with OCD had mounted inside her, pressurizing, as she stood amidst the laughter, moments from losing her polished demeanor.

Van tilted his head. "You looked up images on the Internet, right? You would've seen how completely normal your cunt is."

She wobbled on the counter, nodding. "Those pictures made me feel worse. Outside of the few deformities posted on medical sites, the Internet is full of porn and beauty and perfection. Normal thirty-year-old women don't post those kinds of images." She tried to close her legs, and his grip on her thighs stopped her.

"Then you recognize the difference between a deformity and an eighteen-year-old porn twat." His hands found her fingers and moved them to her inner thighs, holding them there. "What did you say to Brent after the surgery comment?"

Van's nonjudgmental interest bolstered her, and she sat taller, less shakier. "It was clear he had described my vagina to a room packed with my colleagues, people who could make or break my career. In that single lonely heartbeat, I woke up. I realized he didn't love me. How could he? You don't treat someone you love with such vicious cruelty."

Van shifted against her, and a swallow sounded in his throat. "Love and hate are closely related expressions of the same intensity. Both require passion, and neither follows logic. If he didn't love you, he would've treated you with shrugging detachment."

His response resonated with what she knew of his own volatile behavior. She didn't *know* him, but she imagined he could love someone as fiercely as he hurt them. It would take a strong, willing person to survive his brand of passion.

With his hands caressing her fingers and thighs and his face nuzzling her shoulder, his affection momentarily eclipsed his earlier abuse. But he would hurt her again. She needed to pin that to the forefront of her mind and never confuse possessiveness and control with love. The way she had with Brent.

A glance at her pussy transported her back to the ballroom, and the remembered shock of what happened dragged her tongue over numb words. "The beer I held out dropped to the floor as I repeated out loud, 'Flapping wings.' It was the first time I'd heard that particular insult, and I wish I would've yelled it, owned it, with fucking venom. Brent didn't bother to turn around, simply glanced over his shoulder and told me to fetch him another beer."

Van's fingers wove through hers, digging into her thighs, and his breaths grew sharper, faster. "Amber—"

"Let me finish." She wanted to relive her anger, feel it thrash through her body and feed on its strength. "Tawny leaned back in her chair beside him and asked with drunken liveliness, 'Your lips are so stretched you can fly with them? Really, Amber? You gonna fly across the stage tomorrow and collect the crown with a sweeping vaginal thrust?'"

Van's eyes flashed to hers in the mirror. "I hope you smacked the mouth off that whore."

She flinched. "She was drunk." Tawny had a sick mother just like her and would always be her sister, the girl she raised and loved unconditionally. Even when Tawny stood by Brent during the divorce. And after. The heavy, achy weight of responsibility pressed down on her chest. "You promised not to hurt her."

"I won't." His gaze didn't waver from hers. "Unless you ask me to."

"Never." She unloaded the gravity of her heart in that single impassioned word.

His arms fell away, his body heat gone. She watched his reflection pace the large bathroom, hands in his hair, red splotches creeping from the neck of his t-shirt. Even when irritated, he moved with a swagger in his step. The lift of his arms raised the hem of his shirt, exposing the cut *V* of his abs and the bounce and flex of cotton-stretching muscle. His jeans rode so low on his trim hips a dark line of hair surfaced above his belt.

On the next pass, he slipped a toothpick in his mouth and stopped behind her, his expression turbulent. He gripped her thighs, holding her legs open, and gave her the full potency of his silver eyes and growly voice. "You should've yanked up your dress and showed those fuckers your beautiful pussy."

Oh God, he was fuming. On *her* behalf. It should've scared her, but in that fleeting moment, she trusted he wouldn't turn his anger on her. "I did. I removed my panties and ripped my designer gown from ankles to waist, right up the middle."

His eyes widened, and his mouth hung open, the toothpick protruding from the corner. She liked that. When his lips tilted in a lopsided grin, she loved it, so much so she wanted to smile with him. But she could still feel her fury from that night, her blood simmering at the surface, scorching her skin.

"I gathered the satin fabric behind me, turned in a circle, and let the room have their fill of my flapping wings." Brent's face had turned ashen, but she'd been too heartbroken to care. Somehow, she'd managed to grab her panties from the floor and walk out of there with the confidence of a beauty queen, head high, long strides, one heel before the other, hands relaxed at her sides. The nervous laughter of two hundred people had followed her out the door. "I left Brent that night. I was disqualified. Tried to enter other pageants for the next year. I never stepped on stage again."

"Your disqualification remains a mystery on the Internet. No one talked to the press? No camera phone shots of you in your ripped gown?"

Every nerve in her body bristled on high alert. Of course, he'd researched her. He was a *stalker.* "The event was an invite-only affair for the semi-finalists. Since the pageant hadn't aired yet, the attendees were confidential. No cameras allowed. After, the pageant officials were tenacious about keeping the details hushed." They hadn't wanted to tarnish their reputation with the disgrace of a contestant.

Van's palms slid down her thighs and paused an inch from her outer lips. "No one has seen this since that night?"

She shook her head. "Not even a doctor," she said absently, distracted by the view of her pussy framed with the thumbs and fingers of his huge hands. It looked the same but strangely...protected. What if Van had been there that night, standing beside her with his broad shoulders, alluring scar, and intimidating eyes? Would they have laughed then? Would she have cared what they thought? Such an absurd, disturbing notion, yet imagining it sparked a burst of warmth in her chest.

"When I look at your tiny pink lips," he said softly, "I want to slide my tongue between them and suck the sweetness from your tight hole. I crave your taste, the velvety feel of you in my mouth and around my cock." His eyes found hers in the mirror, a smoldering collision. His pupils dilated into bottomless pools of danger, pulling her in. "Your pussy is exquisite, Amber. A perfect mold of flesh and fantasy, of throbbing blood and healthy life. Nothing compares to the grip of your wet heat. *Nothing.*"

He ground his erection against her back, but she didn't think he was trying to be lewd. Nor did she believe he'd force her to have sex on the heels of revealing her humiliating story. He was merely proving his words the one way he knew how, and she wanted to believe them.

When he stepped away and handed her the towel, she knotted it around her and stared at his outstretched hand. *Don't let your guard down.* With a steady breath, she gripped his fingers and followed him out of the bathroom to the kitchen.

The drapes on all the ground-level windows kept her breathing at an even tempo, but the layers of dust on the furniture, the crusty dishes on the counter and in the sink, and black smudges on the tiles ratcheted her pulse to ear-ringing anxiety. She pulled away from his hand and sprinted to the sink, the tremors in her legs numbing her feet.

Where to start? Oh God, she would never get this place clean enough. She ducked her head, searching for the soap, the scrub brushes, the dishwasher... Where were the damned—?

His hand wrapped around her throat and yanked her back. Deep grooves formed in his forehead, his eyes narrowed and steely. "Sit the fuck down." He shoved her by her neck until her ass hit a chair at the table, seating her.

Utensils and canisters cluttered the counters in no logical order. Streaks of grime coated the cabinet doors. God only knew what she'd find if she opened them. Her lungs tightened, her inhales shallowing, coming faster.

His fingers returned to her throat, forcing her chin up. Frustration hardened his eyes, but it didn't channel to the soft rumble of his voice. "There's no way a room full of shallow fuckwads turned you into this. When did it start?"

Nothing was that simple with her. "I have—" She choked around his grip, and he dropped his hand to her lap, squatting before her. She coughed, glaring at him. "I have a genetic connection to agoraphobia, OCD, and substance abuse." *Don't look at the burnt splashes of food on the stove. Don't look at it.* "My mother predisposed me to some nasty traits." And she was seconds away from having a full-on freak-out amidst his nuclear level of disgusting clutter. She leaned into his face, her chest pumping with heavy breaths. "You should probably return me. I'm no good."

His jaw set. "If you lose your shit, I'm tossing you on the porch." He stabbed a finger at the front door.

In that moment, she despised him. Her eyes and chest ached, and she wanted nothing more than to stick it to him by stepping over that porch and running to safety. But there was no safety out there. Her safe place was unreachable, and once the mortgage foreclosed, it would be gone.

He stood. "You're going to sit there and tell me about the anxiety while I fix dinner."

When his back turned, she closed her eyes, shielding herself from the cluster-fuck-chaos of his kitchen, and drew a ragged breath. "Eighty percent of patients with my conditions have first degree relatives who suffer from panic attacks. My mother is a doozy of mental illnesses and was committed to Austin State Hospital when I was twenty-two. Tawny was twelve when I took her in."

The glide of his feet over tiles drifted toward the fridge. "Does your sister have these conditions?"

"She has her own obsessions, but nothing like my mom and me." Strange how she could talk about this with a man who would hit her as readily as kiss her. It took twelve phone calls with Dr. Michaels before she'd opened up. Probably because she wasn't trying to impress Van. He'd brought her crazy into his home, so he could suffer the ugly details or fuck off.

"Where's your dad?" he asked.

"He left when Tawny was a baby. He couldn't handle it." She didn't blame him for leaving her mother, but leaving her and Tawny? That was unforgivable.

She rested her closed eyes on her hands, elbows propped on the table. "I used to manage the anxiety with medication until I became addicted to the pills. With the help of one of my therapists, I learned how to focus it outward. Pageantry and modeling was a distraction." Though not a healthy one.

Dishes and silverware clattered behind her. Then the microwave beeped four times, grounding her.

"After the night in the ballroom, I held myself together for three months. Brent and Tawny had been my only potential support network, and when I lost them, I had no one. Still, I bought that house, applied for competitions, and taught myself leather-crafting to keep busy." To keep herself sane. She crossed and uncrossed her legs beneath the table. "Then the panic attacks started. The first one happened in a clothing boutique where I ran into a group of models who had been there that night. When they saw me, they laughed and whispered. But they made sure I heard what they were saying."

The panic attack had left her crippled and sobbing on the floor for hours. The manager had to drive her home. "I never returned to that store or any other boutique again. One by one, the attacks surfaced in different places. I'd see someone leer at me at the gym, smell something in a store that reminded me of that night, and an attack would drop me to my knees. I couldn't go back to those places, and my world grew smaller and smaller. Eventually, I stopped going anywhere."

The chair beside her screeched across the floor, and the scent of chopped onion, peppers, and cilantro tickled her nose. She opened her eyes to find a platter of folded shells resembling enchiladas.

"Enfrijoladas." He cut into a corner with a fork and held it to her mouth. "Corn tortillas dipped in bean sauce. Open."

"You just made this?" He could cook?

"Last night. For you."

A shiver licked down her spine, a reminder that he'd been stalking her, planning her capture. "I'm not hungry." How many calories were in the shavings of white cheese alone? Two days worth, at least.

"This" —he wiggled the fork— "or the door."

She slammed her teeth together. She was a captor's dream. No steel bars needed here. Just threaten her with an open door, and she would fall at his feet. Well, she wouldn't make it that easy for him. "Four bites."

He smirked and pushed a glass of water across the table so she could reach it. "Three."

Tension vibrated her shoulders. Three was fewer calories, but it wasn't *four*. His smirk meant he knew how much she depended on that number. So much for being difficult. She opened her mouth, too tired to dwell on numbers or the fact that he was creeping her out by feeding her.

He slid the fork between her lips, and a zest of full-bodied seasonings mingled over her tongue. Spicy but not too hot, the taste of Mexico melted in her mouth. He watched her with an expectant expression as she chewed.

His last name was Quiso. His pale gray eyes looked European, but with his dark hair and tanned skin, he could easily have a little Mexican in his woodpile.

After he fed her two more bites, she asked, "Did your mother teach you how to cook?"

He laughed, but there was no humor in the clipped tumble of huffs. "If Isadora couldn't smoke it or inject it, she didn't bake it."

Oh. He'd said she was dead. She gripped the towel covering her lap, curiosity scrabbling at her tongue. "Your father—"

The fork clanked against the plate. He stared at the table, eyes shuttering as his silence tightened around her. She tensed for the impact of his fist. But what he hit her with was far more jarring.

"He was a human trafficker like me." His empty voice coiled the tension in the room. "Brought me into the business when I was twenty-five." He looked up. "When Austin appointed him Chief of Police."

She stopped breathing, her head spinning with the biggest news story to come out of Austin. *Police Chief linked to the kidnapping and rape of two missing persons.*

"Eli Eary," she whispered.

"Good ol' Dad. Quality role model for Austin's youth." Disgust and sarcasm layered his tone, but it also held an edge of sadness.

His father trafficked slaves. His mother was a drug addict. She looked at him, *really looked* into his insidious silver eyes. What must they have seen in his thirty-something years? Had he spent his entire life in a dark light, dragging the sins of his parents behind him? How could he not be anything but fucked up?

Don't make excuses for him, Amber.

He dug into the food and spoke while he chewed. "You followed the news story?"

"Some. He kidnapped that girl and held her for years. And the football player from Baylor." Enslaved them in a suburban house doing unimaginable things to them. "They shot him."

"Yep." He leaned back in the chair and leveled her with his luminescent gaze. "Don't remember their names, do you?"

She shook her head, dread creeping into her bones.

He chewed, swallowed. "Liv Reed and Joshua Carter."

Liv and Joshua got away. They all got away.

The trembling started in her chest and rippled to her arms and legs. They lived right next door all this time? The reason he was on her porch?

She could guess why he'd returned for them, and it slammed her heart into a laborious frenzy. Even if she could return home and save her mortgage, would she feel safe living beside Liv and Joshua? Van would come back for them. For her.

"You should really get out more." He raised a glass of water to his lips, grinning.

She choked, wanting to argue this unbelievable story. "The news reports said he worked alone." Her voice strangled, rising in pitch. "There wasn't any mention of a son."

He drained the glass, set it down, and leaned in to stroke her jaw. "Because I don't exist."

As Amber paled and scooted her ass away inch by inch, Van questioned the brilliance of telling her who he was. He put his elbows on the kitchen table and rubbed his aching head. Despite how familiar he'd become with her strained fearful look, she now stared at him through new eyes. He already told her he'd trafficked slaves. Apparently, connecting him to the infamous Eli Eary had sent her over the edge. Literally.

She'd scooted so far, she fell over the side of the chair and crashed to the floor, giving him a glorious view of all her taut little lines and curves beneath the splayed towel. He bit his lip, halting his grin. Her clumsiness in these frazzled moments was such a contrast to the image of her decorously posed on a stage.

With a huff, she jumped to her feet and retied the knot at her chest. "What do you mean, you don't exist?"

Here we go. He'd opened the door. Might as well give her a tour of the shit hole. He dug a toothpick from his pocket and slid it between his teeth. "Eli Eary—we called him Mr. E—never mentioned me to anyone in his lawful life."

"Why not? You're his son."

"The bastard son of his first *slave*. Not something you brag about over donuts at the police station." He gnawed on the toothpick. "And in his criminal life, I only existed to the slave buyers—who don't talk because they're dead. And the slaves—who don't talk because they killed the buyers."

She touched her throat, her voice disbelieving. "That's how the others got away?"

Should he worry about her connecting Liv's escape with hope for her own way out? Nah. She couldn't even look at the windows, let alone step outside. And by the time she overcame the agoraphobia, she would be too attached to him to leave. "Yep." Liv had been a very naughty girl, but her ability to outsmart him and Mr. E lifted his chest with pride. "I didn't know Liv had freed the others until I started watching her."

"*Stalking* her." She flashed him a reproving glower. For long moments, she didn't move, but she seemed to be calming herself. It was a fascinating thing to watch. The heave of her torso slowed, and her hands loosened around the knot of the towel. She had no idea how strong she was. "You said you were twenty-five when he brought you into the...business. Does that mean you and your mom had escaped before that?"

Not quite. He smiled as his acidic existence burned him from the inside out. "Mr. E took my mother from a US-Mexican border ghetto when she was sixteen. He broke her, impregnated her, and returned her where he'd found her." She'd been his first, after all. His guinea pig. And a pregnant slave, so far beyond mentally ruined, had no value on the market. So he'd thrown her away like a used condom.

She stepped toward the kitchen table and sat two chairs away. "And you went with her?"

"Yeah." The unwanted spawn. He rolled the toothpick with his tongue and relaxed against the chair back as every organ inside him twisted and turned. He'd only ever shared this with Liv, and he'd been weak from her bullet when the truth spilled out with his blood.

Her slim eyebrows pulled in, her face pinched in thought. "What did her family do when she returned? Wasn't there retaliation? An investigation?"

He laughed and shook his head. "My mother was a run away, and we lived in a *colonia*. The dumping grounds for America's uneducated, discarded waste. No drinking water, no working sewers, no *law*, and certainly no care for someone else's problems." A wave of bitterness tightened his muscles. It was no wonder he took pleasure in human suffering.

She gripped the knuckles of one hand. He waited for the four cracking pops, a mechanism he'd noticed she turned to when she was upset. But they never came. She flattened her palms over her thighs, staring at them, and spoke quietly. "You were cursed at birth to be fucked-up. Just like me." A ragged inhale. "Honestly, I'm surprised you're so..." She closed her eyes.

He leaned toward her, his heart knocking at his ribs with anticipation to hear the rest of that thought. "I'm so...what?"

Her eyes cut to his, and she shrugged. "You're smart."

The compliment curled through him, loosening his shoulders and thickening his tongue. He'd never considered himself smart. He researched anything and everything that interested him, but he certainly wasn't educated in the traditional sense. "Mr. E taught me what I needed to know." How to read expressions, lure the unsuspecting, calculate human reaction, and how to break the strongest will. "But I couldn't tell you what the square root of sixteen is."

She moved her mouth as if tasting her precious number. Then her eyes glimmered. "Liar."

True, but that was the extent of his math skills. Feeling playful, he smirked. "You know what the square root of *us* is?"

She cocked her head and wrinkled her nose. Then her lips curved, dimpling her cheeks. "Fucked-up." The strength of her brilliant smile hit him smack in the chest with a shimmering burst of warmth and connection.

He was so fucking tempted to grab his chest and trap the feeling there, that strange exuberant joy. Whatever his expression held made her lips soften. The seam of her mouth slowly separated, the rosy flesh clinging together then letting go. Something was inching its way into the air, energizing the space between them, and she was two chairs too far away.

Carefully, he slid back from the table. Her shoulders tightened, and her chest expanded on an inhale. He stood and covered the distance between them with lazy deliberate steps, marking her subtle breaths. When he reached her, he lowered to his knees.

Her gaze dipped to his mouth, and her tongue darted out to tap her upper lip. "What's with the toothpicks?"

The question stiffened his back. He'd acquired the habit as a means to intimidate. Nothing conveyed *scary motherfucker* like removing something from his mouth, something he would've appeared to be concentrating on, to focus all of his attention on a frightened little slave.

No way would he remind her what he was and ruin the moment. "It used to be a tree trunk. I'm so badass I chewed it down to a toothpick."

She shook her head, gifting him with another sweeping smile.

His dick swelled. He flexed his thighs but couldn't shake the grip of his arousal. It surged blood down the length of his cock and lowered his voice to a gruff rumble. "Admit it. Ain't nothing sexier than me on your ass, gnawing a toothpick."

She reached up and flicked the protruding end, making it quiver like an arrow. Then she exploded with laughter. "Yeah, you're soooo hot when you have wood in your mouth."

Aw God, the husky rhythm of her laugh could light a fire in a cold dead heart. "I'd rather have *you* in my mouth. Specifically, your perfect, tight cunt."

A flush crept across her cheeks, but her touch lingered, brushing against the toothpick and slipping to the corner of his lips. Her fingernails scraped the stubble on his cheek, and her eyes followed the movement, lashes heavy and dark against her glowing skin.

This tenderness...it was like nothing he'd ever experienced. It made his heart race and his fingers shake. It both alarmed and invigorated him. He didn't want it to end.

He held still, aching for her kiss. Not to take her lips but to give her his, just to experience a moment of surrender, to be at her mercy. Throughout the toxic span of his sexual history, he'd only had one relationship, and Liv had fought him through every damned interaction. He'd never allowed another to initiate a kiss, not even when he was used as a boy or later as a whore. What would it feel like to receive genuine affection?

Her face neared, perhaps an unconscious movement, and her exhales caressed his chin. He knew what this was. Stockholm Syndrome was a foregone conclusion, a symptom of being captured. But that didn't stop him from parting his mouth, hoping for something that couldn't be explained away by a criminal psychologist. The toothpick dangled between his teeth, seconds from falling. She plucked it away and replaced it with her lips.

Every cell in his body zeroed in on the soft glide of her mouth, the gentle suckle of his lower lip, and the taste of spices and honey swirling over his tongue. His entire fucking world flipped inside out, everything he knew about intimacy crumbling away to be replaced by something softer, farther-reaching, and intensely terrifying.

He tried not to fall, told himself it was dangerous, but her kiss grew in confidence, demanding more, stretching so fucking deep she was swallowing him whole. If she reached his soul, he would've given it to her. If the cabin burned down around him, he wouldn't have noticed. He was a goner.

Her jaw stretched wider, and he opened his, letting her explore his mouth with licks and nibbles. Her little bites stroked a feverish heat over his skin, and his brain melted into useless mush. Soon, he couldn't feel his body at all, didn't know where he was, as every sensation concentrated on the warmth of her lips, the dance of her tongue, the beat of her pulse beneath his palm.

Ah, there were his hands, wrapped around her neck, his fingers a restraint made of flesh and bone. He savored the acceleration of blood pumping through her carotid, the delicate sinews yielding to his will, his grip immovable yet soft and cherishing.

His experiment in surrender over, he moved on autopilot, reclining back and taking her with him. As he wrapped her legs around his waist, she tried to break the kiss, but he was in charge now. His mouth was insistent, his tongue holding hers down. His hands found her ass beneath the towel, and his fingers curled into hard, hot muscle.

No doubt she would fight him. Her muscles would go rigid, her jaw would stiffen, and—

Whoa. Her body liquefied against his chest, her arms folding around his shoulders. Her tongue followed his, and a quiet moan vibrated in her throat.

Fuck him, but her submissiveness was her most powerful compulsion, one that would haunt him and possess him until he owned her body, soul, and tangled mind. He ground his hips against the bared apex of her thighs, dragging her closer with his hands on her hips.

They kissed for a delirious eternity, their breaths fusing in a caress of wet licks over heated flesh. He wanted more, his cock wanted in her, and his groan vocalized his need. He flexed his ass and rocked his erection against his zipper, against her cunt, his jeans too damned itchy and tight.

She wriggled in his lap and sucked on his tongue, seemingly as lost as he was. Until she tensed, silencing their smacking sounds.

No telling where her mind just went. His thoughts floated somewhere between *Fuck her now* and *Don't fuck her up*. He let her pull back and grimaced as she shifted on his aching, swollen cock.

Her lips, glistening and swollen, taunted him as she spoke. "What are your plans for Liv and Joshua?"

A sour taste hit the back of his throat. He stalked them because he was sick. Obsessed. Lonely. But more than that, because they had access to a life he wanted. *Sweet, round face. Brown curls. Precious. Innocent. His only living blood.*

He couldn't admit to Amber how much a relationship with his daughter meant to him, how Livana was the only pure thing that had come from his miserable life. Maybe Amber wouldn't say anything out loud, but he didn't want to see the doubt in her eyes, the glaring rebuttal. *You're just like Mr. E. You're not good enough to be a father.*

A fission of pain ripped open behind his eyes. "I wasn't going to take them. Or hurt them." He hated the desperate edge in his voice, the frantic need for her to believe him. He gripped her neck. "I told you I'm out of the slave business."

"Then what am I?"

What *was* she? Broken like him but better, brighter, an unexpected discovery, like the gems in her shattered crowns. "The greater half of fucked-up squared."

She sighed. "I think your math needs some work." She glanced down at the flat expanse of her tummy where it lay bare beneath the separation of the towel.

The cleft of her pussy pressed so seductively against the ridge of his strained jeans. She ran a hand down her torso, and her shoulders bunched. A frown gripped her face, the only warning he had, before she shoved off his lap and stumbled back.

What the fuck just happened? "What's wrong with you?"

Her face twisted, and she hugged herself. "My stomach hurts."

He studied her tightening posture, bent spine, and defensive tuck of her arms. "Maybe you need to take a shit."

She cringed. "You did *not* just say that."

He'd bet his right testicle she'd never so much as farted in front of her ex, let alone discussed her bowel movements with him. He shrugged. "A good dump always makes me feel better."

"You seriously don't have any boundaries."

Boundaries were for the scared and weak. "At least I'm not constipated. Want a laxative?"

"I'm not—" She stomped a bare foot on the floor four times and squeezed her arms around her abdomen. "You're right. I need to go to the restroom."

Because he didn't have an iota of desire to watch her shit, he stood outside the closed bathroom door and gave her some privacy—the *only* privacy he would ever allow her. Hands in his pockets, mind at peace, he marveled at how much warmer the cabin felt with her presence. Someday, she might consider it her home, her safe place, with him. But it would take time to trust her not to hurt herself, to not harm him.

As he waited, that thought began to niggle. Nothing in the bathroom could be used as a weapon, and the door didn't have a lock, but something didn't feel right. She hadn't just asked to use the bathroom. She'd scowled at her body and triggered some thought that had her hugging her belly.

He grabbed the knob and hit the door open with his hip.

She was bent over the toilet, hacking quietly, too softly, as if she'd invented the art of graceful barfing. Even then, he might've blamed his cooking if she hadn't lowered her eyes to the floor and pawed at her hair with anxious hands. If she were truly sick, she would've ignored him, too focused on the pain.

She solidified his suspicion when she opened her mouth. "You trying to poison me?"

Her tone was too inwardly focused, too ashamed. If she thought he'd put something in the food, she would've gone at him with fire in her eyes.

His hands clenched and unclenched. He should've known. She was too fucking thin. "You're a puker."

She wiped her mouth with the back of her hand and said to the floor, "I never asked you to take me." She looked up and shouted, "Or my fucked-up problems!"

Fuck that. She was *his* to care for, to revere and keep safe. He didn't care what her *problems* were. He wouldn't allow her to treat her body this way. "Where is the girl who had enough pride in herself to stand on a stage and invite judgment? I *demand* more from you."

"Let me give you a quick lesson on vanity." She seethed through her teeth. "It's sensitive and shallow. If you overfeed it, you'll make it puke."

That mouth would get her nowhere. If she was going to behave like a brat, he'd treat her like one. He released a frustrated breath, calming himself, and removed her toothbrush from the drawer. "Brush your teeth."

She gave him a nasty little glare then did as she was told. She must've been counting in her head, because she muttered "Four" around the foam of toothpaste each time she moved the bristles to a new tooth.

He pinched the bridge of his nose. She was fucking exhausting, and he hadn't even begun the discipline that was coming for her unacceptable behavior.

When she finished rinsing, he yanked the towel from her body. Before she could protest, he threw her over his shoulder and hauled her out of the bathroom with a firm grip on her ass and thigh. She kicked and punched as he carried her through the sitting room. Her tiny fists hammered his back, propelling him through the kitchen and into the mudroom.

The tall cabinet held everything he needed. Pinning her tiny, bucking body to his shoulder with one arm, he gathered rope, cuffs, condoms, and his favorite whip. Then he reached for the door that led to the woods out back.

A painful wail tore from her lungs, her nails clawing his back. "What...what are you— No, I can't. Can't go out." Her breathing came in choking stops and starts. "What are...you doing?"

He'd spent seven years breaking people. Could the same methods un-break someone? It would certainly make her think twice before puking again. "Punishment, darling." He threw open the door and stepped outside.

She convulsed in his arms, totally missing out on the surreal skyscape, the fading mist of violet clouds, and the full moon ascending above the horizon of timber. As she strangled on her breathless protests, he strode toward the tree line and into the twilight of what might be the longest night of her life.

Amber's screams clawed their way into Van's heart as she flailed and sobbed in her wrist bindings. Fucking hell, why did he care? He wasn't an unfeeling man, but his emotions usually resulted in a ruthless, more external reaction, like a black eye on the person who caused them. This unexpected compassion smacked the damned sense out of him. What the hell was he supposed to do with that?

He cinched the last knot around the tree and recalled what he'd read about agoraphobia. Systematic desensitization was the term many articles used, and his takeaway was simple. *Expose her to the phobia. Let her panic, watch her freak out, and don't let her give in to her response, which is avoidance.*

It was supposed to be a gradual process, but easing into things wasn't his style. And while he could've handled Amber's punishment inside the cabin, she needed to learn how to cope with and overcome the fear. He wanted to become the *habitual response* she turned to.

His own purpose hadn't wavered. Helping her would help him. A whole, recovered Amber would prove he was a better man, that he could be a good father. If he succeeded, she would stand by his side and maybe even *hold his hand* when he met his daughter for the first time.

Hanging from a massive horizontal branch by her arms, she kicked her feet through the dirt, contorting her torso and gulping for air as if each breath were her last. A string of hyperventilating shrieks followed. Spasms shook her body, and the demon returned in the form of flinging spit and snapping teeth. "I hate you." More heaving. "Fuck you." Her teeth chomped at the air between sputtered insults.

He'd managed to dodge the majority of her rabid bites, but she'd sunk her canines into his arm twice before he'd securely tied her to the branch. She'd burrowed beneath his skin in more ways than one, and he couldn't help but treasure the imprints she'd left on him.

Her arms wrenched against the restraints, and her eyes rolled back in her head. "Oh God, it hurts. Take me back." A howling wail. "Need inside, inside, inside..."

Her chant ebbed into a mumbo jumbo of hiccupping sobs and indiscernible words. He'd read that panic attacks could last anywhere from minutes to hours. Sooner or later, she'd wear herself out. Or pass out. The latter wouldn't save her. Not anymore.

When her ankles were locked down with rope and tied to the trees on either side with two feet of space between her feet, he checked her limbs for blood flow, making sure the cuffs weren't cutting skin. Then he stood before her in the spotlight of the full moon, made brighter by the beams of floodlights illuminating the yard.

Her body faced the woods, her back exposed to the swath of lawn between the cabin and the tree line. The placement gave him enough visibility and room to maneuver. He'd also hear the house alarm if the perimeter wires were tripped.

Strangled noises coughed in her bucking chest. She was beyond speech now, seemingly lost to the frenzy in her head. Brown ropes of hair clung to her frame in sweaty strands, her eyes bulging as she fought for every rasping breath.

Seeing her dark hair and agonized features flared a deep, long-buried memory. His mother used to wear the same defeated look before the drugged haze of detachment had permanently emptied her expression. He would *not* allow the same thing to happen to Amber.

He paced out eight steps behind her and tested the weight of the whip's handle. Shaking out the fall, he let the six-foot thong ripple over the ground. His target, in all her magnificent nudity, shook wildly before him. Her arms stretched over her head, secured by wrist cuffs and rope, and the muscles in her back bounced beneath the unblemished canvas of her skin. The stunning sight took his breath away.

He delayed a moment to clear his mind and refill his lungs. Then he bent and locked his elbow, moving his arm upward and flowing the whip out behind him. At the twelve o'clock position, he relaxed his arm straight down and released the plaited leather through the air with a *crack*.

The fall landed with pinpoint accuracy, raising a pink bite just above her ass cheek. She flinched, and her violent thrashing slammed to a stop. Shock? It only lasted a heartbeat before she flung herself forward, caught by the rope, and cried out loudly and mournfully.

In the past, those pained howls would've hardened his cock into a burning steel rod. He would've imagined beating the shit out of the weak boy he'd once been and gotten off on it—as vile as that was. But his dick didn't jerk, his body pliant and cool, his mind completely focused on what she needed. Too many fears were coming at her all at once, probably faster, harder, and more intensely than anything she'd experienced. He wanted to shelter her from the onslaught. He wanted to see her eyes shine bright and protect that light. He wanted to free her.

A swallow lodged in his throat, and the handle shook in his hand. Where were these thoughts coming from? And what if he made her worse?

If the whip brought her unfathomable pain, she would avoid the outside more, *unless* she was able to engage with the pain and connect it with pleasure and arousal. It was the response he hoped for. Otherwise, this would end in disaster.

With his feet spaced shoulder-width apart and the grass tickling his toes, he shifted his left foot forward. Hips loose, left hand up and out for balance, he settled into a relaxed stance and waited for the shaking to stop.

For the span of a dozen pummeling heartbeats, his uncertainty shifted. His dominant hand warmed and strengthened as it held the whip *selflessly* for the first time. Until now, it had struck only because it felt good, because it satisfied a craving. He tightened his fingers around the stiff leather grip as Amber's panting cries surrounded him, begging wordlessly for his help.

He let the whip fly. Over and over, the lashes kissed her back, her ass, and her trembling legs. Whether he wanted to deliver a light sting or a muscle-bruising blow, his body knew what to do, his attention centering on her responses. The uncurling of her fingers, the loosening of her knees, the clench of her thighs, every answer contrasted with and complemented his strikes, each stumbling sigh playing different tones of the same melody. The song of unbidden surrender.

As the physical pain overpowered the emotional, her body liquefied. Nerves, muscles, and vocal chords, once stressed to their max, appeared to be softening, dissolving into a gentle sway of limbs and hushed moans.

His arm burned with exertion, his t-shirt soaked with sweat. He lowered the whip, catching his breath, and angled his head. The moon cast a globe of light on the glistening arousal slicking her inner thighs.

Pride lifted the corners of his mouth and expanded his lungs. He was the Master of a glowing red ass and a soaking pussy, of an agoraphobic who hung naked in the woods with a sigh on her lips. Damn straight, he owned that.

He set down the whip and approached her back, pausing close enough to let her feel his body heat without touching. Not one lash had broken the skin. He'd gone easy on her, though she probably wouldn't thank him for it. "What are you feeling, Amber?"

Her head rolled forward, and a shiver rippled her shoulders.

He walked a wide circle around to her front, slowly, confidently, his gait a habit of lethal charisma, as her heavy eyes tracked his movements. A kiss away, he cupped her face and raised her chin. "Tell me."

She licked her lips, her eyelids half-mast. "I...I need..."

She'd better say *him*. He *needed* her to say it.

Holding her jaw with one hand, he dropped the other to a taut nipple, brushing it with a knuckle in teasing strokes. "What do you need?"

She arched her spine, pressing her heavy tit against his palm. Her eyes rose to his, brightening with unspoken thoughts, then drifted over his shoulder and widened. Her next inhale caught in her throat. "Take me inside." She sucked in sharply, her jaw stiffening, her voice rushed. "Need to go back. Oh God. Now."

Panic gripped him, and he twisted his neck, scanning the timber behind, his muscles swelling to attack. But nothing moved amidst the skeletal silhouettes of the sleepy woods.

A throb lit behind his eyes. Shit, her phobia was contagious, and of course, it was still there between them, a gasping fucking presence. What had he expected? A miraculous cure beneath his whip?

He checked his blooming anger and kept his tone calm yet authoritative. "Focus on me, Amber. On my hands." He flicked her nipple and trailed the pads of his fingers around the curves of her breast, lifting the warm, dense weight. "Fucking love your tits. The velvety texture, the little hard buds." He pinched a nipple, made it harder.

Her eyes shifted, and when they found his, they softened. She leaned toward him, her arms trembling in the cuffs.

"Focus on my lips." He took her mouth, and after a few coaxing nips, she melted into him. He kissed her with a deep ache in his chest, a burning need for her total attention. Sucking and licking, he dominated her mouth, fingers plunging into her hair, angling her head to deepen the kiss.

The phobia might've slipped in, but she was still entranced in subspace. All the endorphins and adrenaline that had been released with the pain would be buzzing through her body, floating her in a warm, drifty cosmos that gravitated toward her Master.

As their tongues swirled together, tangling and tasting, his hands edged around her breasts, down her flat belly, and tiptoed over her hipbones. Her skin prickled with goose bumps, her pelvis lifting toward his, enthralling him.

He continued his caress to the creases between her mound and hips, sliding down her inner thighs, and returning to her waist. A vibration thrummed beneath her flesh, heating with circulating blood. He knew how to toy with her, when to ease off, teasing the anticipation by touching everywhere but the one place that would send her into a blissful spiral. He broke the kiss. "Tell me what you need now."

A visible tremor skated over her. She tried to bend her elbows, unable to budge the rope, and dropped her head to his chest. "I...I'm scared."

Quiet, desperate, her admission shivered through him. He needed to hold her, to assure her. If he released the cuffs, would she try to run? Doubtful, but if he was wrong, he'd catch her.

With years of practice in rope work, he freed the French bowline knots in seconds. He caught her wobbly descent, mindful of the welts, and carried her to the thick carpet of grass. When he laid her on her side, she curled in on herself, her face distorted in terror, and her body wrenched into the violent throes of panic.

It happened so damned fast, locking her muscles and pinching her breaths. He watched helplessly, gripping the back of his neck. He could take her inside—*avoidance*. Or he could try something else—*distraction*.

He rolled her to her back and blanketed her body with his, bracing his legs and arms on the outside of hers, caging her in, knowing the coolness of the grass would soothe the lashes. "No one can see you. Look. You're completely covered beneath me." Not that a soul would dare step foot on his land. The *Fuck Off* signs he'd posted had been anything but welcoming.

She grabbed at his ribs with rigid fingers and pulled him closer, rooting her body into the core of his while fighting for breath. Fuck him, but he wanted to be her security, her anchor, her fucking everything. Not as her captor but as her lover.

As she burrowed deeper beneath him, her fingers stumbled against the waistband of his jeans. Maybe it was accidental, but she didn't jerk them away, rather they inched inward along his tightening abs.

A heady rush of exhilaration connected his spinning emotions to his groin. His cock, instantly hard and hungry, strained against the zipper. He ground the aching thing into the dip of her clenched thighs, and she responded in kind, bucking and gasping as her fingernails dug into his stomach.

His heart raced. He wasn't alone in these feelings. She needed him as much as he needed her, physically as much as emotionally.

He ducked his head and captured her mouth, kissing her deeply and thoroughly. She met him, her tongue sliding against his, but her breathing didn't slow its sharp, shallow rhythm.

The grass was cold and damp beneath his forearms where they bracketed her head. He ran his hands through her hair and gathered the thick mass, using it to hold her still while he plunged his tongue between her sweet lips.

The panic hadn't fully tapered, evidenced in the heave of her chest and the jerking of her body against him. She kept her elbows tucked in and her shoulders curled between his as if she truly believed he was shielding her from her biggest fear.

He strengthened the kiss, fucking her mouth with his tongue, stealing her breaths and, hopefully, the noise in her head. The earthy scent of soil and the musk of their mingled sweat bathed his inhalations as he chased her tongue, pinning it and releasing it in a sensual dance.

As her breathing slowed from anxious to aroused, he wedged a hand between their bodies, caressing her belly and lifting his hips to glide lower. When he reached the hood of her clit, he watched with awe as her eyes closed and her chin rose, exposing her neck.

Warmth sifted through him, lifting his broken soul to the surface. Where was the temptation to jump on that vulnerable throat and crush it with a ruthless hand? He wanted to own her, but not if it scarred her. She was his weakness, and with a confidence that punctuated every revelation he'd come to accept since he'd taken her, there wasn't a damned thing he'd do to change it.

Stretching his fingers to slide along her slit, he inhaled her heavy exhale, taking in the minty scent of toothpaste. Each twitch in her body sizzled along his nerve-endings, and his cock throbbed to shove itself inside her hot little cunt.

When his fingers furrowed through her damp flesh, she tensed. He removed his hand and touched her cheek, drawing her eyes to his. As she focused on him, her mouth parted and her expression gentled, but he could see the memory of him raping her straining that sensual, seductive-looking gaze.

Guilt, intense and agonizing, shredded his insides. His stomach hardened, and he dropped his forehead to hers. He'd fucked up when he'd forced himself on her, scaring her in a way he wished he could take back. “I'm sorry.”

Whatever she heard in his voice, perhaps the reedy vulnerability in his otherwise controlled tone, brought her hands out from beneath him to grip his jaw and guide his face into the light.

She stared up at him for a long, terrifying moment, her eyes searching, her lips rolling together. Then her fingers moved to his temples, combing through the hair over his ears, tenderly, lovingly, in a way he didn't deserve. Her gaze didn't waver from his as she swallowed. “I will never forget. But maybe someday, I might be able to forgive.”

A surge of emotion pulled at his jaw and gathered in his throat. “I don’t deserve forgiveness.”

She tugged on his ears, drawing his mouth to hers, and gave him her assurance in a kiss. He answered it, furiously and passionately, as a fire swept over his skin. Their mouths slid together for a blissful forever, exploring and learning, giving and taking, and still, it wasn't enough.

With her thighs imprisoned between his legs, her chest safely covered by the width of his torso, she seemed stable. Relaxed even. Her hands and arms had returned to their tucked concealment between their bodies, which put her fingers at the perfect position to bump against the swollen bulge in his jeans.

Given all the kissing and foreplay, she had to know where this was leading. Without releasing her mouth, he slipped a hand over her silky abs, sliding downward to the heat of her cunt. She didn't flinch. In fact, her kisses grew hungrier, breathier. Her nipples hardened, dragging against his chest.

A testing reach just inside the folds of her pussy soaked his finger. He pulled back his hand and brushed the hair from her face with steady fingers while his insides shook with profane need. His cock jumped, so fucking painful in its bent position it slammed his teeth together. His whole body seemed to know she was ready. As badly as he wanted to tug himself out and shove inside her, he couldn't.

He should ask first and heed her answer. Fuck, had he ever done such a thing? And open himself to rejection? Hell no. His jaw stiffened.

But if she didn't say 'No,' if she accepted him into her body through a will of her own, it would invite trust and maybe a deeper connection.

Which could expose him to a different kind of pain, a hurt far worse than Liv's bullet in his shoulder.

He stroked her cheek, her chin, and her waiting lips. "I want to fuck you, Amber. But I won't take you again without permission." And there hovered the most frightening thing he'd ever uttered. What if she never gave him permission?

She stared into his eyes, her mouth squeezed shut as if to trap the noisy breaths flaring her nostrils. Christ, the wait was torturous. Her rejection scared him as much as he had scared her. Then she spoke. "I need you inside of me."

He stilled as her words pinged through him like raindrops striking tin. Steady rain on a rusted tin roof, with his doll safe and unbroken in his lap, his mother sitting beside him, a warm breeze lifting her hair and brushing it against his face. And maybe she patted his leg as if she wasn't bothered by his company. Yeah. Amber's words were as consoling as that, his single happy memory.

He stared back at her, wanting to ask if she was sure and not daring enough to open his mouth. But her expression said it all. Firm eye contact, a soft blush, and parting lips that built into a gentle smile.

With shaky fingers, he fumbled for his buckle, loosening it and tackling the button, the zipper. His breaths caught, impatient and awkward. Holding his body over hers to maintain her veil of security, he tugged a condom from his pocket and rolled it on.

His cock jutted out, hard and ready, nudging the valley of her thighs. The position of her legs, pressed together between his, would limit his thrusts. He didn't care. He wanted to fuck her right there, outside, knowing he would love it, that she would, too.

He pressed the swollen head against her slick pussy, leaned down, and thrust his hips forward, slamming into her tight body. The hot flesh of her sheath rippled around him, squeezing, welcoming, fucking consuming him. His head fell back on his shoulders, a moan sighing from his gaping mouth.

Ah God, nothing was grotesque about her cunt. Its pretty shape, its gripping strength, there was no place he'd rather be.

He stroked in and out, her velvety warmth sucking and releasing him, shooting sparks of electricity over his skin. She flexed her hips upwards to meet his thrusts, pulling a groan from deep inside him.

His hand cupped the fullness of her breast, his palm rolling over the hard bud of her nipple. Too soon, his release rushed forward. He held it off, angling his pelvis to grind against her clit. With a few hard rotations, her breathing changed, growing faster, more shallow.

She didn't cry out as the climax took her, but he felt it throb around his cock, tightening every muscle in her body. Her fingernails scratched at his ribs. Her heels scraped through the grass between his feet.

His overwhelming satisfaction burst into exploding ecstasy. He ejaculated so hard and long stars invaded his vision. He might've thought he died if not for the kisses she peppered over his chest, grounding him.

He couldn't speak, couldn't breathe, couldn't *move*. When he finally found his voice, he stuttered with stupidity. "I can't even...that was..."

"What mutual pleasure feels like?" Her voice was husky. And bratty.

He sank his teeth into her shoulder, not to break skin but hard enough to leave a pretty bruise.

She screeched and writhed beneath him until he let go. "What was that for?" Her gaze was wide and shiny, glaring up at him, but a smile twinkled at the edges.

"For being a brat." He grinned, floating on a cloud of lingering bliss, and rolled off to free her of his weight and remove the condom.

Her choking gasps were the first indication of his fuck up. Her hands flew to her chest, her eyes darting wildly around her.

He rolled back, landing atop her and covering her thrashing body as best as he could. But he knew he'd lost her the instant she grew rigid. A scream roared from her throat, cut off, and she bucked in his arms.

Just like that, she was back to square one.

Shadows crept from the woods, inch-by-inch, breath by ragged breath, closing in and swallowing Amber's ability to run, to crawl, to scream. The ground spun beneath her, tossing her body and splintering her chest. Her lungs burned, and her bones melted into icy liquid. Too helpless. Too exposed. *Nowhere to hide.*

The earth began to suck her in, twisting oxygen-depriving tendrils around her neck. As she struggled against the chokehold, a heavy presence grabbed her and pulled her into a prison of strength and darkness.

She curled into that shelter. It felt safe, beautiful, and she didn't want to leave it. How could that be? Maybe it stemmed from her belief that every man possessed the ability to cause wonderment—even dangerous, vicious men. As she flailed through her mind, searching for escape, she found Van's wonder, his hand, reaching out through the terrible noise.

It lifted her, yanking her farther away from the horrors of outside and into a quiet cradle of warmth. His arms folded beneath her back and legs, and his chest flexed against her cheek as he carried her, his body propelling forward.

Overhead, the moon shone bright and full. The sight of it was startling, wonderfully overwhelming, and her emotions poured out in a burst of sobs.

He sped up, running now, as fast, as hard as his breaths. Through the door and up the stairs, he held her like glass. Like her aquarium, fragile and transparent, brimming with brokenness.

The world stopped spinning as the mattress caught her limp body, but her mind continued to trip. She tried to organize the mess of her thoughts, floating through them, unsure where to begin. Where had her brain been the last hour? Skipping around in a nutter's wonderland of slippery delusions? She lay there, numb and empty, as if she'd just been ripped from a drunken haze.

The cool conditioned air bit over her skin, intensifying the heat in the lashes on her back and legs. She was grateful he'd brought her inside, but she needed to lay into him for whipping her.

Maybe later. She couldn't find the energy to be pissed. Exhaustion pulled at her muscles and burned her gritty eyes. But something else muted her anger as well. Curiosity? Or shame.

Once the initial shock of his whip had faded, her body had drifted into a strange weightless suspension of time and place, her mind so centered on the next strike, all the threats of outside had evaporated from her senses.

The crack of the whip had stung, sure, but the pain had been fleeting, hypnotic. Nothing like the agony of a panic attack. Even more confusing, it had turned her on.

A jolt of remembered pleasure zinged up her inner thighs. All those floaty feelings had orbited around Van. She'd wanted him so badly, she'd fucked him. No, not fucked. She'd welcomed him like a wanton thing, grinding against his erection, begging. And he'd given it to her, a deeply physical and soulful connection, so unlike the cruelty of the rape. In fact, none of her sexual experiences compared. Not even with Brent. Especially not with Brent.

Had Van whipped his other captors? Surely, they hadn't felt the same profound intoxication? Had he fucked them, too? Her neck stiffened, and her chest ached with an irrationally selfish emotion. They had been sex slaves, normal people forced into a horrible situation, where she was...she was just sick.

The mattress jostled with his movements behind her. He kept the light on as he shifted toward her back. When he touched her, it was with cool, wet fingers. Whatever he was rubbing into the welts was tingly, soothing, and there was way too much care in those gentle strokes.

It hurt to swallow, her throat raw from screaming, so she closed her eyes, relaxing into his touch. Her head grew heavy on the pillow, the aftershocks of the last panic attack still trembling through her veins. Too soon, his fingers disappeared. But he replaced them with his body heat as he tugged the covers up and tucked them in.

Two years of shutting off the lights and closing the shades, and she hadn't been able to conquer the fear. Maybe it needed to be whipped out of her. *Inside the house.* No doubt he would do it again. She should just wrap her arms around it and embrace it.

With the same illogical impulse that had propelled her to kiss him in the kitchen, she rolled to face him, first to her belly then to her side. When she met a broad hairless chest, her heart stuttered. Had he removed his pants as well? The wall of muscle an inch from her nose tempted her to follow the dusting of hair below his abs and find out.

His arm slipped around her, and his thumb glided lazily over her nape. He smelled of earth and warmth and virility. His pecs twitched and rippled beneath golden skin, each brawny brick of his torso chiseled in a uniform sculpture of strength. Jesus, the man's body didn't know when to quit.

Apparently, hers didn't either, given the sudden throb of heat between her legs. She clenched her inner muscles and shivered. His unlawful beauty and sneaky moments of tenderness both scared and captivated her, but more than that, he compelled her.

She wedged a hand between his bicep and ribs, snaking it around his back and inching closer, so close there was no question about his state of dress.

The short hairs on his thighs tickled as his strong legs intertwined with hers. His cock, soft and thick, laid against her hip. She shivered again and knew he'd felt it when he released a soft hum.

She pressed her lips to his hard chest and savored the catch in his breath. His skin tasted salty, his raw outdoorsy scent chasing the spice of his cologne. He was quiet, perhaps thoughtful, as he snuggled against her, seemingly content with her affection, neither dismissing it nor demanding more. Laid-back, unassuming Van was irresistible.

She wriggled upward along his body, kissing his sternum, the side of his neck, and lingered on the dime-sized scar on his shoulder. A bullet wound? Had one of the slaves or the buyers shot him? Or were there other fragments of his criminal life she knew nothing about? "How did you get this?"

"Not tonight, sweetheart." The tired rumble of his voice settled over her, and the caress of his thumb moved from her neck, down her spine, pausing mid-way. To avoid the welts?

Leaning back, she peered up into his eyes and found the silvery depths tinged with lazy fatigue. She loved that look on him, but it couldn't be trusted. "My back doesn't hurt."

"It will tomorrow, brat. You need to drink water." He reached behind him and grabbed a plastic cup from the nightstand, knocking random clutter to the floor. He didn't bother picking it up. He simply rolled back and held out the cup with a raised brow.

God, what must the floor look like? Clothing and crap scattered with no order and configuration? "The mess—"

"The mess is mine. Drink."

She gritted her teeth. "Last time you told me to drink—"

"I won't drug you, because I'm not taking you anywhere." He leaned in and kissed her forehead. "You're exactly where I want you."

Her heart thumped, the foolish, gullible thing. She narrowed her eyes. "Why?"

"Because I like you."

She expected a charming grin, but what he gave her was an expression etched with honesty.

"Jesus, you look so beautiful right now." His timbre was rough, throaty.

Her mouth fell open. She was a fucking mess. Mental issues aside, she didn't wear a stitch of makeup, and her hair tangled around her neck and shoulders from rolling in the grass. She wanted to point this out, but he regarded her with such intense focus, it was easier to drop the subject. She glanced at the waiting cup.

How long had it been sitting on the table, amongst watches and hangers and discarded candy wrappers? Was there dust and bacteria in it? She wrinkled her nose. "How fresh is that?"

His eyes hardened into steel blades. "Too damned tired for this, Amber. Don't test me."

Just like that, his command was back, a reminder of his volatile nature. She accepted the cup, draining the lukewarm water, her throat tightening in pain and revulsion with each swallow. He took it from her, tossing it somewhere on the floor. With all the other mounting debris. Where there were no lines, no structure, no routine.

Her scalp tingled with rising anxiety. *Stop thinking about it.* "I'm going to make your life hell."

His head lowered to the pillow, his eyes closed. "My life is already hell. An eternal dark walk of the damned."

A bit dramatic, but no question he was damned, as was she. But there was warmth in his dark walk. Intense warmth with rock hard arms that held her close. She couldn't figure him out and, at the moment, didn't have the strength to try.

"Did you count the swings of the whip?" he murmured against her forehead. "In little groups of four?"

Her head jerked back. Count the—? No, it hadn't occurred to her. Her teeth clamped down on the inside of her cheek, sparking a burn in her eyes. How could she have forgotten to count? She'd been so scared of the woods stretched out before her, gawking at her nudity. Then the sting of the whip came, and her mind had just...blanked. He'd distracted her in a way no one else had been able to do.

"Didn't think so." His face was softly vacant, but a smile lightened his tone. "Twenty-three lashes. Not twenty. Not twenty-four."

Twenty-three marks on her body. An uneven number without balance or special meaning. Her pulse raced. The fucking prick did it on purpose! "Give me another whack of your whip. Just one." She leaned up, patting his whiskered cheek, but he wouldn't open his eyes. "It'll be quick. We can do it right here." She cringed at the frantic pitch in her voice.

"Begging already?" His lips bowed up beneath her fingers, his eyelids smooth and closed. "Go to sleep."

She glared at him, fingers itching to slap his peaceful face. What would he do? Give her another twenty-three lashes? Pin her down and fuck her? Take her outside? The last thought jerked her hand away.

The longer she studied him, the more conflicted she became. The sharp angles of his jaw, the slope of his perfect nose, the fringes of dark lashes, and the jagged edge of the scar that cut so deep into his cheek it must've hit bone. He was stunning, painfully so, but nothing in his features revealed *who* he was.

His lips relaxed, the muscles in his face loosened, and soon his chest settled into an even rise and fall of sleep.

For the next hour, she deliberated over what to do. She was a captive to this man. She should've been plotting her escape with fearful breath. Only she didn't feel scared, and *that* should've scared her the most. Instead, she was enraged, dreaming up ways to stick it up his ass and rotate it because he'd refused her a twenty-fourth mark. So yeah... All kinds of logical reasoning going on.

The bedside clock flipped to 12:04. It had only been twelve hours since she'd sent Zach away. No one would've noticed her disappearance yet. Or ever. No missing woman reports. No investigations. She was a nobody and had no one to blame for that but herself.

Van hadn't moved in his sleep, his heavy arm hanging limply around her. How could he have let his guard down so easily?

Because he knew she didn't have the balls to leave the house.

Well, fuck him. He was possessive and controlling, and she couldn't mistake that for care or concern. Everything he did was calculated, and all she had to combat him with were her wits and courage.

Courage?

Right. With a long inhale, she dug deep, pulling it from somewhere, certainly not from her hammering heart or queasy stomach. Then she shimmied out from beneath his arm. When her hair caught in his fingers, she bit down on her lip, her pulse thundering in her ears.

He didn't stir.

Slowly, breathlessly, she unwound the strands from his grip and slipped to the floor. Peeking over the edge of the mattress, she watched his breathing for a long, agonizing minute. Then she glared at the clutter. *Don't pick it up.*

With the grace of a queen balancing in six-inch heels, she tiptoed around the mess, stopped to remove a casual halter dress from one of her bags on the floor, and gave her aquarium a longing look. *Come on, Amber. You can't take it with you.*

She hugged the dress to her chest and dashed down the stairs on silent toes. In the bathroom, she pulled on the knee-length halter, ran a brush through her hair, and scoured the cabinet. Lotions, soaps, toothbrushes, and tampons filled the drawers, but no makeup.

She gripped the edge of the counter. He'd grabbed all these things from her house but not the one thing she needed to escape. How could she go outside without her cosmetic armor?

A skitter of panic seized her muscles as her reflection glared back in the mirror. Pallid skin, dark shadows beneath dull eyes, and lips twisted with disgust. She couldn't let anyone see her like that.

Excuses. She didn't need to look her beauty pageant best. She just needed a goddamned backbone. What kind of captive dolled herself up before making her great escape?

The stalling, crazy kind. God, she really annoyed herself sometimes.

She crept through the stillness of the house, the windows closed up, and the loft looming above like a watchtower. Was he watching her? Not a flicker in the soft lamp light on his nightstand.

Releasing a thready exhale, she moved to the kitchen. No cell phones or phone jacks. No knives or scissors in the drawers or on the butcher block. Not that she could've found a goddamned thing in the junk overflowing from every cobwebbed cranny. People really lived like this? Thankfully, Brent had been tidy, though thinking on it, she'd stayed on his heels, fixing everything he'd touched. And hadn't cleanliness been a point of contention between her father and OCD mother, one of the many reasons he'd left?

She opened the silverware drawer, at least the semblance of one. It also held oily screws, toothpicks, and pencils. She grabbed a fork and held it up.

What was she going to do with that? Hell, what would she do with a knife? Wasn't that something an escapee would carry while running for her life?

Until she had a meltdown, stumbled over her feet, and stabbed herself.

She abandoned the weapon idea and considered the cluttered drawer. She could put a really good dent in this while he slept. She'd start with the utensils and realign them in their appropriate sections. First, she'd have to find the sections, remove the crumbs, scrub the bottom, and—

Shit, she was doing it again. She was supposed to be escaping. As she continued to mentally clean and organize the drawer, she backed away from it and took the final steps to the mudroom.

Inside were two solid doors. One leading out back, and the other? A garage and maybe a getaway car?

Gripping her knuckles, she popped through the joints, working herself into a frenzy of indecision. Fuck, she hadn't driven in two years. And wouldn't he hear the garage doors go up?

She approached the back door and stopped a foot away. When her toes curled, she looked down in shock. She wasn't wearing shoes. *Brilliant, Amber.* No makeup, no jewelry, her hair unwashed and uncurled, she wasn't even close to being put together. Then there was the fact she had no clue what she'd do if she actually made it off the porch and encountered another person. Would she ask for help?

If she didn't face plant in a full-on breakdown, she'd spazz out over her appearance and run in the opposite direction, as pointless as that would be. But where would she go? She didn't even know where she was. Could she go home? He'd track her down, of that she was certain.

Assuming he was still asleep, she'd have a head start. She touched the knob, gripping it with a sweaty hand as her nerves flared tremors down her spine.

God, she'd rather be sleeping with him, nuzzled up against his hard body, soaking in his warmth. She could stay...

To what end? She'd heard about the psychological effects of captivity, how capture-bonding could fabricate emotional ties. He'd hit her, whipped her, raped her. *Don't fucking forget how dark he can be.*

But his darkness had showed her the moon for the first time in two years.

The tarnished metal grew slick beneath her palm. Her brain told her heart she needed to leave, but her hand wouldn't turn the knob.

Her chin trembled, and her grief rushed forward in a riptide of shaking limbs and burning tears. Dammit, she was so tired, so emotionally mixed-up. She wasn't strong enough to open that door. Not now, maybe not ever.

Deep down, she knew she'd never make it off that porch, but fuck, her pathetic self couldn't even try.

Her knees gave out, and she slid to the floor, so fucking dramatic in her misery. How had she ended up here? Not in this house, but at this level of utter weakness?

Dr. Michaels had said the *how* wasn't important. It was the *now* that mattered. *Does the* now *stop you from eating, sleeping, smiling, interacting...living?*

Van seemed to encourage all those things. She folded her arms on her bent knees, head on her forearms, and stared at the gray tiles between her feet. Gray like his eyes, the perfect blend of light and dark.

She sat there, displaced and achingly tired, until her tailbone complained and her eyes grew heavy. *What's it gonna be, Amber?* A life under his roof or a life filled with puking, sleeping pills, deliverymen, and loneliness?

She could always leave later, on another day. No, the unmade decision would linger and taunt her and drive her crazy.

For a girl who lost her shit when a sock found its way into the wrong drawer, she wasn't foaming at the mouth right now, in this house of clutter. Maybe there wasn't such a thing as a *wrong* drawer. Maybe *here* wasn't wrong. With different drawers. A different routine. With a man who might be able to love *her* as fiercely as he hurt.

She rubbed her eyes along her arms, wiping away stray tears. Lifting her weary head, her gaze crawled across the floor to the kitchen and froze.

Leaning against the fridge opposite the mudroom, he stood in the dim glow of the stove light. Wearing black athletic pants, legs crossed at the ankles, arms folded across his bare chest, he studied her with a calm, unreadable expression. She swallowed hard and dropped her eyes. Jesus, even his bare feet were intimidating.

Who knew how long he'd been standing there, watching her? She'd been so caught up in her pity party he could've been there the whole time.

He didn't move or speak, his stillness thick enough to strangle the air. What if he made her leave?

That was when she felt it, deep inside, breaking free. Her missing backbone. It straightened her back and invigorated her with a thrilling rush of strength. If he didn't want her, he could...he could go climb a wall of stretched-out vaginas.

She met his eyes. Pale, piercing eyes that told her he knew her next four steps before she did. With her eyes, she said, *Bet you didn't see this one coming.*

She rose—gracefully and steadily, despite the burning in her legs—and walked to him. The proximity forced her to look up to hold his gaze. Arms relaxed at her sides, posture strong and proud, she smiled without force or agenda. She smiled because it felt right. "I've decided to stay."

"Uh huh." The corner of his mouth ticked up. "Too scary out there?"

She glanced over her shoulder, acknowledging the door, and looked back at him. "Well, there's that. And while I could continue to fight through it and maybe someday make it beyond the porch, I've lost interest in escaping." She put the strength of her backbone in her voice so he would hear her earnestness in the most absurd, childish, fucked-up reason ever. "Because I like you, too."

Van had perfected the pose of lazy nonchalance years ago, but as he leaned against the fridge, he embraced it for no other reason than fucking exhaustion. Of course, Amber would pit her fear of him against the agoraphobia. But the first night? Good thing he'd wound her hair around his fingers like little trip wires.

No one could say she wasn't tenacious, especially considering her willingness to risk another panic attack so soon after the last one. No sweat off his balls, though. He'd been too curious to stop her. Besides, it moved her a step closer toward acceptance of her new life.

So he'd followed her down the stairs, blending into the shadowed corners of the cabin as she fought her demons in the bathroom and kitchen. When she'd opened the silverware drawer, he'd been ready to stop whatever cleaning fest she might've been envisioning. Honestly, his cabin could use a good scrub, but not at the expense of the OCD thing. He wanted to shake up the disorder, not enable it.

Big brown eyes glared up at him, her expression expectant, and challenge evident in the lift of her chin. Damn, she was willful and tireless. He was a year younger than she was, yet her energy ran circles around him. Apparently, he needed to workout more.

Judging by the fists that now moved to her hips, she was waiting for him to respond to her announcement. Impatient little twit. He'd already picked through her words, not only what she'd said but how she said it.

I've lost interest in escaping.

The steady resolve in her voice and her unwavering eye contact had been convincing. But her revelation wouldn't keep her from going outside. He'd make sure of that.

Because I like you, too.

Five easy words, but the promise they imparted filled him with fierce belonging. And an uncomfortable amount of sentimentality. He rubbed the back of his neck. He needed sleep. They both did.

"How about you *like me* upstairs...while we sleep." He added that last part to make his intentions clear. Though he could be up for something else with a little coaxing.

She smiled, and the illumination of her eyes flooded the kitchen with light. "Yeah, okay. I'm beat." Her voice hardened on the last syllable, asserting her disapproval of his heavy hand.

Bring it, baby. Fuck, he looked forward to her fight. After a good night's rest.

He let her lead up the spiraled stairs because really, how could he refuse an opportunity to be eye-level with her backside? And fuck him gently with a two-by-four, she flexed that ass with the grace of the gods. The sight of her round cheeks straining the fabric of her dress would chase his dreams for an eternity.

Then he remembered he hadn't packed any of her panties. Christ, she was too damned tempting. Halfway through the climb, he shoved the dress up to her waist, found two unmarred spots of supple flesh, and pinched the hell out of them with both hands.

Her shriek echoed through the cabin. "Hands off my ass!" She reached back, wriggling to his delight, her fingers curling around his wrists. "I mean it."

He released her, chuckling. "Darling, my hands and your ass are meant to be together. Don't fuck with destiny."

She sighed, adjusting the dress, but he didn't miss the smile dimpling her face.

"You're insufferable." She shook her head, then flew up the remaining steps, and vanished into the loft, leaving him standing there grinning like a fool. A deliriously happy fool.

The scar on his face bristled with his smile, itching. His lips fell, his fingers rubbing his cheek. She could cut him far deeper than a bullet or a knife.

He clenched his jaw and gripped the railing. He couldn't fathom backing away from whatever this was. There was so much about her, her unpredictability and her routines, her strength and her brokenness, that made him want to go all the way, wherever that might take him.

Tonight, he would sleep with her in his arms. She deserved someone better, but at the very least, he could come to bed freshly showered.

Her footsteps pattered around in the loft. All the dangerous weapons were locked up. He dashed to the bathroom and grabbed a five-minute shower.

When he climbed the stairs again, it was with renewed purpose. At the top, he found her digging through her bags. "What are you looking for?"

"Pajamas." She moved to another bag.

He hadn't packed those, either. "Wasting your time." He shed the towel around his waist and stretched out on the bed, arms folded behind his head, blissfully naked. "We both know you sleep like this."

She didn't look at him, but her arms stopped moving, elbows deep in a bag. "I hate that you know that."

He could see how the stalking stuff might bug her, but... "I won't apologize for that." His obsessive habit had led him to her. "Come to bed."

He anticipated another fight, one where she would refuse to undress and he would win because, well, he always won. But in bewitching Amber-fashion, she shocked him again.

Rising to her feet, she faced him with her hands on the hem at her thighs and tugged it up and over her head. Gorgeously nude in the glow of the lamp, she walked to the hamper, folded the dress, and placed it on the pile of dirty clothes. She stared at it for several heartbeats with her lips pursed and her eyebrows pulled in.

He shifted to his side, lifting on an elbow. Was it the sight of her laundry mixed with his? Or maybe she had some kind of ritual that involved sorting clothes in multiple hampers? Would the absence of her system trigger another breakdown? He refused to go to her. He wanted her to come to him when she was upset. "Amber?"

She looked up, and her fingers flew to her knuckles. *Crack-Crack—*

"Amber." He put force in his voice and grabbed the edge of the blanket, pulling it over his lower half and holding it up in invitation.

Her eyes darted to his face then lowered to his sleepy dick. She continued to stare, cracking her knuckles, as he recited the U.S. Presidents. "Washington, Adams, Jefferson" *—Madison—* "Mac...No, uh, Roe—"

"What are you doing?" She lowered her hands and approached the bed, head cocked.

Good girl. Keep walking.

His arm was growing tired of holding up the blanket. "Who was the fourth president?"

"Madison." She blinked. "Why?"

He was bored a couple years ago, in between slaves, and passed the time by memorizing all the presidents, first ladies, and trivial facts about each. Now he used it to distract her from a meltdown, as well as to keep his dick from hardening and scaring her away.

"Takes my mind off things." He glanced down at his flaccid cock and could feel the weight of her eyes there, too.

In the next breath, the lamp clicked off, and her knee landed beside him. Before he could catch his breath, she curled around him, arm hooked at his back and leg nudging between his.

Christ Almighty, what a goddamned fulfilling feeling, her hard feminine muscles and soft curves all up against him. He rolled to his back and savored the warm weight of her tight body pressed against his side. She felt fucking amazing, all relaxed and accepting, holding him as if she appreciated the intimacy as much as he did.

This was his new favorite position, and his dick wasn't even inside her. Hell, he wasn't even hard.

How was it that just twelve hours ago he'd held her at gunpoint, drugged her, and forced himself inside her. How could she have admitted she liked him or have any desire to snuggle against his body? But she had, and she was.

She wasn't normal.

He released a long, conflicted breath. They would never be normal. It just wasn't in their blood. He gripped her thigh, hooking it over his, and coiled his fingers around her hair. Fuck normal.

Her exhale warmed his neck, and the pad of her thumb traced his collarbone. "When was the last time you slept beside someone?"

"More than a year ago." Which didn't exactly conjure sweet memories. On those rare occasions when Liv actually stayed in his bed, he'd never felt so alone. "She was the only one. What about you?"

"Brent was the first and last." Her tits pushed against his ribs as she breathed in. "What was her name?"

"Liv."

Her fingers jerked against his chest, but her lips pressed a soft peck on his shoulder, just beside the bullet wound. He'd tell her about that, about all of it, eventually. The idea of keeping anything from her was ludicrous. And so unlike his relationship with Liv, which had died at the hand of secrets.

Tonight had been the first night he didn't drive to Liv's neighborhood in over six months, and he hadn't even thought about it till now. Thinking of her tended to stir up a turmoil of conflicting emotions. But at the moment, all he felt was a dim ache somewhere behind his heart.

"Do you love her? Is that why you were on my porch?"

There were no quick responses to that. "I'm going to delay the answer to your last question because we're both tired. As for the first, I like to think of it as a seven-year fever." Which had burned into a hotheaded, delusion-inducing illness.

His admission hovered in the darkness, smothering like a miasma he'd accidentally let in.

Her quiet voice scattered the thick air. "My fever lasted fourteen years."

Fourteen years. That sleazy asshat didn't deserve fourteen seconds with her. "You know how to treat a fever?"

"Mm. I'm too tired to think of something witty. Go ahead."

"Rest and lots of *fluids.*" He lowered his voice. "Obviously, not at the same time."

"Oh my God." Her groan dissolved into a soft lullaby of laughter. As it whispered through him, he realized the reason his days felt so empty was because they hadn't been filled with that sound.

He touched his lips to the top of her head, grinning. What a sentimental asshole.

For the second time that night, he waited for her breaths to tumble into sleep. This time, they did, pulling him along with a smile on his face.

The next morning, he woke wearing that same damned smile. But it didn't last. He was alone in the bed and the loft.

He shot up, his feet tripping over the floor. Only he wasn't tripping on a goddamned thing. Not a shirt or a magazine or a discarded pack of cigarettes in sight.

Fuuuuck. She'd been up for awhile.

The bedside clock read 10:43. He released a relieved breath. It was still early. He raked his hands through his hair. That was early, right? Jesus, what time did she normally wake?

He dug through the hamper, pulled out a pair of jeans, sniffed them, tossed them, and dug again until he found a fresher pair. Laundry was on the agenda at some point in the near future.

Tugging on the jeans, half-walking, half-hopping, he didn't bother with the zipper or button as he sharpened his attention on the stifling quiet downstairs. Would she have left? *Could* she?

A rush of blood heated his neck and face, his fingers curling into his palms. He plucked a toothpick from a holder on the dresser and sprinted down the stairs.

Halfway down the stairs, the scent of lemon and bleach reached Van's nose. Damn, damn, damn. He quickened his descent on silent feet. At the bottom, his gaze landed on the shiny kitchen counters, small appliances and canisters sparkling in a neat row, and Amber's ass hanging out of the fridge in her bend to scrub the deepest corner.

He pinched the bridge of his nose and let his frustration wave off his back. As much as he loved the sight of her in those little shorts cleaning his house, he wanted her to do it for *him*, not for her illness.

Shoulders back and chest out, he moved to the kitchen with heavy, wide steps. By the time he reached her, she was organizing condiments in the fridge door.

She spun when his footfalls landed behind her. He held his head down, his hand casually rotating the toothpick in his mouth. When her toes flexed against the tiles, he removed the pick, slowly placing it on the counter, and gave her the full force of his eyes.

She tensed, her pupils widening, her lips pinched in a line. The overhead light reflected a metallic glow around her, her dark hair freshly washed and dried. She drew in a lungful of air and grinned with overly bright eyes. "Morning. Sleep well?"

Apparently, he'd slept too well. He hadn't even heard her shower or run the hairdryer. But did the little vixen really think her pleasantries would distract him from the hand that was adjusting the mustard label in the fridge door behind her?

He stifled the laugh bubbling up inside him. Jesus, from the booty shorts and tit-hugging tank top to the fluttering eyelashes and saucy attitude, the whole package was cute as fuck. *And defiant.*

"Best sleep of my life. You?" He turned away, feigning disinterest in his now spotless kitchen, and reached into the overhead cabinet. His bare feet didn't stick to the tiles like they usually did. She'd been awake for a long-ass time.

"I slept well." She hadn't moved from her position by the fridge. If she was wary of him, she had every right to be.

He removed a box of Froot Loops and opened the package with intentional slowness as his mind sped through the next ten steps. "Have you eaten?"

"Nope." A casual response, yet it vibrated with caginess.

He kept his back to her but could feel the heat of her eyes stroking the muscles he'd worked hard to maintain. "How about some cereal?" Froot Loops was a midnight snack. No way would he feed her that junk. Nutritious meals only. Eggs and bacon, fucking protein and shit.

"Uhm. Sure."

Without turning around, he held the open box over the floor and dumped it upside down. Colorful *O*'s tumbled around his feet. He stepped side-to-side, crunching them into a satisfying dust of sugar.

Her breathing grew loud and rushed behind him. "Oh my God." Then louder. "Why?" She released an ear-splitting shriek. "I just mopped the floor!"

And he would clean it later. He wasn't a damned slob. Sure, he slacked on the laundry and didn't give a fuck which shelves the cups went on. But she wouldn't find moldy food or mouse droppings or hoarding stashes of crap falling out of the closets. He pivoted slowly to check on her.

Pressed into the gap of the open fridge door, arms wrapped around her rib cage, shoulders curled in, and eyes wildly darting over the floor, she definitely struggled to hold it together. He was about to make it worse.

He emptied the last of the box, tossed it on the mess, and strode toward her with an air of calm and focus. His unyielding grip on her elbow shuffled her sideways as he closed the fridge. Then he backed her into the counter and put his face into hers. "You will *not* clean up after me."

Her strong-willed chin appeared, jutting up and out, ready to fight. "I can't live like this. This" —she thrust a trembling finger at the floor— "is *not* okay."

"That's right. So here's how it's going to be." He clutched the counter on either side of her hips, arms straight, with two feet of tension rotating between them. "As long as you are obsessively clean, I'm going to be obsessively *not clean*. For every inch you give, I'll match it. We'll eventually meet in the middle." He lowered his head so she could see his eyes. "Got me?"

She didn't look at him, her gaze locked-and-loaded on the floor as if waiting for the crumbs to sprout hundreds of tiny stingers and attack. He knew what was coming, tipped off by the slow deep inhale and the twitch below her eye, and he let it happen.

Her knees bent fast, her body dropping to the floor. Free from the corral of his arms, she scrambled to the mess, sweeping and scooping, her breaths rushing in her frenzy to shove tiny handfuls into the box.

With an even pulse and loose muscles, he lowered to sit beside the huffing tornado. Cereal crumbled beneath his ass and legs as he leaned his back against the cabinet. She didn't seem to notice him, too consumed with black and white, linear numbers, and clean floors...her tragic need to perfect everything.

He'd had enough. She didn't weigh more than a buck-ten soaking wet, so it didn't take much effort to drag her, chest-down, across his thighs. With his forearms braced on her back and legs, she was effectively pinned.

Furious eyes flashed over her shoulder, and her legs kicked uselessly against the floor. "Let me go," she snarled, her fists still clutching handfuls of cereal.

Without moving the arm on her back, he yanked her shorts to her knees. Beautiful, bare, and blotched with tiny pink bruises, her ass flexed and prickled with goose bumps. The arnica gel he'd rubbed into her muscles the previous night would've reduced a lot of the swelling and stiffness. But he caressed a palm over the silky skin to make sure.

Her glutes didn't flinch, her fight still concentrated in the thrashing of her arms and legs. And what a fight, all muscle and soft skin and seductive curves writhing on his lap, her ass right there for the taking.

He was already hard—it was inevitable. He shifted her hips so that her clit lay directly over the swell of his erection through the open zipper, ensuring that every wriggle would stimulate her. *And him.* Then he waited for the next buck of her ass.

It rose. Fell. She gasped as her clit hit his dick. *Fuck.*

He swung his arm, laying into her round cheek with a solid, stinging smack. She writhed, the movement grinding her bundle of nerves against him, tormenting him. He spanked her again, over and over. Her flesh heated beneath his hand, her breathing catching and releasing, growing louder, and staggering into a chorus of moans, hers and his.

After the fifth whack of his hand, he trailed the tips of his fingers over the glowing burn. "Who am I, Amber?"

Her arms slid across the floor, the cereal evidently forgotten beneath them, as she snarled with a thick voice, "Van Quiso. Filthy spawn of the devil."

He gave her five more fiery strokes of his palm, harder and more concentrated than the first five. Then he pinched the heated sore flesh. "Try again."

She released a hiccupping wail, her attempt to squirm away from his grip fruitless. "Mm-m-master."

"Good girl." He glided a finger between her legs, slipping through her slick heat and thrusting to the knuckle. Tight, pulsating muscles gripped him, sucking him in, speeding his pulse.

Bound by his arm on her back, she could only kick her legs and accept the pleasure he allowed her. In turn, her responsive cries propelled him to a euphoric state of lust.

He added another finger and banged her cunt, twisting his wrist and massaging her G-spot as she groaned and rubbed her clit against the sensitive ridges of his cock.

Christ in heaven, the need to fuck her was a raging thing inside him, tearing him to shreds in its attempt to rip out and shove in her. But he couldn't force her.

He bit down on his lip, tasting blood, and dropped his hands to the floor.

Panting, she lifted her head, looked up into his face with heated eyes, then at his hands, back at his face. Her expression fell, and she slid off his lap. "Why?"

Why did he spank her? Or why did he stop? He grabbed her shorts, halting her attempt to pull them up. "I control this." He gripped his dick with his free hand, squeezing hard to dull the ache, and lowered his voice. "And this." He released his cock and gestured around them, encompassing the cereal, the covered windows, the overhead lights, and her gorgeously flushed body. "I control all of it."

She studied him for a silent moment then slipped her legs out of the shorts in his grip and rose. His muscles stiffened to chase, but she didn't run. She backed up until her ass hit the fridge, nude from the waist down, nipples pressing against her tank top. Her heavy-lidded eyes locked with his, her jaw lowered and closed with a whispering inhale. A wordless *Yes*. An undeniable plea.

Climbing to his feet, he tucked himself into his jeans and pulled up the zipper. Then he stalked toward her, mirroring the tilt of her head, knees and shoulders loose, and his gaze holding her prisoner. A breath away, he paused, soaking in the subtleties of her tipped-up chin, parted lips, and glossy but resolute eyes.

With the next breath, he lunged, hands on her jaw, fingers spread around the back of her head. His elbows dropped, shoulders raised, and he yanked her to him, lifting her on tiptoes, guiding her mouth, taking it. His grip twisted through her hair as he drew in her upper lip and shoved her against the fridge, following her with the weight of his body.

The kiss went fucking wild, their lips mashing in a frantic battle. His tongue plunged her mouth, attacking, thrusting in and out, possessing her movements, owning her. Breath for breath, lick after lick, he ate at her mouth, tasting, devouring.

He dropped his hands to her breasts, squeezing ruthlessly as he rolled his cock against her cunt. His tongue tingled, his skin burned, and his head swam. God, she was a drug, and he was so fucking high.

She gripped his biceps, bit at his lips, and threw her arms over his shoulders, her fingers scratching the fuck out of his back. He shuddered, loving it, but he was in control.

Reaching back, he grabbed her wrists and slammed them above her head. Their bodies ground together, his forearms pressing hers to the fridge, their tongues dancing and clashing. Chest-to-chest, hips fused together, he flexed his ass, dry humping her like a horny teenager.

Jesus, fuck, he didn't care. He wanted her.

He leaned back to study her face and found strong smoldering eyes, sharp breaths, and swollen wet lips. Whatever she saw in his expression made her mouth chase his and her fingers curl around his hands. They kissed endlessly, fueling the fire and pushing his control long past the point of discomfort before pulling back and starting all over again.

When he broke the kiss with a hand on her jaw, they panted as one, mouths open and so close their bottom lips brushed. She peered at him through lowered lashes, and he stared back in awe. What trembled between them wasn't an *if?* Or even a *how hard?* Those were foregone. The question they shared was simple.

Ready?

With his body holding her weight against the fridge and her arms restrained by his hand overhead, she lifted her calves, sliding them up his legs. Her feet dug into the back of his thighs, pulling him impossibly closer and trapping his cock between them.

She kissed his lips and leaned back as her gaze caught on the overhead light and froze. Along with her breath.

The goddamned lights. How could she not be over that?

His fingers fell from her rigid face. Fuck him, he was in hell.

Amber squeezed her eyes shut, stomach tightening with nausea, and tried to pull free of Van's grip. Her hands wouldn't budge, held by one of his above her head. "The lights."

"Jesus, Amber. I've seen every gorgeous inch of you." His breath was so close, heating her cheek and vibrating with frustration. "Open your fucking eyes."

She stared up at his striking face and attempted a confident expression. But his gaze immobilized her much more effectively than she could pin him. His pillowy lips semi-puckered with sulkiness, and his intense eyes creased at the corners. Irritation? Uncertainty, too, given the grooves in his forehead and the twitch in his jaw. It was a raw look for him, one that ripped at the places she was already torn and stitched her back up with stronger seams.

Too many terrifying possibilities bounced between them, tingling over her scalp. She could give him a physical connection in the dark, her method of maneuvering through lovers. It would keep her heart safe and her mind focused on the real dynamic of their relationship. She might've decided to stay, but she was still his captive.

As she dropped her toes from his thighs to the floor, he crowded in, melding their bodies together, his feet on the outside of hers.

He gripped her jaw roughly. "You've been in the dark too damned long. The lights. Stay. *On*. Why does that scare you?"

Her heart cramped in its thundering torment against her ribs. As he glanced down at her most intimate places, he didn't seem disgusted. But her filter questioned it. He would get halfway through fucking her and see a flaw he hadn't noticed, an unsavory part of her body brought to light. "It's...I don't...God, this is hard." She breathed in deeply. "I feel exposed. I can't...I don't handle rejection well."

His eyes flashed, and his nostrils flared. He released her and backed away, but his gaze stayed with her. "Your piece of shit ex abused that beautifully unique part of you that needs to be accepted."

Said the former sex trafficker. She shook her head, unsure how to respond to that.

He gripped the zipper on his jeans and dragged it down, slowly, torturingly, his eyes heated and locked on hers. Without looking away, he hooked his thumbs in the waistband, shoved them down, and kicked the pants to the side. His cock stood hard and swollen between his legs. A curl of heat twitched through her, and her pussy clenched.

He reclined on his back amidst the destruction of Froot Loops and propped up on his elbows. "Now I'm exposed, too. Waiting for *your* acceptance."

There was something changing inside him. She couldn't name it, but she could see it creeping to the surface in the stiffness of his muscles and the clench of his fists as he lay on the floor. It seemed to be feeding on feelings that gravitated around *her*. Was he aware of it? She wanted him to know she could *see* him, that she wanted to accept him.

"You look uncomfortable." She cringed at the stupidity of her statement.

"Yeah, well, this position doesn't bring out the best in me. I'm not a bottom, babe." His eyes darted away as he blew out a long ripple of air then looked back at her. "And you're not the only one susceptible to rejection."

Who would've rejected *him*? She wouldn't, not anymore, but he was covered in cereal. It stuck all over his skin in multicolored crumbs. Who knew what other nooks and crannies it was finding its way into? Just looking at it made her itchy and sweaty.

The other post-Brent men she'd slept with had been so much easier to deal with. They didn't ask questions, didn't pay attention, and certainly didn't fuck her on a crumb-encrusted floor. They pounced; then they bounced. On her terms. "Can we go upstairs?"

"How about you follow your nose down here and taste the rainbow?"

Her heart pounded anxiously at the thought of rolling around in that, but the pleading expression on his face splintered her anxiety painfully down the middle.

She knelt beside him, shuddering as cereal adhered to her legs. Picking off four pieces, she searched for the box to discard them. It would only take a sec—

"Amber." His demanding tone made her drop the crumbs. His long, skillful fingers drummed on the tiles in such a seductive way she might've leaned down and sucked one into her mouth if not for her repulsion at the crumby floor.

The spilled cereal beckoned her, her mind grouping the *O*'s in fours. She'd scoop them up in those groups then clear the crumbs away from the grout lines. "You ask for a lot. Lights *and* dirt."

"I'm not asking. We are going to have lit-up, dirty sex because you are *not allowed* to look at the mess."

Her gaze flicked to his. "I...I don't kn—"

"You are going to straddle my cock because you need to come. And you deserve that release because you won't be looking at the mess ever again." His glare was as fierce and unwavering as his tone. "Not once. Understand?"

No one had ever talked to her like that, and it gnawed away a chunk of her anxiety. "Okay."

"I'll be right here the whole time." He lowered his back to the tiles and opened his arms, his eyes potent and knowing. He *saw* her yet didn't utter a single hateful word.

Her heart raced as if being chased, hunted. He could catch it, take it, right now, and she wouldn't stop him.

She straddled one of his thighs, a compromise, and nestled into his waiting arms. His relief was palpable in the sighing embrace he gave her. She breathed it in, wanting him, and suddenly determined to give him something she hadn't given a man in two years.

Wriggling out of his arms and down his leg, she didn't look at the crumbs grinding into her knees because he'd commanded her not to. He'd given her the liberty to ignore it. And though his arms were no longer around her, she felt him holding her as she obeyed his order.

A thrill of pride ran through her, as if she'd never ignored untidiness before. She probably hadn't.

She bent over his hard length and wrapped her fingers around it. Satiny skin over rigid steel heated her palm. He was big, not overly so, but he looked massive in her tiny hand. He felt empowering in her grip.

She ducked her head and took his cock into her mouth. His choked breath spurred her to draw him deeper, her fingers pumping the root in sync with her sucking. Pools of heat collected between her legs, simmering to a needy throb. She started to close her thighs to dull the ache, but he lifted his knee, rolling it against her pussy.

His hands flew to her head, digging into her scalp. His hips bucked and his hard body trembled violently beneath her, reducing his rugged timbre to throaty grunts. Seeing him so painfully aroused, so vulnerable in her mouth, was addictive. And she held the power to relieve him.

This was what control felt like. She licked and nuzzled his glans and slid his length over her lips and cheeks, smearing saliva and pre-come across her face. It was liberating.

The hands on her head clenched, and he yanked her off of him. "Condom."

"I don't..." She glanced around the kitchen, knowing full well there were no condoms. She'd been through every shelf and drawer. "Where?"

His eyes closed, and his face twisted in agony. "Check the pockets of my jeans. Hurry."

Sliding off his leg, she snagged his jeans and found a condom in the front pocket. Did he always keep rubbers on him? Given the relaxed wear of the denim, he'd likely grabbed the jeans from the hamper, stocked with a condom. "Got one."

He fisted his cock, stroking it, root to tip. His knuckles flexed in his exertion, his eyes burning with silver flames.

Sweet mother, that image hit her right between the legs, sending her inner muscles into a hot spasm. She ripped open the package, rolled on the rubber, and straddled him, his cock a long, stiff invitation against her pussy.

He leaned up, and she met him halfway in a sweeping of lips. He grabbed the back of her neck and pulled her to him as he dropped against the floor. Their tongues tangled, and their hands slid everywhere, bumping and caressing in urgent exploration, kindling her arousal from a low burn to a wildfire.

She shoved her fingers through his hair, her hips working into an electrifying grind against him, each flex hitting her clit against the head of his cock, the smooth hardness of his length sliding between her labium. Fuck, what would he feel like without the rubber in the way?

"Aw God, put me in," he groaned against her mouth.

The sound of him begging surged heat through her blood. She reached between them with shaky fingers, positioned his cock, and the hard tip pushed through her opening.

His head fell back, and the cords of his neck strained as she slid down his length. He stretched her deliciously as she worked him in, sinking inch by inch, until he was buried to the root. So deep, so full, her needy flesh rippled around him, shooting sparks of pleasure through her body.

She attacked his mouth as she rolled her hips, ravenous and impatient, sucking on his lips, nipping at him. Her fingers found his hair, stroking and pulling as he fucked her. His large hands on her hips held her in place, his thrusts rocking into her in long, powerful strokes.

He was merciless, his muscles flexing beneath her, his balls slapping her ass with every drive of his cock. His hands moved to her breasts and pinched her nipples so hard the sharp pain sent her over, so fast and explosive, she hadn't felt its approach.

The orgasm slammed into her, and she pushed up, back bowing, riding the wave after wave of ecstasy. Her head fell back, mind empty, her body soaring through the tingling sensations.

He let out an unintelligible curse, thrusting hard and fast. His hands dropped to her waist in a bruising grip as his strokes jerked, lost rhythm, and slammed deep inside her. "Unnngh." His jaw hung open with short, ragged exhales. "Uh...ungh..." He shuddered as he spent his seed, his heavy grunts rumbling into a throaty growl.

The kitchen rotated around them, heaving with the sounds of their heavy breaths. Eternal seconds passed before feeling returned to her fingers and toes.

He looked up at her, his eyes dilated and heavy-lidded. "C'mere."

She lowered her body, her arms winding around his broad shoulders and his heart pounding against her ear on his chest. He hugged her to him, his cock growing soft inside her.

"Ready to eat?"

She released a sated laugh. "Such a man. Sex and food."

"Life's two main ingredients."

After they brushed the crumbs from their bodies and dressed, she sat at the table and watched him scramble eggs and fry bacon. She and food had a hate-hate relationship, so she'd never bothered to learn how to cook. He didn't seem to mind, seeing how he'd told her to sit and rest.

The smell of grease filled her nose and roused her hunger. By the time he brought the plate and two glasses of milk to the table, a rumble had gripped her stomach.

One plate. One fork. He perched before her, his thighs on the outside of hers, lifted a forkful of eggs, and held it to her lips. She accepted willingly, wantonly.

He broke off a piece of bacon. "You didn't look at the mess on the floor while I cooked."

It wasn't a question. He knew she hadn't. She chewed, swallowed, and opened her mouth for the bacon bite. When her lips wrapped around his fingers, he drew them out slowly and stroked a knuckle across her cheek.

"What does the anxiety feel like?" he asked, softly.

She sipped the milk to clear her throat. "When it's bad, I don't have control of my body. It feels like something huge and chaotic is wearing my skin, thrashing around in it, stretching it, and I'm stuck in there with it, helpless."

He fed her another bite, thoughtful, listening. Maybe he didn't understand, but he seemed to be trying.

"Sometimes it's subtle, just there beneath the surface. If I'm distracted, I won't identify it until it's passed. I've tried to study it as it happens, to better understand it. If I lay still and really focus, I can almost grab hold of it. It's as if my brain has its very own body and something is brushing up against it, something that shouldn't be there."

"Do you feel it right now?" He watched her with those perceptive eyes that could reach deeper inside her than any other part of his body.

"I feel..." Panicked? No. Troubled? Not exactly. "Out of alignment."

His eyes glimmered. He liked that answer, and it made her insides flutter.

As he finished off the breakfast, she realized she'd stopped counting the bites when he prompted her to talk. Probably his intention. He didn't seem to do anything without an agenda.

There were still a few bites left, but her stomach hardened, way too bloated. She shook her head at the next forkful. "Tell me something about you. Something that's hard for you to talk about."

The fork paused then lowered to the table. He glanced at the mudroom and back at her, his thumb moving restlessly along the edge of the plate. Then it stilled. "I'll show you."

He stood, and without waiting for her, strode to the mudroom, opened the garage door, and stared into the dark hush, his features empty and distinct.

His expressions would never expose *who* he was, but judging by his sudden remoteness, whatever waited in the garage would.

A cold sweat broke out over her skin, but she rose to follow him, determined to know him. As she walked right through the middle of the smashed cereal without looking at it, her head tilted back, her arms relaxed at her sides, and her strides carried her to him with grace.

He glanced at her with cool, unreadable eyes, and she curled her fingers around his limp hand. Then she followed him through the door.

The fluorescents overhead buzzed in the darkness a half second before the garage flooded with light. Amber blinked rapidly, her lungs tightened, and her hand released Van's fingers with a jerk.

Where she expected chains, whips, torture equipment, and hell, maybe a car was something much more startling.

Dolls and mannequins in every size and state of repair lined workbenches and shelves, hung from walls, and overflowed crates and boxes. Detached arms and legs scattered the floor. Headless bodies slumped in piles with limbs tangled together, the hinged eyes and painted faces frozen in apathy.

The humidity in the two-bay garage stifled her breath, and a chill settled into her bones as she took in the largest collection of mannequins she'd ever seen. There was something very sad about their condition, the way they were tossed aside, neglected...yet *kept* all the same. A graveyard for broken dolls? Or some kind of a sick tribute?

He left her side and strode toward a large table in the center of the garage, its surface cluttered with paints and tiny tools and doll parts.

She didn't follow but instead walked a wide circuit around him on shaky legs, hands at her sides, her attention imprisoned by the horde of soulless faces. What would a man as virile and rugged and *manly* as Van want with dolls?

Her steps took her through a maze of baby dolls, toddler-sized dolls, and nipple-less mannequins, all bald and naked, most damaged beyond repair. Her stomach turned, but she wanted to understand the source of her apprehension. He didn't seem to have any friends or family. Were these...things a distraction from the loneliness when he wasn't abducting people?

The agony of being alone and feeling unwanted was a cruel affliction. It could make one desperate for any kind of connection. Maybe even a connection with the plastic replicas of the real thing. Or with deliverymen in the dark.

Had all those men she'd slept with been some kind of coping mechanism for her loneliness? That might've been part of it. Like a fourth of it. Yeah, and the other three-fourths of the reason was simply payment for her deliveries. It'd been a fair trade. She hadn't been using them, right? Her ribs squeezed, and she shoved that thought away.

She passed a tall display cabinet with a glass door, the only one like it in the room. The two dolls inside... What the hell?

A plastic woman sat nude on a chair. She was similar to Amber's height and held a child-sized doll in a red-checkered dress. The woman's brown marbled eyes stared with a glassy, far-away look. Even more eerie was the red line hand-drawn from one glass eye to the pink painted mouth. A scar drawn exactly like the one on his face. She shuddered, gasping, and covered her mouth with her hand.

The dolls in the cabinet were the only two in the garage with hair, the strands intricately woven together in various shades of brown. Why weren't they damaged like the others? Why were they the only ones safely displayed behind glass? What did they mean to him?

They held answers. Shivering curiosity drew her hand to the knob on the glass door.

"Don't touch those."

His harsh voice made her jump, and she yanked her hand back. Shit. She shook off her nerves and turned to face him. "You collect dolls." *Hollow-eyed, creepy-ass plastic people.*

Perching on a wheeled stool, he rolled toward the table and placed his palms on the surface, staring blankly at the clutter around his hands. "I make them, collect them, and...break them."

An emotionless response, but layers hummed beneath the words. He leaned back, knees spread, hands folded between his strong thighs. He watched her from beneath dark eyebrows, his full lips relaxed and pouty. He was somewhat childlike, surrounded by dolls, sulking and rolling on the stool. Yet he commanded the room with the intensity of his sullen temperament, all that muscle, and...the stretch of his jeans cupping his cock so erotically.

She jerked her gaze up. The man was fucking sexy as hell, doll fetish notwithstanding. She swallowed and continued her exploration around the perimeter, attempting to make sense of it. As she wandered, she peeked back every now and then, finding him tracking her every movement with hooded eyes.

A weight bench sat at one end, surrounded by a mess of mismatched dumbbells. She hoped to learn a lot more about him than the location of his damned workouts. When she reached the farthest corner, she faced him again. "Why do you break them? You don't sell them?"

His huge hands cradled a small headless body, his thumb moving over a two-inch hole punched through the torso. "I'm more interested in quality control." He tossed it behind him.

She flinched as the doll skidded across the cement floor. He broke dolls for fun. Her heart crashed into a roaring panic. Had he harmed a real child at some point? Was this his way of dealing with that? Or maybe he had been the child?

Her spine crawled with millions of icy pinpricks. Her feet stuck to the floor, the span of the garage separating her from the darkness surrounding the man she might've gravely misjudged. "Why do the dolls need quality control?" Fear quivered in her voice despite her best attempts to stifle it.

He rose from the stool and walked toward a box of undamaged bodies with a terrifying calmness. Paralyzed, she watched as he yanked out the plastic mold of a baby—its limbs attached—and dropped it on the floor. Then his bare foot came down, smashing the body with one stomp.

She stopped breathing. Was this some kind of reenactment? Horrified, she wanted to look away, but she couldn't. She had to know.

The torso cracked beneath his foot, and the head popped off. Dizziness swarmed her head, sending her ears ringing in a frenzied pulse.

With hands on his hips and his head tipped down, hard eyes rolled up and locked on her. "That's why."

She wrapped her arms around her waist, her fingers sticky and trembling. Quality control meant he was looking for flaws, right? Was he looking for a doll that could survive a heavy foot? That didn't make any sense. Oh God, she didn't want it to make sense.

Breathing deeply from her diaphragm, she smothered her dread with a strong voice. "I don't understand. Why are you smashing them like that?"

He looked away, his lips in a flat line, seemingly refusing to answer. But he wanted to. She could see it in the rise and fall of his chest and in the shift of his eyes as they studied the collection, searching for the words.

Endless seconds passed, the stillness strangling, before his Adam's apple bobbed and his fingers twitched on his hips. "It was the first and last toy I owned. A goddamned doll." He laughed nervously, his hand lifting to rub the back of his neck. "I don't even know how I got it. Probably from one of those missionaries who would pop in to deliver food and Jesus pamphlets."

A clot of emotion gathered in her throat. Something had happened *to* him. She lowered her hands to her shorts, gripping them. "This was when you lived in the *colonia*?"

He nodded and crouched over the broken doll, glaring at it. "I was a nine-year-old boy. What the fuck was I doing with a doll?"

His tone was angry, at odds with the tender way his finger traced the jagged hole in the doll's torso at his feet. He seemed to be lost in memory, his silence hardening the lump she couldn't swallow. She stepped forward, aching to erase the distance, but the jerk of his shoulders halted her approach.

"He was a huge man. My mother was a whore, sold herself for the needle, and he was just some random john, but he was the first one I remember. He fucked her right there in front of me. She was so fucking high I don't think she was conscious." A tremor shook his body, and he sat back, legs folded against his chest, his arms wrapped around his knees. "And there I was, curled up in the damned corner, hugging that doll, kissing her ratty hair like she was my only friend. Hell, she *was* my only friend."

He put his hands over his face, and his shoulders hunched like a scared little boy. Her heart clenched painfully, and her eyes burned. She wanted to hold that little boy so damned badly.

Straightening the legs of her shorts, she moved with fast, quiet steps. Then she dropped before him and mirrored his pose with her arms around her knees.

His hands lowered and dangled between them. He didn't look up, didn't acknowledge her at all. "When he was done with my mother, he turned to me. I wouldn't let go of that doll. He was so goddamned strong I couldn't stop him from ripping Isadora out of my hands."

"Isadora? Your mother?"

His head cocked, and his eyes narrowed in confusion on the broken doll between their feet. He squeezed his legs tighter against his chest, his body curling inward. He was shutting down.

In a bold gesture, she reached out and placed her hand on his cheek, stroking her fingers through the thick hair above his ear.

He shook his head, eyes on the floor, then leaned into her touch. "I'd named the doll after my mother."

There was no embarrassment or resentment in his tone, just...sadness. He loved his mother, that much was clear, and evidently that love wasn't reciprocated.

A burn seared through her nose. She envied his devotion. She didn't know her mother well enough to love her. There'd been no connection, no relationship. Just illness. She rocked forward to her knees and wrapped her arms around his shoulders.

His legs dropped, and he pulled her against his chest, speaking softly into her hair. "When he stomped on the doll, her body split in half, and the arms and legs tore off. Just like that, she was dead."

She rubbed his rigid back, her own muscles stiff with anguish. The attachment he must've felt for that doll amidst such a neglected, fucked-up upbringing... God, he must've mourned her. The doll. His mother. She glanced over his shoulder and took in the menagerie of brokenness with new eyes.

It was tragic and beautiful and inspiring. She didn't know the depth of his suffering, but the coping, the struggle to self-medicate? She knew all about that. The memory of his doll had stuck with him, and he'd recreated his appreciation for it, clinging to the notion that he could somehow repair what had happened, that he could fix the past with the present.

She didn't think that was possible, but what did she know? Just because she hadn't been successful at taking back her own life didn't mean he couldn't find some kind of peace in creating an indestructible doll.

He adjusted her legs so that she straddled his lap and squeezed her chest to his. His arms were strong and immovable around her, his body a powerhouse of muscle. But she felt the scared boy in the hunch of his shoulders and the restlessness of his fingers gripping at the shirt covering her back. That little boy felt like her insides, fractured and hurting, lonely and scared, but brimming with the desire to love something or someone and to be loved.

His cheek rubbed against hers, but his arms turned to stone and his chest expanded with a long, tense inhale. "After he smashed the doll, he pressed my face into the dirt and fucked me." Her heart crushed instantly at the emptiness in his voice and the impact of his words. He released a slow breath and kissed her brow. "I came to grips with that a long time ago. He was the first but certainly not the last. For the next four years, many of her drug dealers turned to me when she was too stoned to put out. She OD'd when I was thirteen."

Amber held him tightly, her hug expressing what she couldn't with her voice. When he leaned back, his eyes were clear and searching. His gentle expression filled her with heartache, but she also felt a strong surge of something else. "I'm proud of you."

He cupped her face, his thumbs caressing her cheeks as his eyes followed the movement. "Mm. Not much to be proud of, Amber. By age thirteen, I was a whore just like her."

Her jaw stiffened, her words rushed and heated. "You were young. It was all you knew. And you broke free from it. You didn't let it kill you."

"Don't make excuses for it." His eyes sparked. "I don't."

She wanted to argue, but his hard, domineering glare was back. She bit her lip, her mind swimming through everything he'd told her. "So you're trying to make a doll that doesn't break?"

His gaze traveled through the garage, probing the broken body parts. "I've tried. They all break eventually." He laughed. "I'm convinced their hollow bodies are filled with mysterious energy, just waiting to cave in. Like dark matter. Can't fuck with science."

She stroked a finger over his jaw, savoring the connection. "Dark matter holds the universe together."

His lips twitched. "It also threatens to destroy it."

Were they talking about the dolls or him? She pointed at the plastic woman and child sitting in the cabinet. "What about those two? They're not broken."

His eyes closed, opened, and he patted her leg, lifting her to her feet as he stood. "That's enough for one day. I've got shit to do."

More secrets then. She stared at their shiny blank faces, and they stared back, trapping their story behind painted lips. "You'll tell me when you're ready?"

He nodded and led her to the door with light steps as if he'd shed the weight of the world. So why did she feel so heavy? It was admirable what he was doing, making and breaking dolls to redeem his childhood. To redeem his mother.

But she wouldn't dress it up. He was her mirror in a way. They both carried a million cracks beneath the skin. Even under the stark light of the fluorescents, it was hard to see which of them was more broken. But for the first time, she felt like she had to vanquish her mental illness not for herself but for someone else. Because she was broken *with him*, and if she fixed herself, maybe she could make him a little less broken, too.

The first twenty-four hours in Van's cabin had been both terrifying and eye opening. Amber's surroundings and the man she shared them with challenged the routine and order she desperately clung to. Her world had become a state of nonlinear catastrophic exasperation.

As the hours bled into days, the next three weeks were very much the same. Every day was just like the first, the punishments and the tenderness, the panic attacks and the sex. She made his life hell, and he whipped her for it. She adored him, when she didn't hate him.

He followed through on his promise to be as messy as she was clean. When she scrubbed the shower walls, he coated them with motor oil. When she picked up his socks, he decorated the house with tampons, tying the strings in knots so complicated she couldn't undo them.

Three weeks with him made her fear a little less. She still couldn't face the outdoors, yet every day he forced her out. Sometimes, he required a single step on the porch. Most days, he hauled her kicking and screaming to the tree where he whipped her and fucked her into an adrenaline-induced state of elation.

But as the weeks passed, she could still feel that intangible thing in her head, scratching against her brain like it wanted out. Something else lived in there, too, making her anxious. Her dependency on routine and straight lines was shifting. She was becoming too centered on Van.

She was aware of it, knew it was unhealthy, and still she listened for his footsteps and watched his expressions with a pounding heart. Whenever he left the house to jog in the woods or run errands, she awaited his return with an uneasy amount of panic.

Then there were his secrets. How did he get his scars? Why did he keep those dolls in the glass cabinet? Why wouldn't he tell her? She'd developed a new obsession, a dangerous one.

On day twenty-four, she sat alone in the garage at the worktable and tied off the final stitches on a doll. The body was made of leather, strong and durable, and stuffed with wool batting. She'd glued and sewed the plastic limbs and head to the leather torso. Van had painted the face with red puckered lips and twinkling blue eyes. The long straw-colored hair had taken him hours to weave.

She finished it off by dressing it in a blue gown with yellow bows. When she held it up for inspection, a feeling of breathlessness came over her as heat radiated through her chest. *Try to break this one, Van.*

She hopped up, carrying the doll with her, and stopped at the display cabinet. The angle of the light cast her reflection in the glass door. She guiltily tugged up her shirt and revealed her tummy. Having neglected her purging habit in Van's ever-watchful presence, she'd gained weight. At least six pounds, maybe more.

Bile simmered in her throat. She tucked the doll under her arm and pinched her hip, a repulsive hunk of flesh. Saliva burst through her mouth, overwhelming her with the sudden need to spit. She clamped her lips closed, fighting it.

Maybe he wasn't telling her his secrets because he'd lost interest in her. She hadn't made much progress combating the OCD, and she fought him every day when he dragged her outside. That must've been it. He was tired of her.

With her self-berating thoughts banging in her head, she left the garage in search of him. To show him the doll, to hold him, kiss him, talk with him, it didn't matter. She needed his strength and their connection.

When she stepped into the kitchen, she slammed to a halt. He leaned against the counter, sipping a glass of tequila, dressed in a suit. His strong, freshly-shaven jaw and thick, dark hair were just two of the countless traits that made him painfully attractive. He wore a narrow black tie and black button-up shirt beneath a suit that matched the striking color of his pale gray eyes.

The spice of his cologne reached her nose, seductively tempting her arousal. And taunting her insecurities.

Did he want to go on a date? He knew she couldn't. Oh God, she couldn't. She bit down on her cheek. *Stop being so self-absorbed.* Maybe this had nothing to do with her.

She swallowed her dread. "You look...Wow." She wanted to eat him. She laid the doll on the counter and reached up, adjusting his collar and stroking her knuckles over his jaw. Then she slid her palm down his tie. "Why are you dressed up?"

He drained the glass of tequila and set it beside the doll. "I'm going out."

A cold fever flashed through her cheeks. Dressed like that? A date with someone else? Her hands shook, and she gripped them behind her back. "Where?"

His eyes, *God those eyes*, pierced through her like knives. Then he sharpened the cut with his answer. "I'm going to see Liv."

Probably an inappropriate time for Van's cock to get hard, but fuck him, Amber's jealousy was as sexy as her tight little body. He leaned against the kitchen counter, shoved a hand in his pocket, and gave his dick a firm pinch, not that it helped.

Her jealousy, however, was bred from her poor self-worth, which was the root of the bulimia, the need for perfection, and the avoidance of outside.

She held her composure admirably, but that didn't mean her insecurities weren't bursting at the seams. Her hands were behind her back, so he leaned in, straining to hear the crack of her knuckles. The popping didn't come, but her cheeks flushed a lovely shade of pink. And was that a growl in her throat?

Somehow, she pulled off a pleasant voice. "Why would you need to see her?"

Because his daughter was growing up without him. Because his infrequent visits to Liv's window over the past three weeks weren't turning up any information. There'd been nothing on her possible connections with the cartel or FBI; nothing to tell if she was using those connections to trap him in the event he attempted to contact their daughter.

His involvement in Mr. E's operation was still unknown to authorities. If he surfaced, it would threaten his freedom and ironically Amber's. Liv would rat him out if she sensed even a hint of danger with regard to their daughter. Prison was *not* an option.

The one thing he wouldn't do was take Livana from her stable life with Mr. E's widow. Despite his history with kidnapping, he would *never* do that to his daughter. Fuck, he just wanted to be a part of her life and needed to make sure Liv understood that.

He turned the glass of tequila on the counter round and round as he collected his thoughts. Telling Amber about his purpose with Liv meant revealing his parenthood and exposing the looming reason he'd taken Amber, why he'd worked so hard to help her conquer the disorders. She would eventually find out his intention to use her as a character reference with Liv. How would she react to that? Would she think he was using her? Was he?

He used her body for his pleasure, and he depended on her strength to be a better man. But most days, it was a damned struggle to reconcile his goal with all the sentimental crud sticking to his heart. He was so wrapped up in Amber, adrift in the most thrilling moments of his life, he'd lost his bearings.

Amber's health and happiness were as important to him as his daughter's was. In fact, his goals with Livana had become secondary to his relationship with Amber. And that scared him to fucking death.

As he stared into the worried brown eyes of the woman he'd come to adore more than any person in the world, he realized she owned him as much as he owned her. He clung to that heady, full-body feeling because it infused his every thought with hope.

It was also turning him into a cherry-scented, floaty-hearted sissy fuck.

Why did he need to see Liv? He twisted his lips into a charming smile, but the effort hurt. "She has something I want."

At an arm's length away, she glanced down at her tits, then her hips, and looked away with a pained expression. No doubt she'd filtered his words into something like *Liv has something you don't have.* She was oblivious to the effect she had on him. How could a woman so fucking beautiful be so damned blind?

Good thing he had some time before he needed to leave. "You'll be punished for that."

Her gaze jerked back, and she crossed her arms. "What the fuck did *I* do?"

"I want *you* to answer that question, and after your punishment, I might" —he drew out a long breath, letting her mind flicker through the possibilities— "allow you to come."

"You're an asshole."

"Noted." He was delaying the eminent conversation regarding Liv, but toying with her was a delicious distraction. He rested his ass against the counter, tilted his head back, and stared at the ceiling with a dramatic amount of interest in the white brush-strokes. She would tell him why he was punishing her eventually.

She tapped her fingernails on the counter, blew out some heavy exhales, and stomped her foot twice. *Not four times.* "Fine. I don't know what you want from Liv, but it makes me feel" —she groaned— "inadequate."

He awarded her honesty with the full commitment of his gaze. "Be specific."

She pinned her lips together, fisted her hands on her hips, and glared at her feet. "Jesus, you're annoying." She peered up at him, then back at her feet, and mumbled, "My boobs—"

"I can't hear you."

She huffed then hardened her voice. "My boobs are fake and plasticky. She's probably beautifully natural."

He hooked a knuckle beneath her chin, lifting her face to capture her eyes. "She's both beautiful and natural" —her jaw stiffened, and he squeezed it— "but she's got jack shit on a beauty queen."

Her chin pressed down on his hand, stubbornly and uselessly.

"What else?"

She shifted her weight from foot to foot. "My hips are fat." Her voice wobbled into a seething shout. "And that's *your* fault!"

There it was. He'd been waiting for it. Bulimia was the quietest of the disorders, the one they hadn't discussed since her first day here. But he never left her alone until her food settled, strictly limiting her opportunities to puke.

He crouched at her feet and gripped her thighs beneath the short skirt, lifting the hem to her waist with the slide of his hands. "You're done with your calorie-counting world of size zero."

"There's nothing wrong with size zero. Runway models—"

"If you want to look like a starving creature, you better have drool clinging to your chin and your mouth reaching for my cock." He leaned forward and sank his teeth into the flesh on her thigh.

She jerked in his hold, and he bit down ruthlessly into her flexing quad. If she'd gained any weight at all, it was muscle. She was a fucking machine during their morning workouts.

He kissed the two half-moon indentions he'd given her and pressed his nose against her bare pussy. Christ, he loved that she didn't have panties at his house. As he breathed in her sweet scent, her hips trembled beneath his grip. It had only been two hours since he'd fucked her, yet his cock was as stiff as the night he'd met her.

He lowered the skirt and stood. "Wipe your mind of all your preconceived notions of how you think I see you." He touched her cheek and really looked at her, the glow of her skin, the dark fall of hair around her shoulders, her sultry fuck-me lips, and the rise of her full tits. Defined biceps, slender throat, petite nose, everything about her ensnared him. He could stare at her for hours, losing himself in her beauty. He brushed her hair behind her ear. "How do I see you, Amber?"

Her eyes were bright and glassy, peeking up at him through dense lashes. "You think I'm...pretty."

Not the word he would've chosen for the exquisite view before him, but it pointed her the right direction. "Good girl." He kissed her softly, happily, humming his contentment. "Now you can ask your questions."

She fingered the lapels of his suit jacket, sliding her hands up and down the folds of finely woven wool. "What does Liv have that you want?"

"Mm." He fisted his hands behind his back. *Stop delaying, dickhead.* "It's time to visit that display cabinet."

She arched her eyebrows. "You're ready to tell me?"

Fuck no. "Yeah."

He led her to the garage, loosening the tie and rubbing his tight neck. He'd practiced how he would tell her for weeks, but as they stood before the lifelike reminders of the family he'd longed for, his carefully composed speech disintegrated, and his polluted heart clawed out of his throat.

"In thirty-three years, there have only been four people I've given a shit about, that I'd even consider putting before myself." He opened the glass door, his mouth dry. "The first two didn't love me back."

"Your mother and Liv." She stated it not as a question but as a realization as she stared at the dolls, her elbows tucked to her sides, her fingers trembling on her bottom lip.

He touched the hair on the mannequin, his token of Liv. But as the soft strands slipped through his caress, he didn't feel the usual heaviness in his chest. Instead, his pulse raced with nervousness. He hadn't intended on telling her about the hair, but he longed for her to accept *all* the ugly parts of him.

"I made this with Liv's real hair. Collected it for years from her pillow, her hairbrush, and directly from her scalp." At the time, he didn't know why. A compulsion maybe? A sick one. He removed his hand and shoved it in his pocket.

"Oh, Van, I can't even..." Her voice strained with disbelief, and she cleared her throat. "Why?"

He was damaged, in the most irredeemable way. He brought shaky fingers to his forehead and gave her his back. He hated this feeling, this fucking vulnerability. "This was a mistake."

"Van Quiso." Her clipped tone vibrated with impatience. "You put me on that bathroom counter with my legs spread and made me talk about some scary shit. You owe me." She sucked in a long breath and softened her voice. "I want to understand why you kept her hair. I want to know everything about you."

Her words moved him. And the sudden support of her arms wrapping around his waist and her chest against his back found him and held him.

"I have a memory of my mother under the tin roof of our makeshift shelter. She wasn't crying or stoned. She was just sitting there, *being*." He placed his hands over Amber's on his abs, absorbing her warmth. "She was sitting so close her hair touched my face and shoulder, and I imagined maybe that was what her fingertips would feel like or her kisses." His voice thickened, his chest aching. He coughed into his fist.

She slipped under his arm and cupped his face with fire in her eyes. "My mother couldn't look at me because I reminded her of her illness. She gave birth to me, this child who embodied the worst of her sickness, and nothing I could've done would change that." She caressed his chest. "I guess what I'm saying is...I get it. I wanted you to know I understand."

He coiled his fingers through her hair and put his lips on her forehead. He was his mother's repulsive reminder of her slavery. Of course, he knew that, which was why he needed a relationship with his daughter. To show her she wasn't a thing he resented. To give her a father's love. "The third one doesn't know I exist."

"The third?" Her brow wrinkled beneath his lips. She pulled back and peered around his shoulder at the display cabinet. "The small doll is the third person you...she's..." She swallowed, hard.

"Livana will be eight next month." Another birthday he wouldn't be a part of. His throat burned with painful frustration.

She nodded, a jerky movement, as her gaze shifted over the doll, swimming with thoughts. "Livana. Liv and Van."

Livana. The name he'd given to the child that was snatched away the moment she was born. Mr. E hadn't even allowed him to hold her.

He touched the scar on his cheek. "Mr. E gave us matching scars when I got her pregnant."

Her eyes squinted, probably narrowing on the hand-drawn scar on the mannequin.

With his hands on her waist, he turned them to face the cabinet, standing behind her with his arms around her mid-section, holding her tightly in case she ran. "Mr. E and his wife raised Livana." His voice clogged, thick with painful memories. "My father prohibited us from seeing her outside of the videos he sent."

"Videos?"

"His *incentives.* To ensure we didn't fuck up the meetings with his slave buyers."

"My God—"

"I knew where Livana was the whole time and kept it from Liv." Though he'd never been allowed contact, he'd secretly watched his daughter from a distance. "Liv would've gone after her. It was too risky."

His stomach hardened with guilt. He could've helped her get their daughter, but in doing so, he would've lost Liv. In the end, he lost her anyway. He closed his eyes, breathing in the clean scent of Amber's hair, and opened them. That same end had brought him a woman he would never deserve. "When she shot me, I told her everything. I'd planned on telling her anyway. Mr. E killed her mother, and I knew Livana was next."

"Jesus." She pivoted in his arms and ran her palm across his shoulder, over the bullet wound. "She shot you and your father." She chewed on her lip, watching the caress of her hand. "And she escaped. So why did she never mention you to the police?"

"She'd killed seven slave buyers. She thought she killed me. And she hasn't heard from me since the day I wired her six of the seven million we'd earned in trafficking."

She stepped away from him and paced along the wall of doll parts. "A payoff?"

"An apology."

She pinched her bottom lip, wearing a pensive expression. "And she has something you want. Which was why you were on my porch."

"Mr. E's widow has my daughter. But I know Liv has unrestricted access to her."

"You're a stalker." She reached up and traced the gnarled seam of a doll arm. "You're also a fugitive, and your daughter lives with the Police Chief's widow." She dropped her hand and looked at him with confusion etching her beautiful face. "I'm sorry, Van, but I don't understand what you hope to gain by seeking out Liv."

He put his hands in his pockets to hide his shaking fingers. "She could bring me along on her visitations with Livana. She could introduce me as a friend or an uncle, and someday, when Livana's old enough, when she trusts me, I could tell her."

Her lips tilted into a frown, her eyes downcast and glossy as she shook her head. "Why would Liv agree to that? Van, she must be terrified of you. She'd never let you near Livana."

His pulse sped up, his voice hard. "I'll convince her I can be a good father, that I'm not a threat." He moved toward her with determined steps and gripped her head, tilting it back, trapping her gaze. "You're doing so well, going outside every day. You could tell her how much I've helped you and convince her I've changed." Adamant resolve strengthened his posture, and he channeled that strength to his eyes. "Come with me."

The flash of Amber's eyes and the set of her jaw made Van's stomach drop. Fuck, his words had come out all wrong. They clotted the space between them, shoving them apart.

She yanked her head from his hands. "*That's* why you've been forcing me outside? You thought you could fix me, that I could vouch for you?"

The sadness in her voice ripped him in half, but he refused to let go of her or give up on this. He grabbed her wrists and held them against his chest. "You could tell her I'd be a good father, that I would never hurt my daughter."

A tremble skittered across her chin. Her arms twisted in his hands, her fingers clutching his jacket. Then, in an unexpected move, she lifted on tiptoes and pressed her mouth against his.

The beat of his heart stumbled as she kissed him without resentment or anger or any of the reactions he'd feared. He was numb with shock, dizzy with lust, swirling his tongue over her lips. Fuck him, *those lips.* He needed them on his body, on his cock. He needed to tug it out and shove it inside her, to bury himself in the place she accepted him.

She broke the kiss and spoke quietly. "I don't think you'd hurt your daughter like you've harmed all the other women in your life." He opened his mouth to agree, and she pressed a finger over his lips. "In fact, I think you're done treating women that way."

"I am—"

"Shh." She dropped her hand. "You would be a great father. Fierce and protective and attentive."

God, that felt good to hear. He pressed his lips tight to keep from smiling like an asshole.

Her eyes darted away, and she leaned back. "But I can't be the one to confirm that, Van. I can't..." She shook her head. "I can't leave. I'm not fixed."

There lay the crux of his conflict over the last few weeks. He didn't just want her fixed for his purpose. He pulled her back to him with her forearms pinned against his chest. "That's not why I want you. I just want...I need you to *want* to be by my side."

She sniffed, her eyes closing then cutting back to him. "You said there were four? Four people you cared about?"

Ah, there was his little *count*ress. He might've grinned if his chest didn't hurt so badly. "Number four..." He blew out a breath, lowered his brow to hers, and told her the truth. "When I met her, I wanted to pick apart her mind and play with the pieces. I wanted to become her obsession, her solitary devotion, her fear." She tensed and so did he. "But along the way, *she* picked *me* apart. I'm the one who is obsessed, devoted...scared. Come with me to see Liv?"

She wrenched from his hold and backed up. "I can't."

He prowled after her. "You handle the agoraphobia just fine while hanging from a tree in subspace." She stumbled against the wall, and he closed in, blocking her on either side with his arms. "You don't even know you're outside when I'm fucking you beneath the shelter of my body."

"Right." She straightened her spine, hands clenched at her sides. "So you plan on whipping and fucking me during this meeting with Liv? 'Cause I'm not sure that'll help your fatherly image."

"No. I'm just saying you can do this without the mental distractions. I won't leave your side, Amber, and I would never let anything out there harm you in any way."

She shoved against his chest with a shriek and slipped beneath his arm, shuffling backward. "My enemy isn't out there, Van." She thrust a finger at the garage doors. "It's here." She gripped her head. "Right here. I sit in this house day after day and tell myself I'm strong, that I'm better than this. But once I step outside, something takes over. Something more powerful than me invades my body and I can't fight it. I try." She sobbed. "I fucking try. But it brings me to my fucking knees. Every. Time."

He reached her in two strides and lifted her into his arms. His chest was so fucking tight it felt like his heart was shrinking. He couldn't fail her. He wouldn't. He carried her out of the garage and through the house. "When you're ready" —he climbed the stairs— "you'll be there with me."

With a heavy sigh, she hugged his neck. "So you won't go see her? You won't leave?"

God, she sounded so relieved, and he was about to steal that away. He set her on her feet beside the railing in the loft. "Liv is singing in a bar tonight. It's neutral ground, a good place for me to feel her out."

"What?" She gripped his hair and pulled his face to hers. "You can't. She'll turn you in, Van. You can't go."

He removed her hands from his head, walked to the nightstand, and grabbed a length of rope. "Do you need to go to the bathroom?"

She gaped at him. "No. Why?"

"On your knees." With the rope taut between his fists, he returned to her with a clear sense of purpose in his strides. He promised her a punishment, and he expected her to remember. She must've read the intention in his eyes because she lowered to the floor.

"Arms up and together."

She obeyed, but of course, she couldn't keep her mouth shut. "You can't punish me for having thoughts, Van. They're just thoughts!"

Insidious thoughts that fed an eating disorder. He wound the rope around her wrists—nineteen times because she'd told him once it was her least favorite *anti-number*—and tied it off at the base of a banister beam on the railing. An anchor hitch knot she wouldn't be able to undo with her bound hands.

The restraints were just preliminary, to prime her for the punishment she would receive when he returned. The rope prevented her from standing and leaping to her death, but she could lie down. Which was a mercy because she would be there awhile.

He left her with a lingering kiss and adjusted his tie on the way to the front door. A sudden thought veered his path toward the kitchen counter, to the doll she'd left there. He picked it up and lifted the gown, pressing his thumbs against the seams in the leather torso.

"Stomp on it." Her voice drifted down from the loft.

He spun and met her gentle eyes peering through the railing overhead. When she gave him an encouraging nod, he set the doll on the floor and slammed his loafer into the soft belly. The limbs bounced but remained attached. He cocked his head, heart thundering. With an unsteady hand, he scooped it up and raised the gown. No holes. Every stitch intact.

The tingling started in his hands and spread out through his entire body in a warm feeling of weightlessness. "You did it," he whispered then raised his voice. "You fucking did it."

When he looked up, her gorgeous, teary smile lifted him on his toes. He wanted to tell her that she had to come with him, that he needed her because he loved her, that she found him and released him with a fixable doll, and maybe, just maybe, she could fix him, too.

But the warmth that nuzzled every tattered shred of his being didn't come from some doll. It was brought to life by her unfathomable understanding. She could have called him a creeper and spit on his collection. Instead, she supported it by devoting thought and effort to make it better, not for herself but *for him.*

He wanted to tell her this, wanted her to know how much her actions moved him. But as she sat back and pulled her bound wrists to her chest, her smile soft, her lashes lowered, she seemed to already know. So he settled on a thickly uttered "Thank you."

"You're welcome."

He placed the doll in a paper bag and tucked it under his arm. With one last glance at Amber, he squared his shoulders and hardened his expression. "I'm whipping your ass when I get home."

She nodded, her eyes gleaming with an inner light. "I know. Just come home."

Fuck, he loved her so much it hurt. If anything happened to him, if he wasn't able to return, would she die of starvation? He shoved a hand through his hair, his fingers clenching. "I promise."

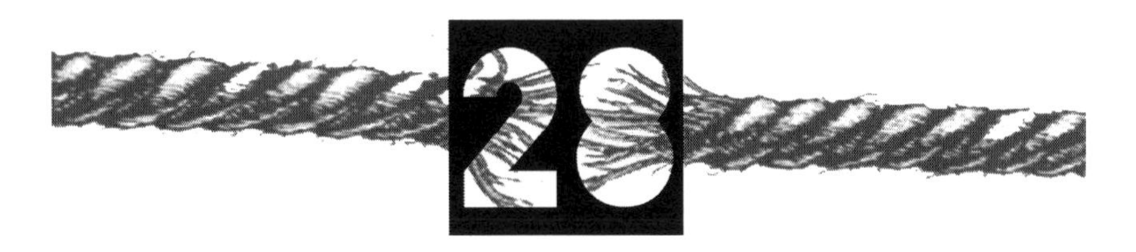

Van stepped into the thick black foyer of the *Curie Lounge* in downtown Austin. Pockets of dim light flickered above the tables. Every chair in the house was filled, maybe a hundred or more live-music enthusiasts sitting back, enjoying a drink and a sexy voice. They wouldn't be disappointed in the latter.

Humming through the speakers was the sound that had haunted him for years. There were no instruments. Just the terraced rippling of her voice, reverberating seductive notes along a man's cock, reaching deep inside him, the only warning she gave before she ate his soul and spit it out. He shivered.

She stood beneath a spotlight in the corner of the large room, eyes closed and sheathed tits to feet in a black gown as she sang a bluesy melody with a sultry sway of her hips.

Remarkable how he didn't entertain a single obsessive thought for the woman. Amber had truly cured his fever.

Pinching the paper bag between his arm and side, he scanned the lounge for her clunkier half and his gaze collided with Joshua Carter's wide eyes at the far end. The man shot from his chair, all six-foot-two of him, his expression shifting from shock to fury. The burly linebacker glanced at Liv, ten feet away, and back again.

Joshua wasn't a bad looking guy. Age twenty-two or twenty-three with black hair, he had that chiseled jaw women loved and green eyes, which were really narrowed and pissed right now. But even so, Van would've gladly fucked him if he didn't have something better waiting for him at home.

And that something was tied to his banister, waiting for his cock. Damn, he needed to speed this along.

As Joshua strode toward him, choosing a path that blocked his view of Liv, he let his gaze rest on those furious flames of green sparking in the dim light. A year ago, he'd been Joshua's captor. He hadn't fucked him, but there'd been some non-consensual kissing and dick stroking. A friendly greeting was probably too much to ask.

Because of the money he'd wired Liv, Joshua knew he'd survived the gunshot wound. Beyond that, did his former slave assume he was still trafficking slaves? What were the chances they'd even hear him out?

He slid a toothpick between his lips and closed the distance. This should be fun.

As Van approached the charging ex-football player, it reminded him of a game of chicken. Who would yield first? Or the worst possible outcome, neither of them. Amidst a crowded bar of patrons, the confrontation needed to be handled delicately, which wasn't a strength he'd mastered.

At the center of the room, Joshua's hand landed on his shoulder in a hard grip, those tightly pinned lips lowering to his ear. The voice he'd heard groaning orgasmically through his mics for six months was now harsh and clipped. "What do you want?"

Van leaned back, deliberately removed the toothpick, and glared at the hand on his shoulder until it dropped. "What, no hello kiss? Afraid my tongue might make you come again?"

A sharp inhale. "Go back to whatever hole you crawled out of. Right now."

So much anger in those eyes. He didn't remember wrangling that much of a reaction when the man was bound and nude in his attic. "Down, boy. I'm not here to fuck you or your girl. I just need to talk with her."

Joshua glanced over his shoulder at Liv, and Van used the opportunity to catch her eyes.

As her gaze clashed with his, she belted her voice through an eerie cascade of notes, the scar on her cheek a shadowed line beneath the angle of the lighting. She excelled at hiding her emotions beneath a cool facade, her intentions well disguised through cunning and underhandedness. She appeared to be lost in song, but she was probably planning the hundred and one ways he would die when she finished the set.

Whether it was by coincidence or design, she ended the melody with a hum, and stepped out of the spotlight, heading directly for them amidst the rise of applause.

When she reached them, her hip-swishing gait carried her right on by and to an isolated table in the corner. Joshua trailed her like an obedient puppy, and they slid into one side of the booth.

Returning the toothpick to his mouth, Van took the opposite seat and set the doll beside him. Liv knew he'd collected dolls over the years. The night she'd shot him, he let her see replicas made with her hair for the first time. He hadn't seen her reaction. No doubt it was one of horror. He'd never explained what they meant to him. Maybe someday he could trust her enough to tell her.

Folding her hands on the table, she appraised him with God-knew-what swirling in her dark brown eyes. Her hair was shorter now, shoulder-length and fringed around her pale face. She was still beautiful. In an inhuman, callous kind of way.

Once upon a time, he'd been turned on by the perplexity of her masked expressions. Now, he felt strained to his limits. A twinge lit behind his eyes.

She tilted her head. "I see you haven't lost the toothpick."

He rolled it between his lips and grinned. "I see you haven't lost your puppy." He glanced at Joshua's scowl and back at her.

"Where's the hoodie?" The bubbled pink gash on her cheek moved with her lips.

His own scar itched, but not with the same tingling connection he'd once felt. Maybe he'd imagined that bond. Perhaps their shared pain hadn't really been shared at all. He slid a palm down his tie and tapped the heel of his leather loafer beneath the table. Fuck, he was sweating already. He needed to lose the jacket. "People change."

She held herself so impassive, so stock-still, one might question if she were breathing. "Why are you here?"

Typical Liv, skipping past friendliness and shoving straight to the facts. He could only blame himself for her coldness. Beneath that defensive shield lay the warm and caring woman she was, the girl who existed before he'd taken her.

The year that separated them should've tempered her visage, and maybe it had. Most likely, she wore her protective mask now because of *him.* His stomach sank. He was there to change that.

"I've stumbled upon something incredible" —someone with a wealth of spirit and strength, someone he *hadn't* ruined— "that has put all my mistakes in perspective. I've found a reason to try harder. To be a better man." Ah, there it was. A flicker of warmth beneath her frozen face. "I *know* I'll be a good father."

Her thawing expression hardened into ice. "Absolutely not."

Joshua grabbed her folded hands and squeezed. "Hear him out, Liv." Green eyes locked with his. "You found someone?"

More like she found him. His very soul lay in the palms of her bound hands. He nodded. "I love her."

Liv's lips twitched, barely a tic, but it could've been a smile. "Does she know what you've done? Did you tell her about us, all *nine* of us, and your father?"

He tapped the toothpick with his tongue and reclined against the seat back. "She knows everything."

"I'm happy for you, Van." It was undetectable in her tone, but a glimmer of sincerity touched her eyes. Then it was gone. "If she loves you in return."

"She loves me."

"So where is she? You're hardly a man who would leave his girl unattended. Why isn't she with you?" Her emotionless voice set his molars together. Worse was the diligence in her questioning. She didn't believe the relationship was consensual. She would've been right two months ago.

He held her unwavering gaze. "She's agoraphobic. She can't leave the house."

"Convenient." She inhaled a subtle breath, and her tone hardened. "Cut the crap, Van. No manipulations. No bullshit. Tell me what you want."

He held his hands still on his lap and maintained strong eye contact. If he showed any sign of nervousness, she'd jump on it. "I want to meet Livana. Take me with you on one of your visitations."

Joshua bent forward, his dark brows lowering over narrowed eyes. "You know about the visitations? You've been watching Liv?"

"Of course he has." Liv stared back without a hint of surprise on her face. She was smart. She had to have known or at least suspected. "Stalking and abducting is what he does."

His cheeks burned, and his body tensed. Yeah, he had been stalking. "She's my daughter, too." How could he explain?

"Do you have someone tied up in your house right now?" she asked.

Fuck yes, and he was two seconds from shoving out of there to be with the one person who had faith in him.

She leaned closer and lowered her voice. "How many times a day do you beat her and make her suck your cock?"

He launched toward her, mirroring her pose. "Asks the hypocrite who fucks her slave boy on the kitchen table with a strap-on."

She put a hand on Joshua's suddenly heaving chest and sat back with a satisfied smile. "Only one way you'd know that. Some people *don't* change."

The toothpick snapped between his teeth. He spit it on the floor and faced her again. "Come to my house. You can meet my girlfriend. She'll validate everything I've said."

A waitress appeared at the table, beaming a smile at Liv. "That was an incredible performance, Miss Reed. The manager wants to meet with you before you leave to discuss a regular schedule."

Liv nodded. "Thank you."

"Can I get y'all any drinks?"

"No, we're good. Thanks." Joshua waved her off and folded his forearms on the table. "Why on earth do you think I'd ever allow Liv to step foot in your house?" He continued in a harsh whisper. "You blackmailed her for seven years. Beat her. Raped her. Gave her no choice but to train and sell slaves." His voice pitched in a state of disbelief. "You kept her daughter from her."

"Besides that," Liv cut in, "Van has a *talent* for training people to obey. I'm sure a sweet submissive girlfriend would say just about anything."

He tightened his fists beneath the table and whispered furiously, "That's logical *if* I were trying to con anyone else. But you have both been there. You'd recognize coercion from a mile away." He turned to Joshua. "And you read people better than anyone I know." He flicked a hand at Liv. "If you can see through her fucking masks, you should damn well be able to see through mine and my girlfriend's."

His former slaves stared at him with furrowed brows as if they were considering his words.

"I'm just asking for a chance." His words rushed forth with the pump of his heart. "I've done some horrible things, and I want a chance to protect her from the kind of man I used to be. I grew up without a father's love, and I want to fucking be there to give her that."

Their silence wore on. He scrubbed his hands over his face, and when he looked up, her expression sent a chill down his spine. Not her usual detached frigidness. In its place were soft, sympathetic features that didn't belong there. He didn't want her looking at him like that. She was about to break his heart, and he couldn't bear to hear it.

"No," she said. One soft, excruciating word.

The pain exploded in his chest, and he struggled to breathe through it.

She wasn't done. "You coerced me for seven years, and I let you. But this isn't about me. It's about Livana. I can't let you" —her breath hitched, and her jaw stiffened— "I *won't* allow you to fuck with her."

"Liv, I would never—"

"If you go near her, I won't involve the authorities." Her eyes blazed with rage. "I'll kill you myself, and when I dispose of your body, no one will ever find it."

His heart pounded, and his stomach soured with regret. He'd told her the same thing once.

Her voice dropped to a heartless rasp. "You know why?"

The answer he'd given her a year ago about her own death crawled from his thick throat. "Because no one will care enough to search for it." *Or wouldn't be able to cross the porch to search for it.*

Joshua wrapped his arm around her shoulders. She leaned against his chest, her eyes closing not with satisfaction but with heavy sadness.

He should've stood and walked out of there, but he needed to know his options. "You won't kill me."

Her eyes flew open. "No? How do you think I freed eight slaves and ended your father's operation?"

The real question was how she disposed of the buyers' bodies. "How did you come by your cartel connections? It was Camila, wasn't it?"

He hadn't been able to confirm the connections, let alone link them to the first slave they'd kidnapped together. But her averted gaze validated it.

Fuck.

Liv had cartel connections through Camila. If he approached Livana, he was a dead man. His pulse thrashed, and he yanked at his collar. Fuck, fuck, fuck, fuuuuuuck!

He felt sick, his throat tightening. He reached for the paper bag beside him, removed the doll with a shaking hand, and held it out. "My girlfriend and I made this. Will you give it to Livana?"

She cringed. "Ugh, you still have those things?" Her face distorted with disgust as she climbed over Joshua's lap and strode away.

Fucking moronic how he'd thought bringing a doll to the meeting in place of Amber could've proved anything. Didn't matter that it was handcrafted, beautifully detailed, and made with so much goddamned hope. His daughter would never see it. His gut clenched.

Joshua gave him a pitying look. "Van..."

Fuck him. He shoved the doll back into the bag and got the fuck out of there.

The leaded weight of his feet dragged through the parking lot, the humid air pushing down on his shoulders. When he reached the Mustang, he stripped the jacket and tossed it in the back seat. With his hands clenched around the wheel and the doll in his lap, the weight of the night came surging in, burning his eyes, clotting his throat, and filling up every splintered crack inside him with thick, oily crap. Yet he felt so fucking empty.

He opened the glove box and shoved the doll inside. Then he slammed it shut and numbly stared at the closed door.

A knock on the driver's side window kicked the air from his lungs, and he jumped.

Joshua stood beside the car, bent at the waist with his hands on his knees. "Roll down the window."

He rubbed the ache in his chest and turned the window crank, offering the man a bored expression.

"You had a look about you in there," Joshua said, "when you talked about your girlfriend. A peaceful look."

Joshua was a charging protector as much as a touchy-feeler, a reminder he was going to be a preacher before Liv took him. He was hardwired to see the good in people.

And Van wasn't in the mood for it. "Get to the point."

"Get your shit together, man. You've got a month. Meet us at this restaurant. I jotted down the date and time." Joshua shook the napkin. "Liv will feel less threatened if your girl is with you. So don't show up without her."

He didn't like this numbnut dictating his schedule, but he buried his arrogance. "Liv won't agree to this."

"She's scared, Van. But she'll be there. I'll make sure of it." Joshua's mouth tilted in a half-smile.

Well damn. Their relationship dynamic was baffling. Clearly, Joshua was a sexual submissive, but maybe he wore the pants when he didn't have a dildo in his ass.

He reached for the napkin, and Joshua snatched it back, eyes hard and assertive. "And stop stalking my girlfriend."

"I don't need to." Nor did he want to. He grabbed the napkin and rolled up the window on the fucker's gloomy face.

Hope. It was just a tiny twitch in his chest, but it was there.

As he drove back to the cabin in Cedar Creek, that hope dwindled by the mile. He had a month to slay Amber's beast. His ears pounded. The more he thought about it, the more he wanted to slay it literally.

He turned off the exit and drove to the suburban house in Austin he'd visited a few times in the last three weeks. She might've been predisposed to the disorders, but they hadn't taken over her life until her stupid motherfuckering ex brutalized her from the inside out.

He parked in front of the two-story house and shut off the car. Residence of Brent and Tawny Piselli, insurance salesman and aspiring model. Proud owners of two yappy dogs and a sprinkler system. Only thing missing was the white picket fence.

He cracked his neck from side to side and tried to shake the tension from his hands. He wanted to kill both of them, but he'd promised he wouldn't harm her sister.

The picture window glowed with light from the sitting room, flickering with movement inside. Tawny's Audi wasn't in the driveway, and Brent always parked in the garage.

His pulse elevated, driven with a desire for vengeance. He burned for a fight.

My enemy isn't out there, Van. It's here. Right here.

Maybe Brent's death wouldn't help her, but it sure as fuck would release the burning misery built up behind his eyes. He wanted to dominate, to hurt. He wanted to fucking see blood. Fuck the consequences.

He flipped open the glove box, reaching inside for the pistol. His hand brushed the paper bag, crinkling it.

You would be a great father. Fierce and protective and attentive.

He would be a great inmate. A kidnapper, a rapist, a sex trafficker...a murderer.

His head hurt, and his damned body felt like a thousand pounds, every tense inch of it sinking into his stomach. He tore the bag off the doll and bent the legs to sit it on the passenger seat beside him.

You're trying to make a doll that doesn't break?

I've tried. They all break eventually.

Except the one Amber built.

The image of her soft smile and bright eyes shining through the railing invigorated him with a warmth that could only be connected to life.

Not death.

He didn't have to be a kidnapper, rapist, sex trafficker, or murderer. Not anymore.

He slapped the door on the glove box, closing away the gun, and started the car. He had a promise to keep and a sexy ass to beat.

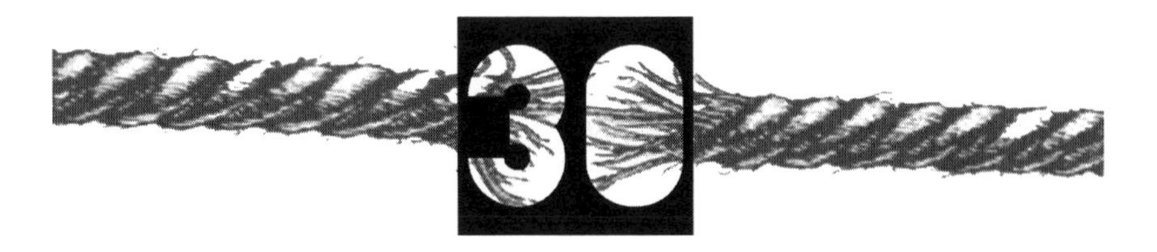

The front door closed with a heart-jolting thunk. *He made it home!* Amber rolled off her back and scrambled on her knees to the railing. Clutching the wood spindles, her fingers ached with the physical and emotional strain of the last few hours.

The steady fall of leather soles on tile swished through her ears, centering her. Liv hadn't turned him over to the police. Huge exhale. Maybe he hadn't gone home with her. Deeper inhale. His beautiful, naked body wasn't in a bed right now, wrapped around the woman who'd given him a seven-year fever. He was home, safe. Hers.

His broad back came into view, and she trembled with anticipation. He'd lost the jacket, the black dress shirt stretching across his shoulders. He must've known she was watching him, but he didn't look up. *Please, look up.*

His casual gait veered through the great room, the tips of his fingers sliding across the sofa back and tapping along the edge of a desk, his powerful legs moving slowly yet systemically. He stopped at the center of the window wall with his back to her and stared at the drapes. His head tilted to the side.

Every muscle in her body turned to ice. "Van?" Her throat convulsed. "Van? How'd it go?" *Oh, God, turn around, turn around. Please stop looking at those drapes.*

He slid his hands into the pockets of his gray suit pants, the fabric hugging his tight, narrow ass. His feet spaced shoulder-width apart, his posture terrifyingly relaxed. "Tell me the worst thoughts you entertained while I was gone."

His vibrating timbre was so low, so commanding, she melted into the floor. "I imagined you hauled off in handcuffs and how I wouldn't be able to come to you."

"What else?" His baritone echoed off the two-story ceiling.

She swallowed. "I thought about..." She swallowed again, aching for him to turn around. "You and her...together."

A twitch rippled across his back. "Say it, Amber."

Her stomach twisted with shame. "I pictured you...making love to her."

"Thank you." His head lowered a millimeter. "Now tell me why *you think* I would do that."

She closed her eyes and tightened her fists around the spindles. "You shared seven years with her. You collected her hair...your matching scars."

Her voice quivered, her eyes opening and clinging to the back of his muscular frame. "You have a child together."

"I haven't touched her in over a year, and tonight I felt no desire to." His back rose with his inhale. "I enslaved her for seven years because I was selfish. The hair, the scars, Livana...all examples of my selfishness. That's not love, Amber, which was why I never thought to free her."

He reached up, tore open the drapes, and wrenched them off the wall. Wheezing, she jerked away from the railing, caught by two feet of rope.

Fabric and metal poles tumbled to the floor as he moved from window to window, ripping and tossing. She curled into a ball, chest heaving, her face buried in her bound arms.

Every clatter of metal and rip of sheet rock made her heart jump in terror. Her breathing reached an all-too-familiar velocity, burning her lungs and beading sweat along her scalp.

Eventually, her breaths were all she heard as silence settled through the cabin, thickening, waiting. No footsteps on the stairs. No commanding voice. Was he waiting for her to pull herself together?

Her limbs shook, and her pulse ripped through her veins, but breath by painful breath, she reined it in. He'd opened the windows because he wanted to free her. He waited patiently because he believed in her.

She gathered all her courage to accept that knowledge and crawled back to the railing on wobbly knees.

He stood at the bottom of the stairs, pinching the button on the shirt cuff at his wrist. As he loosened it and moved to the other wrist, he lifted his eyes, locking them on her. Intense eyes. Dangerously beautiful eyes. She didn't need to look at the windows behind him because she held those eyes, because they told her he loved her.

He didn't look away as he climbed the stairs and rolled up his sleeves. He held her gaze as he reached the loft and removed his belt, dropping it on the wood floor before her. He didn't break eye contact until he knelt at her side and ripped the straps of her tank top.

The openness of the windows crawled on her skin. So she sat on her hip, leaning toward him, and let his touch, his eyes, and his spicy scent swallow her senses. The nylon rope bit into her arms, rubbing against her clammy skin, but she welcomed it, gloried in the restraints he'd given her.

Sliding the shirt to her waist, his fingers stroked a trail of fire down her breastbone, over the lacy bra cups, and across her belly. "Lift your gorgeous ass."

His whisper pulled that fire inward, heating her blood and curling tendrils of warmth through her pussy. She raised her hips, lost in the potency of his hands on her body. There was something unequivocal about pleasing a man as controlling and calculating and *adoring* as Van Quiso. No need to think. She simply obeyed, placing all her pleasure, and her pain, in his strong and capable hands.

His full lips parted as he glided the shirt and skirt down her legs, his sharp silvery gaze totally and completely focused on her. No matter what kind of confrontation he'd just come from, he was here now, gifting her with the command of his concentration.

With only the bra and rope left on her body, she met his eyes comfortably and confidently. "Will you tell me about it?"

"After your punishment." He licked the corner of his mouth, perhaps seeking the toothpick that wasn't there. "On your knees."

She obeyed, eyes glued to the swell of his groin as he stood and unbuttoned his shirt. When he shrugged it off and tossed it somewhere near the closet, she yanked against the restraints to go after it.

He chuckled, damn him. Whatever. She'd pick it up later. Right now, she had something better to do, like take in the sight of his magnificent body.

His abs flexed with his reach for the leather belt on the floor and contracted with his stretch as he straightened. Veins ran beneath the skin of his forearms, bulging over muscle, pumping with the movements of his hands folding the belt.

Her fingers tingled to run down his chest and around his back to feel his taut muscles and absorb the smooth texture of his skin. More than that, she wanted to bask in the heat of his belt on her ass.

Dangling the strap at his side, he unzipped his pants and slid his hand inside. "Do you know how fucking hard you make me?" He removed his hand and grabbed a fistful of her hair. "Spread your knees. Arms up and elbows out. Like you're hugging a six-foot cock."

Her mouth watered, and her pussy throbbed with liquid heat. When she assumed the pose, he stepped into the ring made by her bound arms and yanked her by her hair until her cheek pressed against his hip. The strength of his thigh supported her as he pivoted to face her, his cock hard and pulsing and tenting his slacks an inch from her face.

She slid her cheek against it, reveling in the curved shape and the way it jumped against her touch. Her arms tightened around his thigh, and she ground her clit against his shin, humping his leg and throbbing with need. "Van—"

"Who am I?"

She smiled. "The ruler over lights and porches and window shades and spectacular messes and—" The yank on her hair made her smile harder, and she answered honestly and respectfully. "Master."

He caressed the edge of the belt over her cheek. "Describe your pussy. I want details."

"It's wet, leaking onto my legs. And it hurts. It's clenching like crazy." Her admission intensified the throb. "Van, I need you."

"What does it look like?"

She choked. Dammit, why did he have to go there?

The belt whistled through the air and landed across her ass with a searing sting.

She grunted against his hip. "It's swollen."

"More." He swung again, hitting her other ass cheek.

Her thoughts blurred with shameful images, but she would tell him, and maybe he'd spank her harder. It didn't matter why he belted her as long as he continued to do so. The pain was a need, a distraction, and a connection. "It's stretched, loose, chewed up, and used."

He laid into her, beating her ass just as he'd promised. She didn't count the swings. She never did, too consumed by the fiery sensations blazing through her body, the press of his cock in her face, the exertion of his breath, and the bolster of his leg as she hugged it tighter with every stroke. The pain was binding, an extension of him, an outpouring of his very essence, his darkness and devotion, his damage and strength.

He could whip her against a tree, fuck her beneath the moon, or tie her down on the porch and mar her flesh with the cuts of his teeth. It didn't matter, because wherever he took her, no matter how brutal or dark the destination, there would always be warmth. Because he would be with her.

The belt clattered to the floor. He slipped his leg from her embrace and tackled the knots, unwinding the rope from her arms. The room spun around her, but her world was aligned. Because he was right there, his arms beneath her legs and back, his chest against hers. He lifted her and laid her on the bed.

She melted into the mattress, ass tingling, her pussy spread and soaking and aching to be filled. He stripped his pants, his erection long and thick, as he climbed over the edge of the mattress.

He wedged his shoulders into the gap of her thighs and breathed against her pussy, "I don't see anything here that's stretched, loose, or chewed up. But the last part, well..." He pressed a finger in her opening and stirred it around the edges, shooting pulses of heat through her inner muscles. "It's definitely used. I've made sure of that."

He dragged a slow, torturous lick through her folds, and her hands flew to his hair, her pelvis bucking to meet his mouth.

"Fuck, you taste like heaven. I could eat you all night...*after* you tell me more about this hang-up. That brain-damaged prick you were married to didn't come up with his insult by looking at you. I'm beginning to think he never looked at you at all."

The truth of his words tensed her legs around his shoulders.

He kissed her cunt with an open mouth and a swirling tongue, devouring every inch of her slick flesh. Hot, wet, "No, he picked up on your insecurity and exploited it to get his rocks off." He lapped at her clit. "Tell me the source of your insecurity, and I'll let you come."

His sucking resumed, his lips sliding over her, his tongue thrusting and circling. His skillful mouth smothered her with overwhelming pleasure, and just as the orgasm rose up, he pulled back. Fuck! Then he went at her again, eating and biting and pushing her toward the edge.

She vibrated with need, the urgency to come overwhelming. "He wouldn't go down on me. He...he talked about the girls who ran in my circle, about how tight their cunts must've been and how he wanted to bury his face in that." She blew out a tired breath. "He hadn't gone down on me in years, and I...I thought it was my pubic hair so I shaved. It didn't help, so I decided there was something wrong with me."

He looked up, his lips glistening, his eyes twin flames of silver. "His fucking loss." Then he immersed his face in her folds and blew her fucking mind.

Her legs trembled, and her fingers twisted and yanked his hair. The attack of his teeth and tongue sent her soaring with weightless wings, the release spinning her out of control, her back arching and her toes curling.

When she landed, he caught her, shifting them to their sides, face-to-face. He pulled her thigh over his hip, his cock nudging her opening. "Your pussy belongs to *me*. You're not allowed to insult it. Not in your head or otherwise."

"Okay." She smiled, and it must've looked as loopy and satisfied as she felt.

With a finger gliding around the tip of his shaft and spreading her open, he worked himself in. His hand flew to the back of her head, and he groaned into her hair as he thrust.

The invasion was full and snug, every inch of him warming and stroking her insides. Her muscles contracted around him, all thought, all feeling, centered on where they were joined. He pumped faster, pulling her head back by her hair and taking her mouth. My God, the man could kiss. She could come just from the slide of his tongue.

She opened her eyes and found him watching her with affection and a thrilling amount of lust. He hadn't grown bored with her. He wanted this. He wanted *her*. Not Liv.

As he began to plow into her with intoxicating roughness, she returned to his mouth, biting his lips, her fingers tracing the ridges of flexing muscle along his torso. He slammed into her, grinding against her clit, and pulled out in long strokes, repeatedly, pushing her to the edge, teetering...

He rolled her from her side to her back and deepened the thrusts. His head dropped to the pillow, his softly-shaven cheek rubbing against hers, his breaths sharpening. "Fuck, Amber. So fucking close. You need to come."

She clutched his ass and clamped down around his driving length. Four more grinding rotations, and she let go. "Aaaagggh, God, I'm coming." As strong as the first, the surge lifted and carried her through waves of drugging pleasure.

His hips jerked. "Fuck." He buried his face in her neck, his palm covering the side of her head, his powerful body trembling through jerky thrusts. "Fuck. Me, too. Fuuuuck."

She held him tight as he fell apart above her, his weight a crushing security and his groans quenching her undying need for his appreciation.

As his muscles relaxed and his cock pulsed inside her, a voice whispered at the back of her head. "Van? The condom?"

He barked out a laugh and rolled to his back, taking her with him and slipping out of her, his seed smearing against her thigh. "Little late for that, babe." He reached between them, swiping a finger through the mess on her leg and sliding it into her mouth. The clean salty flavor mingled with his saliva as he kissed her slow and lazily. He leaned back, grinning.

She pinched his ass. "You have a semen fetish."

"I like the way it tastes on our lips, and so do you." He kissed her again. "The test results came back today. You're clean."

She relaxed against him, draped over his body, her cheek on his chest, smiling happily. Not that she'd worried about STDs, but he'd put her on the pill when she arrived—using a no script online pharmacy—and she hadn't had sex without a condom since she'd been married. "No wonder that felt so good."

"Mm." He stroked her hair with one hand and cupped her ass with the other. "I went to Brent and Tawny's house tonight."

Fucking whiplash. She jerked back and collided with his unreadable gaze. "Why?"

He forced her face back to his chest with a strong hand and held her in place. "I drove there to kill him. Decided not to."

Her heart raced. She hadn't even considered the possibility. "You're not a murderer."

A heavy sigh expanded his ribs, and his thumb drew restless circles over her jaw where he held her against him. "A year ago, Liv was brutally raped by a slave buyer. I felt responsible because I'd sent her to him fully fucking aware of what kind of monster he was. When I found out, I shot his wife just to torture him. Then I..." He exhaled. "You don't need to hear the details. I killed him."

Torture. Van had no doubt brought unholy vengeance on that man. His breathing labored, and his hand loosened on her head. She rose up and searched the hard lines of his face. No remorse or horror painted in those lethal features.

"Protective till the end," she whispered.

"The very end, in fact. I packed up after that to leave the operation for good."

"But Liv shot you before you got out?"

He twined their legs together. "Yeah."

"Your avenging-murder days are over?"

"We'll see."

Right. If someone harmed her, all bets were off. The thought filled her with a selfish kind of comfort. She slid a toe up and down his calf. "You're not going to rehang the drapes, are you?"

He laughed. "Nope."

That was a problem she'd worry about in the morning. "What happened with Liv tonight?"

He combed his fingers through her hair and stared at the ceiling. "You were right. She's too scared to trust me. Can't blame her." He lowered his eyes to hers. "They want to meet you. Joshua specifically. The meeting is set a month from today." The fingers in her hair curled, pulling the strands and speeding her pulse. "In a restaurant."

The spectacle played out in her head. A slobbering panic attack, nothing like the little gasping hiccups she'd been having outside the cabin. More like one of those spit-flinging episodes that bucked her body all over the floor and rolled her eyes into the back of her head. Patrons would gape in horror and spill their drinks. The manager would call for an ambulance. And Van would be humiliated.

A silver light focused on her, funneling her feral thoughts back to the loft, the bed, and the hard body cradling her. His eyes glowed with acceptance, hope, faith. He looked at her with the kind of love that would transcend any answer she gave.

With a trembling smile, she nodded. "I'll try."

Amber did try. Hour by hour, day after day, Van watched her tackle her fear till her body gave out. He supported her the best way he knew how, with a commanding presence, a steady hand, and an aching yet prideful heart. But he eased up on pushing and dragging her in his usual way, because dammit, she was hard enough on herself.

Even now, five days away from the meeting with Liv and Joshua, she lay passed-out in the front seat of the Mustang, covered in sweat and dark hair tangled around her. Because she'd demanded he drive her to the edge of the two-hundred acre property.

He paced beside the open passenger door, the gravel driveway crunching beneath his sneakers. Even through muscle spasms and hyperventilation, she'd fought with white knuckles on the dashboard to remain conscious.

The tightening in his gut told him she wouldn't make it inside that restaurant. If she didn't, he would never hold it against her. But how well would *she* accept her failure?

He searched his pockets for a toothpick and came up empty. Fucking hell.

He lowered onto the edge of the seat beside her and stroked the soft, damp skin on her cheek, traced the lashes beneath her closed eyes, and pressed his thumb against her full bottom lip. He yearned to take her back to the house before she woke, but he'd agreed to her plea.

If I pass out, please don't drive me back till I wake. I need to fight through this.

The phobia was so deeply worked into her mind it felt more powerful than the two of them combined. But she *had* made progress. She'd conquered the uncovered windows within one week. Hell, she didn't even mess with her hair anymore when she passed by them.

The bulimia seemed to be subdued because she didn't obsess over her body image anymore. She never tried to cover her body from him, her appetite had grown to a healthy level, and a few times, he'd caught her looking at her reflection, not with disgust, but with approval flickering in her eyes.

The OCD had become a trivial thing. She still counted and popped her knuckles when she was upset, and she would always be an orderly little neat freak. But it didn't control her life. Not like the agoraphobia. Not like *him.*

Her eyes fluttered open, flicking over the surrounding windows, groggily orienting. Her fingers curled in her lap, and her breathing hitched.

He cupped her face to direct her focus on him. When their eyes locked, he was transported back to the first time they met. On her porch, him with his dick in his hand, her all dolled up for a date with the mailbox. Her brown eyes, round as saucers then, had been so terrified.

The very same terror stared back at him now. He tensed, and the surrounding timber stilled, too, waiting for her reaction.

Her breathing tightened, followed by the usual shaking, wheezing, and sweating. Her choking sobs wrenched at the air and weighted his stomach with lead. He crawled into the driver's seat, closed the doors, and sped back to the house, his heart stumbling all over itself. This wasn't working. Nothing was working.

After he fed her lunch, she sat at the kitchen table, staring at the remnants of oyster bisque in the bowl. Her shoulders slumped, her head lowered, and she wouldn't maintain eye contact.

He wore a path on the tiles around her chair, his muscles stiff and his throat tight. Joshua had given him a chance to win Liv's trust. Would this meeting be his only chance? It seemed like an all or nothing kind of opportunity, to prove to Liv he had a girl who wasn't coerced or enslaved.

But her dejected posture made his stomach sink. "Fuck the stupid meeting, Amber. We can attempt another one at a later date. Whenever you're ready."

Her chin hardened. "Where's the man who broke into my house and fucked with all my stuff? Stop being gentle with me. Van. You're the only person who has ever given enough of a shit about me to shove me out the door." She stood, fire sparking in her eyes, and pointed a finger at him. "I need you to shove me across the porch on my face if you have to."

His heart banged against his ribs with furious agreement.

"We're doing this." She squared her shoulders. "*I'm* doing this."

But she was doing it *for him* and only because he would be there. If she failed, her devastation could be self-damaging, and he couldn't allow that to happen.

He pressed his lips together and rubbed his forehead. She was a stunning, naturally-submissive, *housebound*, consensual slave. He should've been out-of-his-mind ecstatic. But if he had one regret in their two-month relationship, it was his stupid, selfish fucking mission to be her obsession. If he hadn't come into her life, maybe she would've lost her house. But more than likely, she would've landed on her feet because she was bullheaded and strong as fuck.

None of that mattered now. He'd fed her, protected her, *controlled* her every damned move, and in doing so, he'd robbed her of her self-reliance and replaced it with an unhealthy dependency. Him.

She blew out a breath and cocked her head, her eyes suddenly bright and mischievous. "I have an idea."

Just like that, she brought a smile to his face. "Does it involve bleach and scrub brushes?"

She tapped her chin. "Hmm. I'm thinking gasoline." Her eyes glimmered. "And fire."

An hour later, he stood beside a well-fueled bonfire roaring twenty-paces from the cabin. The heat from the flames and the aroma of wood smoke had an old-fashioned way of fortifying the spirit and moving the psyche into a place of deep contentment.

He looked up to find her leaning against the doorjamb, just inside the back door. Her arms wrapped around her torso, her expression strained with panic. No doubt she wouldn't be stepping over the threshold. But beneath the fear lay a softness in her eyes, a kind of peaceful resolve.

She'd said the fire could burn away the past, melt the painful memories, and make room for transformation. It was worth the try.

He gave her one more questioning look, arching his eyebrow. *Are you sure?*

At her nod, he lifted the aquarium of tiaras and chucked it into the fire. The flames crackled and sparked, skittering red-hot embers across the ground. Metal and glass wouldn't disintegrate, but it would certainly fuse into an unrecoverable blob.

A glance over his shoulder rewarded him with a view more magnificent than a million fires, her smile as radiant as the iridescent glow of gems melting in her tiaras.

He reached for the garbage bag he'd sneaked outside, her words floating through his head.

It's just stuff attached to broken memories. Burning it will inspire new ones to grow.

By *stuff*, she'd meant her crowns, but he had memories, too. He removed the contents, her *OhmyGod* rippling the air as he fed the blaze with dolls. Two plastic bodies, brown hair, and a red-checkered dress vanished behind a black fog of smoke. It wasn't a cremation. It was simply the end of a life that hadn't been a life at all.

Looping his thumbs in his front pockets, he strode toward her with an easy, unhurried gait. Hope lightened his chest. It had been there for a while, but it strengthened as he took in the promise sparkling in her eyes.

Five days later, Van waited in the kitchen, chewing the ever-loving fuck out of a toothpick. He tossed it in the waste-bin and yanked at the sleeve of his suit. *Come on, Amber.*

That morning, he'd bought makeup, hairstyling crap, a black dress, and heels. And she'd been holed up in the bathroom with that shit for an hour. They needed to leave immediately to arrive at the restaurant on time.

Deep breath. Fuck, he was wound tight. But he wouldn't rush her.

Still, he hoped she was held up by a curling iron and not a change of heart. How could he not be hopeful about what the night could bring? It could crash through the agoraphobia as well as open a door with Livana.

Or it could end in tearful hyperventilation.

The bathroom door opened with a whoosh that sounded like the air rushing from his lungs. Sweet mother of sin, he'd told her cosmetics would defile the natural perfection of her face, but as she lingered in the doorway, shoulders back, arms at her sides, one long leg bent before the other, he stood tongue-tied and stupefied.

The raw, disheveled knockout he drooled over every waking hour had transformed into an untouchable, world-class beauty queen. It was impossible to keep his cock down while admiring her tight body wrapped in hip-hugging silk. Dark hair curled around her face and chest. Deep crimson painted her lips, and her thick lashes went on forever, highlighting her shining eyes.

Toned legs flaunted delectable flesh from thigh to ankle, her feet arched in the black fuck-me heels he hadn't been able to pass up at the boutique, and her smile... Fuck him.

He wanted to lick along the curves of her tits rising above the low neckline and bite the taut nipples pressing against the silk. The view spoiled him, and there wasn't a man on earth who deserved to look at her. "Let's stay home." Christ, he needed to be inside of her.

The smile gracing those red lips widened. "You look good, too, Van." Her gaze roamed his body, turning the stiffness in his pants into a throbbing monster.

Her nostrils flared as if she were trying to smell him from across the room. "So incredibly handsome. Wish I had panties." She twisted to look at her ass. "When I sit down, I'm going to leave a wet spot."

Fuck it. A quickie against the wall wouldn't make them *too* late. He strode toward her and grabbed her hips, leaning in to take her mouth.

His lips crashed into her halting palm. "No kissing." She pinched his chin. "You'll smudge the makeup."

Then she definitely wouldn't be down with what he had in mind. He adjusted his erection and straightened his tie. "We better go or we won't be going at all."

Her easy playfulness vanished instantly, and she cast a fearful look at the front door.

Even a non-agoraphobe would've approached this meeting with a healthy amount of nervousness. Hell, his stomach would be all kinds of fucked up by the time they arrived. With any luck, she would be too anxious about being outside to muster any additional worries about impressing his former slaves. She had enough to focus on.

"Hey." He cupped her face, turning her eyes to him. "I parked the Mustang right outside the door. Just like we practiced."

She nodded with an expression so fearfully hopeful, it hurt to see it. They'd driven to the end of the property every day for the past week. Yesterday was the first day she hadn't fainted during the two-minute drive.

He gripped her hand and led her calmly to the front door. "Your steps are mine, Amber. I won't leave your side."

If they made it out of the driveway, it would be her first time off the property since he'd abducted her two months ago.

Her breath stuttered as they hit the porch. It was spastic by the time they reached the end of the driveway. He rolled to a stop and softened his voice with patience. "How are we doing?"

She popped her knuckles, her eyes squeezed shut, her chest jumping with shallow breaths. "Just keep...going. Don't stop."

She'd told him once how strangers' eyes felt like loaded guns aimed at her head. She was about to face a firing squad, and she'd bravely demanded that he keep going.

He slid his hand around the back of her neck, beneath her hair, and squeezed. "I love you, you crazy woman."

Her head nodded with a jerk, her smile quivering the corner of her mouth. "You, too," she whispered. "Now drive."

He gripped the wheel and began the painful trek toward downtown Austin.

Thirty minutes later, he parked the car in front of a quaint Italian restaurant, his stomach in knots. The sign read *No Parking*, but he didn't give a fuck. The tension in the car had been rolling off her since they'd left, and the combustion was three, maybe four breaths away.

Releasing their seat belts, he twisted toward her and grabbed her ice-cold face. "Amber? Talk to me."

Her eyes were closed. They had been the duration of the drive. Another wave of tension vibrated off of her. She opened her mouth to speak, and her voice cut off with the wheeze of her lungs.

Goddammit, she wasn't ready for this. But if he drove her home without letting her try, it would steal the decision from her. "Look how far you've come. You can do this, sweetheart."

Blindly, her hand fumbled for the door handle. It shook so badly, she wouldn't be able to pull the latch even if she found it.

"I'm going to get out and open your door for you."

She answered with a heart-breaking sob, but he didn't miss the slight nod of her head. With heart-racing strides, he rounded the car in the three seconds. But he was too late.

When he opened the door, the look on her face lanced a new scar, right through his heart. Her eyes were wide and terrified and locked on the restaurant's glass windows, on the patrons inside. Makeup streaked her cheeks, marking the paths of her tears, her complexion ghostly white. Her fingernails dug so deeply into her palms, when he pried them loose, blood smeared over the broken skin.

"I can't...I can't...I can't..." she choked between wheezing breaths.

His blood heated, and his chest tightened. She'd wanted to do this, wanted to be pushed. Well, not like this. No goddamned way. He'd have to carry her inside, and her humiliation from that alone would only cause her more suffering.

He kissed her gasping mouth, hard and angrily, and slammed the door. He'd brought this pain on her. He'd fucking failed her.

On his sprint back to the driver's side, he glanced through the restaurant window. Liv and Joshua sat in a booth in the back corner, heads bowed over a shared menu. His gait slowed, but only for a second. There'd be another time, another chance. And if not, fuck them. He'd find different way, one that didn't destroy Amber.

He climbed behind the wheel and found her slumped over her lap, her head crooked in an awkward angle. The backs of his eyes burned as he reclined her seat back and positioned her limp body beneath the seatbelt. Then he drove his broken doll home.

Hope had a way of leading a guy on, offering tantalizing glimpses of possibilities and enticing him to the edge of belief. But it didn't put out. Van had been on the giving end of such things throughout his criminal history, which made it even more harrowing to watch Amber succumb to hope's cruel disappointment.

A month had passed since the drive to the restaurant, and she'd regressed, immediately and spectacularly.

"Get up." He stood over the bed where she spent the majority of the day, every day.

She rolled to her back, blinking heavy eyelids, and held out her arms. "Make love to me." She dropped her arms and looked away. "Please?"

His body felt cold, his heart weighted down with the ache it had been carrying for too damned long. Maybe her devastation was partly due to her disappointment in herself. But he knew the bigger part was in her inaccurate belief that she'd disappointed him.

He yanked back the sheets and let his weight press down on her nude body. He could never deny her, not even now in her numb state of existence. With a hand on her face, he held her eyes and gave her the words he repeated daily. "I love you, I want you, and I will never ever be disappointed in you."

She kissed him. Her usual response, maybe some kind of coping mechanism.

He matched her licks and nibbles then took over, leading her, controlling this. It was what she wanted and what he needed. He released his belt and opened his jeans, her hands already on his cock, stroking it to readiness.

As he worked himself into her wet heat, her eyes glowed. These were the only moments when he saw that light, the only way he seemed to be able to bring her out of her head. Not the belt nor the whip nor his restraints affected her. Not even when he hauled her outside every night. She'd lost interest in everything but him. And his cock.

It wasn't healthy, and it didn't help her. He was a toxin, polluting her mind and making her worse. If he let this go on, he would destroy her.

He brought her to climax, and as he followed her over the brink of momentary bliss, her words rushed in, punching an agonizing hole through his heart.

You're the only person who has ever given enough of a shit about me to shove me out the door.

As he held her limp body in his arms, the vibrancy in her eyes dulled to blankness. She sank into the mattress, her heat pulling away, and a frigid void slipped between them. It was slow and subtle and perhaps unintentional, but her detachment strained and ripped every nerve-ending in his body.

God, he wanted her light back. He would ejaculate inside her over and over if it could fill her with life. But the sex was fleeting. If anything, she was colder and more despondent after they made love.

He wanted to argue that he loved her too much to *shove her out the door.* Truth was he loved her too much not to. Just like her behavior with the deliverymen, she was only getting by without getting better.

And he'd become another Zachary Kaufman.

Her independence was the key to unlocking the windows and returning the light. Without it, there was no life.

That night, he made the most painful decision he'd ever made. He drugged her dinner, packed up her things, and gave her back her self-sufficiency. He returned her to her house and reinstated her life, a better life, without him.

For hours, he lingered in her bed, wrapped around her unconscious body, immobilized by the gravity of his decision and struggling to breathe through the agony of it. Soon, he would have to rise from her side and give her the only thing he had to offer—life itself.

Death seemed easier than this godawful burden of losing her. But she had a hell of a fight ahead of her, and if she could suffer through that, then he could endure the loneliness that awaited him.

He couldn't stop the tears burning his eyes as he pressed his lips against her unresponsive mouth. He was numb to the violent tremors wobbling his steps as he staggered down the hall without turning around. He squeezed his eyes shut as he stumbled into the garage, the excruciating pain in his chest eclipsing the crash of the concrete floor against his knees.

He left the door opener on the shelf and forced his legs into the minivan. The he backed it onto the driveway and climbed out. Shades covered every window on Liv's house, blatantly shutting him out. Not that he was in any state to give a fuck.

He reached inside Amber's garage and pressed the door button on the wall. His chest burned and his throat ached as he stepped back and wrapped his arms around himself to keep from stopping the doors' descent.

When the garage doors sealed shut, the silent finality of it ripped out his insides and beckoned the enclosing darkness with the sound of his sobs.

Amber woke with an ear-ringing headache. She hadn't even opened her eyes and her body already ached with grief, sagging into the mattress like a useless weight. She'd gone to bed hating herself for what she was doing to Van, and just like every other night, sleep hadn't absolved her.

Her hand slapped over the mattress, searching for the warmth of Van's skin, his strength, their connection. Her fingers collided with papers.

She jerked up on her elbows and rubbed her eyes, blinking against the illumination of a nearby lamp. She rubbed and blinked again.

White walls bled into a shadeless window, glowing with sunlight. Her mouth dried as she soaked in the white carpet, white quilt, the duffel bags by the door... Oh God, her bedroom.

Dread iced through her veins, curling frigid fingers around her throat. The house should've been foreclosed, empty, gone. And where the hell were the shades? She sucked in a shaky breath and shouted, "Van? Van, where are you?"

She scrambled off the bed and raised trembling fingers to her lips, straining to hear his footsteps.

The A/C unit hummed outside the window. The shower down the hall dripped. *Plop-plip. Plop-plip.* The water was on? What the fuck for?

Beside the lamp, the bedside clock glowed 6:19 AM. Electricity, too? Her heart stopped then went ballistic, tightening her skin and firing up her muscles.

She sprinted through the house, searching room by room for answers, for him. Not a single shade on the windows. The fridge and cabinets were filled with food. *Food from the cabin.* She opened the garage door and shivered at the dark, cavernous space. No Mustang. No Van.

Returning to the kitchen, she gripped the edge of the sink and looked up. The window and backyard stared back. Her heart froze, and she dropped to the floor, out of sight. Was he out there? Was he coming back?

Unbidden, his words came rushing in, stabbing through her heart.

I enslaved her for seven years because I was selfish. That's not love, Amber, which was why I never thought to free her.

"Noooooo." A roar burst from her throat, heaving her chest and burning her eyes. That couldn't be it. This wasn't freedom. It was some kind of a mistake, a misunderstanding. Oh Jesus, she needed to talk to him.

She reached up to the counter with a blind hand, found her phone, and swiped through the contacts. No calls. No new numbers. She tossed it across the floor and stared at it, helplessly. She'd never seen him use a phone or e-mail. He probably didn't even have those things.

Because I don't exist.

Her heart rate accelerated. Where was the cabin located? Somewhere outside of Austin. With trees. Lots of trees. Fuck! How could she have never thought to ask?

Because she never intended to leave.

She slammed a fist against the cabinet, rattling the doors. The one and only time she'd traveled the route from the cabin while conscious, she'd kept her damned eyes closed.

Her breath caught. Were there papers on the bed? She ran back to the bedroom and crawled over the mattress. The sight of the folded letters turned and twisted her stomach. Her hand flew to her belly, massaging the anguish there, her fingers brushing cotton. She looked down at the cami and panties that covered her body.

Blood drained from her face, her cheeks numb. He'd dressed her and left her. A quiver gripped her chin. She rubbed it roughly away and gathered the papers.

They shook in her hands as she sat on her heels and flipped through them. The first was a receipt for her mortgage. Zero balance, the house was paid off. A pang rippled through her chest.

Next were printouts of all her credit card statements and utility bills. *Zero balances.* The ache in her chest swelled to her throat.

The following letter showed an unfamiliar bank account in her name, the balance printed in bold font. *$100,000.* Enough to live on for years. Burning pinpricks hammered behind her eyes.

She choked, buckling over her knees. Sobs tumbled out, painful and wretched. Oh God, it hurt. He'd left her. Left her without shades on her windows. Left her with a secure and stable and financially-free life.

To free her.

She gritted her teeth, the papers crumpling in her fists. Stupid, stupid, stupid man. Why would she want any of this if she didn't have *him*?

She opened the last letter, a handwritten note scrawled with loose penmanship.

I will always love you, I will always want you, and I will never ever be disappointed in you. -Van

It was a good-bye. A fist-through-the-fucking-heart goodbye. The tears surged, hard and ugly and agonizing. She flung herself off the bed and staggered through the room with a helpless, rage-filled cry, her arms sweeping everything in her path. The lamp, the TV, and the duffel bags hit the walls and bounced along the floor, thumping and exploding.

Her vision blurred. Her legs crashed into furniture. Her teeth sawed her lips until blood coated her tongue. Her fingernails shredded and ripped in her attack on everything she could destroy.

At 8:27 AM, she sat on the floor with her back against the dresser. Her lungs burned, her cheeks cracked with drying tears, and her heart jabbed at her ribs with each thump of its sharp splintery edges.

"Well done, you crazy fucking bitch." Her voice scratched her raw throat, but she deserved it. "First prize for world's ugliest temper tantrum. Yay."

She took in the aftermath with little interest. Pillow stuffing covered the floor. Dents peppered the sheet rock. The small TV lay on its side with cracks spider-webbing over the screen.

Where was her anxiety for straight lines? Her impulse to tackle the mess?

She dropped her head back against the dresser and closed her eyes. She couldn't think about that right now. Something else was pressing against her brain.

He lived thirty minutes from that restaurant. If she knew which restaurant it was, she could narrow her search for the cabin. She jumped to her feet and strode toward the wall that faced Liv and Joshua's house, pressing her cheek against it. Maybe Van had given them his address? At the very least, they knew the restaurant.

And so her harrowing journey to their house began. By the end of that first night, she was able to peer out of every window without losing control of her breathing.

By day five, she started keeping her front door open, letting in bugs and sunshine and the gawking of neighbors in passing cars. She sat on the threshold, trembling and gasping, but she didn't pass out.

On day nineteen, her ass hit the bench on the front porch for the first time in two years. She'd stumbled into it, actually, in a breathless fall of exhausted, quivering muscles. She might've clapped her hands if they weren't squeezing the weathered slats in a death grip.

But she did manage a smile, the first smile to touch her lips since the night they'd left for the restaurant. God, he'd looked so handsome in his suit. He'd been so nervous and...turned on by her.

Her heart pinched, and her smile wobbled away. She missed him, deeply and painfully. His absence was a constant wrench of every breath as if her lungs could never quite fill without him.

She uncurled a hand and raised the hem of her old t-shirt, wiping the humidity and sweat from her face. He would've been proud of her. Fuck that. *She* was proud of herself.

"I'm sitting on his bench," she announced to the coverage of bushes, the sunlight soaking into her damp hair. She ran her fingers over the wood, hoping to absorb some part of him that might still be there.

She glanced at the closed-up windows on Liv's house and nodded. She'd get there.

That night, she lay on top of the covers in bed, nude and as content as she could be without him beside her. As she fantasized about his heat sliding over her skin and his tongue controlling her mouth, her hands roamed her body.

Her house might've been a mess, but she'd maintained her daily regimen of cardio and strength training, and that effort flexed sensually in the hard hillocks of her ass and firm flesh on her hips. Her muscles and curves felt beautiful beneath her fingertips. And so did her pussy.

She stroked her fingers down her mound and between her folds as her thoughts filled with silver eyes, a thick cock, and seductive lips. The deep, reverberating voice in her head commanded she fuck herself. So she did, with urgent, wanton thrusts of her fingers. When his voice told her to come, she shouted his name to the ceiling.

There was a good chance she'd never find him, that she'd never be able to show him how far she'd come. But as the next two weeks passed, she protected her new self-esteem, nurturing it with every little progressive step. She refused to even consider puking. She made trips to the mailbox, reconnected with Dr. Michaels, and reinstated her leathercraft business, adding leather dolls to her list of merchandise.

She hadn't worked up to leaving the yard yet, but as the weeks passed, conquering the agoraphobia became more about self-reliance and less about finding Van.

Still, night after night, she sat on the bench and waited for him.

She'd always thought it would take a tragic event to rip down the walls of her phobia: her house catching fire, terminal cancer, *abduction and rape.* Yet, on day seventy-six, something unexpected finally propelled her over the property line and onto Liv's porch.

Love guided her shaky legs beneath the luminance of the moon. She loved herself enough to raise a sweat-soaked fist and knock on the door. And she loved him enough to smooth her breathing when a gorgeous brunette poked her head through the crack.

A pink scar, just like Van's, twitched on Liv's cheek as she tilted her head. "Yes?"

She curled her fingers in the fabric of her shorts, relaxed them at her sides, and lifted her eyes. "I...I...uh..." Her voice quivered, and the air thinned. "I live next door. I'm—" She wheezed with burning lungs, and Liv's emotionless expression didn't help her nerves. "Sorry. I'm a bit panicky."

A car motored down the street behind her, and she jumped. *Jesus, get a grip.* "I'm...I *was* Van Quiso's..." What was she? Slave? Girlfriend? Lover?

Those dark eyes turned to stone. "What the fuck did he do?" Liv opened the door all the way and stepped toward her.

Her muscles heated, and her own eyes hardened. And she didn't step back. "He loved me enough to shove me out the door." Oh fuck. *Awkward.* She glanced over her shoulder, cringing at the open space of the shadowed street. "Can I come in?"

Ten minutes later, she sat in a brown leather armchair with a mug of coffee in her trembling hands. Liv and Joshua perched on the couch across from her, Joshua's arm wrapped around Liv's shoulders. No doubt they assumed the worst about Van, and her need to rectify that spilled the words from her mouth.

They listened without comment or expression as she told them her story. The agoraphobia and OCD, the reason Van was on her porch, the abduction and rape, the dolls and the restaurant, his forceful attempts to overpower her disorders, his longing to have a relationship with his daughter, and his final unselfish act. The how and why he shoved her out the door. On the surface, the events were horrific and unsavory, but she spoke of them with a passion that made her eyes burn, her chest swell, and her lips curve upward. "I love him."

"I see that." Liv reclined against the couch back, her denim-clad legs crossed at the knee and hands folded in her lap. "Stockholm Syndrome is an intense—"

"I have an addictive personality, Miss Reed." She set down the mug and faced the woman head on. "If you want to psychoanalyze me, please consider all of my *syndromes.* As well as your own capture-bonding relationship." She flicked her eyes at a grinning Joshua.

A smile bent Liv's otherwise unreadable expression. "Touché."

Her shoulders relaxed. "He healed me in a way none of my therapists had been able to do. He freed me."

Liv hummed, and the soft, reverberating note sent an exquisite chill through the air. "And you want me to allow him contact with Livana?"

She nodded. "I also want you to help me find him. The restaurant you named only limits my search to...oh, the greater Austin area."

"*He'll* find *you.* He's nothing if not dedicated to his stalk—" Liv smiled. "Pursuits."

She left Liv's house with a yearning to believe her. Hell, he wouldn't have to look far.

For the next two months, she waited right on that bench. She'd trimmed the bushes so he wouldn't miss her if he drove by. So she wouldn't miss him.

Often, she lie down on the wood slats and fell asleep under the canopy of stars. During the day, she expanded her business and paid her bills. She kept a routine, but it was *flexible.* One time, she even took a cab to the grocery store. A panic attack cut her shopping trip short, but she'd managed to get herself home without assistance.

She didn't subscribe hope, but she refused to let herself slip by without a constant goal to work toward. Sitting on that bench, night after night, was a full-on confrontation with her fears. For an agoraphobe, that kind of courage was hard to come by. She collected her courage from every tiny advancement she made in her recovery, saving it up and making herself stronger.

If he never came back for her, she *knew* she was brave enough to continue alone.

Not a second went by when Van didn't question the choice he made that night. Every window, every speck of dust, even the bedside lamp was a painful reminder of what he'd given up. The most agonizing choices were the right ones, but acknowledging it didn't make it any less agonizing.

Six months had passed since he'd kissed her drug-slackened lips in a torturous goodbye. He didn't just miss her lips, but goddammit, he missed them so fucking much.

He missed the sound of her knuckles cracking, her little gasps of panic, and her constant bratty comebacks. He missed working out with her in the mornings and making love to her in the afternoon. He missed feeding her and whipping her and studying all the quirky nuances that made her blush and scowl and throw her head back with laughter. And he missed her in his bed, the firm curves of her body all tucked up against him.

The silence of the cabin was excruciating without her. Even the simple act of breathing was met with a hollow echo that left everything cold and empty.

Like most nights, he drove aimlessly up and down the streets of Austin, heading anywhere except back to the lonely cabin. The leather doll she'd made was a permanent passenger on the seat beside him, a reminder to not show up at her house and demand she come back. He held no doubts in her ability to recover. The doll beside him was a symbol of her strength. And he'd made her weaker. As long as he didn't interfere, she would find her tenacity again.

He turned onto a dark, narrow street. Austin didn't have ghettos, and certainly nothing as decrepit as his childhood shacks, but there were pockets that bristled with crime and broken families.

Up ahead, a small silhouette moved on the side of the road, bobbing and darting beneath the canopy of an abandoned gas station. He slowed the Mustang, motoring closer, the street empty and unlit. He turned into the lot, and the headlights flashed over the tiny features of a five- or six-year-old girl sitting against the concrete wall, legs curled against her chest.

Where was her mother? There was no one around, and she was way too young to be out alone at eleven o'clock at night. Hell, he'd spotted a prostitute just two blocks back.

He stopped the car and opened the door to the sound of her soft sniffles. Approaching her cautiously, he asked, "Are you lost?"

She hugged her legs and shook her head.

With a hand on his hip, the other rubbing the back of his neck, he looked around. Apartment buildings, dark commercial properties, and empty parking lots lined the street. "Where's your mom?"

She pointed at the apartment tower down the road and sniveled.

"What's your name?"

"Leslie," she mumbled.

He crouched at her side. "Leslie, how about you head home? It's not safe out here."

Tears burst from her throat as she shuffled away from him.

Fuck. He crossed his arms around his knees to keep from going to her. Last thing he needed was someone accusing him of being a pedophile. "Go home, Leslie."

She shook her head in hard, jerky movements, the whites of her eyes glassy and wet in the headlights.

His skin tightened, and nausea hit his stomach. He knew that look, one bred of abuse and neglect. He forced himself back to the car and sat there for endless minutes, staring straight ahead, his eyes watering. What could he do?

He slammed his hand against the steering wheel. He'd gone through such a long period of feeling nothing, refusing to allow his miserable past to morph into a selfish need to run back to Amber. But his heart was growing frailer by the minute. He fucking needed her.

But he couldn't just leave this little girl. If she were Livana, he'd remove her from her toxic home.

Kidnapping.

Okay, not an option. He snagged the doll and returned to the girl, dropping on one knee before her. "Whatever it is, Leslie, it's not your fault." What else had he wanted to hear at her age? "It's okay to be scared. Your mother loves you."

Jesus, he sounded like an asshole. But when he handed her the doll, she hugged it to her chest. Then she sighed.

It was a tiny thing, that sigh of happiness, but from it breathed a rush of wind that liberated him. He could return to Amber, not as a stalker and rapist but as an honest man. She could love him back or reject him because she deserved to make that choice. The choice he'd wanted so desperately as a child.

He climbed into the car and made an anonymous phone call. Then he moved the Mustang down the street and kept an eye on her. Fifteen minutes later, red and blue lights flashed around the corner. The police wouldn't always be there for her, but maybe they would help her tonight.

He didn't look in the rear-view mirror as he pulled away. Amber was forward, Livana was forward, and that was where he needed to be.

As he made the twenty-minute drive to her porch, his anxiety rose to a level Amber would've been all too familiar with. What if she'd taken another lover? Another deliveryman? What if Livana had moved elsewhere? Christ, he should've kept an eye on them.

With a churning stomach, he passed the side street he usually parked on. A few seconds later, he pulled into Amber's driveway and turned off the car.

Something moved on the porch. A stray cat? No, a person-sized shadow, sitting right there. He strained his eyes through the dark, waiting for them to adjust. Dark hair, wide eyes...Amber? Face frozen in...Panic? Confusion? Shock?

He fumbled for the door handle, catching it on the second pass. His legs shook as he rounded the front bumper, his eyes glued on the woman rising from the bench.

Sliding the hood off his head, he quickened his gait, his heart slamming into his throat. *She's on the porch. Outside. And she's not flipping her shit?*

Fuck him, she did it. A smile stretched across his face. Of course, she fucking did.

She leapt off the porch and ran toward him, her legs flexing in tiny black shorts, her gorgeous tits stretching her t-shirt.

He held out his arms to catch her, his pulse racing in anticipation to hold her body, to kiss her lips—

Her hand landed across his face in a stinging slap. "Six months, Van Quiso." She smacked him again, her eyes blazing. "One hundred and eighty-three fucking days!"

Her tiny fists went crazy, raining down on his torso in pummeling strikes. She got in some bruising punches, but dammit, he couldn't stop grinning. God, he missed her feistiness.

When she lowered her arms and gazed up at him, her beautiful makeup-free face softened beneath the glow of the streetlight. "You came."

Christ, he wanted to kiss her. "You waited."

She raised a finger, pointing at the bench. "Right there. One hundred and sixty-four nights."

His heart squeezed. With pain. With pleasure. "What did you do the other nineteen nights?"

Her lips slid into a foxy grin. "I made little Van voodoo dolls and stabbed them with toothpicks." Her smile fell. "Are you seeing anyone?"

The worry pulling at her expression made him sick to his stomach. He cupped her face and guided her mouth to his, just close enough to kiss. "There's only been you, Amber." He brushed their lips. "If we're not counting my hand."

He captured her mouth, or maybe she took his, but their tongues met with equal hunger, lips mashing through drugging licks. When he tilted his head and demanded deeper entry, she surrendered, melting against him with her fingers in his hair.

His kiss grew punishing, urgent and rough, his hands more so. He found her tits, pinching them hard enough to make her yelp. He sucked on her upper lip, his cock throbbing against his zipper, as he caressed her firm cheeks beneath the shorts. Jesus, he'd missed her ass, and he was going to fuck her right there on the driveway if they didn't move inside.

When he pulled back, she slipped out of his arms. Walking backwards, hips swaying, she gave him a playful smile. "So you haven't had sex in six months?"

He stalked after her. "No, baby. What about you?"

She shook her head—*thank Christ*—then took off toward the front door, vanishing inside the house. He trailed her, his blood pumping from his heart to his dick, his jeans a painful constriction.

A quick scan through the front room gave him a sense of how much had changed, like the single clock on the wall and the way the pillows were strewn across the couch. There was no clutter, no dirt he could see, but the house didn't have the same severity it once had. Perhaps it was the addition of color. A red throw blanket, an orange rug, and a yellow vase in the corner.

He found her in the kitchen, her eyes glimmering right before she slipped out the back door. What was she up to?

Another thing he'd missed were her endless surprises.

He stepped into the backyard, the woodsy smell of hickory scenting his inhales as he prowled toward her. She waited beneath a tall lattice trellis that adhered to the house.

He reached above her head and yanked on it. "This is new."

Lifting her lids, she peered up at him. "When I put it together, I fantasized about you tying me to it, taking my ass with your belt. Then with your cock."

His nostrils flared with a deep, joyful breath, and he kissed her mouth, passionately, letting her feel what her words did to him. "I regret that it's been six months since I've told you I love you." He brushed his tongue inside her lower lip. "I love you. And I *will* whip and fuck your ass against this trellis when we move it to the cabin."

The release of her breath wisped over his lips. She gripped her shirt and yanked it over her head. "I missed the way you make love to my mouth."

What the hell was she doing? Oh shit, there went her shorts. He gripped himself through the jeans and tried to restrain himself. He should scan their surroundings, check for gawking neighbors, but he couldn't drag his eyes from her, too afraid if he looked away, she'd disappear.

She hooked her thumbs into the sides of her panties. "I missed the warm, wet feel of that first slide of your tongue against mine, the way you tease and pull back. Mmmm. Then you take over with your big, manly confidence and control. I miss that, Van."

Her panties slid to her ankles, and she leaned against the trellis passively, submissively, awaiting his command.

His arousal fed so greedily on her submission, there wasn't a chance in hell he could stop this. A glance at Liv's house validated his position was in eyeshot of her back door. Fuck it.

He released the zipper on his jeans, and his already excited cock jumped as he shoved his pants and briefs to his knees. "Still on the pill?"

She nodded, her smoldering gaze fixed on his cock, making him impossibly harder.

"Arms above your head. Press your wrists against the lattice as if my ropes are keeping them there." He watched with his whole body as she obeyed with quivering breaths and an adoring gaze.

His cock twitched with the need to thrust deep inside her. "Describe your pussy."

Her breath sped up. "It's tight, Master. It hasn't been wrapped around anything but my fingers in six months. It's wet and beautiful and yours."

He stared at her with wonder, like a witness to the fall of prison walls and the freeing of a courageous heart that had been trapped inside. She stole his breath.

He covered her mouth with boiling, ravenous kisses as he fingered her cunt, finding her wet and tight and undeniably beautiful. Using the strength of her core muscles, she lifted her legs and twined them around his waist, her eyes as hungry and desperate as he was. He replaced his fingers with his cock, pressing against her opening, and hissed through his teeth as he entered her in one long thrust.

Heat rushed through his body, concentrating on where they were joined. To feel this connection after so goddamned long, Christ, it was like a welcoming song, a homecoming. It shook the very foundation of his soul. "Fuck, Amber. I missed you."

Clutching the diagonal rungs of the lattice, she whimpered against his chest. He ground his hips and flexed his ass to deepen the penetration.

He ran his hands over her full chest and around her curvy hips, pulling her to him with a fury of slamming drives. She didn't lower her legs or let go of the trellis as he gripped her hair, jerked her head back, and bit her below the ear. Despite the threat of outside, her movements were more confident than they'd ever been, her pelvis circling and rocking as she met him thrust for thrust.

His release swelled to the brink of explosion, and he grunted. "Come for me, Amber. I want to hear you."

She threw her head back and let go, her body shaking and her moans warbling into the night sky. It swept him away, wrenching the orgasm from his body in trembling waves.

As he came down, their lips met in a kiss so simple and tender, so honest and familiar, it left him split open and helplessly, shamelessly, filled with devotion. He pulled her to his chest, and they stood in silence, their arms wrapped around each other.

"Told you he'd find you." Liv's voice chimed through the darkness.

He yanked up his jeans and glared at her over his shoulder. "Do you mind?"

"Not at all." She leaned against the deck railing and watched them pull on their clothes. "Stalkers are hard to get rid of." Not a hint of emotion on her face, but a smile lifted her voice. Yeah, Liv had been a stalker once, too.

Amber's arms coiled around his waist, her cheek resting on his chest. "This one's not so bad."

"So you've said." Liv straightened and walked toward her back door. Then she paused, her eyes locked with his. "When you're done there, swing by. You still owe me a meeting."

He tightened his arms around Amber's back and closed his eyes as a weightless rush drifted over him. When he looked up, Liv was gone. But her offer lingered. He pressed his lips against the top of Amber's head. "You've been busy."

She shrugged. "She has something you want."

His pulse raced. "You think she'll—?"

"Go find out."

Ten minutes later, his racing heart neared detonation as he stood outside a spare bedroom in Liv's house. He squeezed Amber's hand and strained his eyes to make out the shadowed shapes within the room.

"She's just staying the night," Liv whispered. "If you wake her, I'll kill you."

He was already moving through the dark room, his mouth dry and adrenaline surging through his blood. Amber lingered in the doorway, her supportive smile holding him upright.

Stunned and hypnotized, he reached the bed and soaked in the shaded blur of Livana's dark eyelashes and dainty features. Her tiny fingers curled around the pillow, her slender frame cocooned in bedding. Christ, she was even more precious in person.

Reaching down, he ran trembling fingers over a wisp of her hair. The soft texture seeped through his touch, vividly bright and so damned real.

He could stand there all night, and he did for a long time, breathless and overcome. A cleared throat in the hallway jerked him into awareness, and slowly, reluctantly, he stepped away.

Liv waited outside the bedroom with Amber and Joshua, rigid in her statue-like posture as she watched him approach. When he reached her, her eyes flickered, right before he yanked her into an embrace.

Her arms hung at her sides, her body stiff and unyielding. Beside her, Joshua leaned against the wall, his gaze soft and thoughtful and fixed on Liv.

Van lowered his forehead to her shoulder. "I'm sorry. For keeping her from you. For taking you from your mother. It's too late for apologies. Fuck, I know this, but I'll do whatever I can to make it up to you."

Tense seconds passed, then her arms rose and folded around his back. She squeezed tighter, her voice thick. "This is a good start."

He raised his head and shared a look with Amber over Liv's shoulder, one that promised new memories. Joyful memories. She pressed a knuckle to her mouth and gave him a tearful smile.

He released Liv and moved to her side, where he belonged, surrounded by the radiance of her presence. As he stared into the brown eyes of the woman who embodied impossible dreams, he felt the future in every cell of his body. It felt crazy and beautiful and decisively unbreakable.

Four years later...

Amber was outrunning him, fucking running circles around him. But really, how could he complain? Watching her ass flex in those painted-on athletic pants took his mind off his burning muscles and overworked lungs.

As the sun disappeared behind the skyline of downtown Austin, the city's towers glinted with the lingering rays of yellow and gold. Too bad the humidity didn't vanish with it. He wiped his forehead with the sweatband on his wrist and quickened his pace to catch up with that gorgeous ass.

Maybe fifty paces ahead of him, she pivoted, running backwards and grinning at him like a goon. "What's the hold up, old man?"

Old man? He was still a year younger than she was, even if she hadn't broken a sweat. Fucking show-off.

Pedestrians and fellow runners scurried out of their way. A dozen teen-aged boys paused their soccer game to watch her run by. He gave the fuckers a threatening glare, and they snapped from their gawking and returned to their scrimmage.

He and Amber could've easily jogged in the woods at the cabin, but the social surroundings were good for her. And there was another reason he'd chosen this park.

In an hour, he would be meeting with one of his former slaves, Camila, on the south side of the pond. He'd learned she was attempting to bring down a new slave ring in Austin and was in over her head. Even with her cartel connections, it had been too ambitious and risky as hell. She needed help, and fuck him, but being a husband and a father fueled him with a crazy amount of protective drive, which included a bloodthirsty need to wipe the city of sex trafficking.

Amber was skittish about his involvement, but she would come around. He wouldn't give her a choice.

Up ahead, an old lady and her Boston Terrier stepped into Amber's backward running path. If Amber didn't turn back around soon, she was going to collide with them.

"Amber." He panted for air. "Watch yourself."

As she spun around, he glimpsed the tightening of her fist and the flinch of her shoulders. No one around her would notice the traces of her anxiety, the way she cracked her knuckles too often, the tiny hiccups in her breathing, and the trickle of sweat between her breasts. They would only see the confident woman she was with a knockout body and face so ethereal it compelled longing glances.

Every day she left the house was a workout for her. The agoraphobia would always be there, but she made it her bitch with an inspiring amount of courage.

He caught up with her on the bend around the pond and ran at her side. Christ, he loved seeing her at his side. Good thing, too, since they worked together every day out of the garage at the cabin. Her leathercraft business had trickled into the doll market, and they were inundated with orders.

When they reached the next bend, his pocket vibrated. He checked the caller ID and grabbed her elbow, veering them off the track.

Slowing to a stop and hunching over with a hand on his knee, he lifted the phone to his ear. "Hey, sweetheart."

A melodic voice tinkled through the phone. "Daddy?"

Damn, he would never get tired of hearing her call him that. And it was the only greeting she gave before charging into the reason for her call. "You can't just go around threat—"

"I'm doing great." He smiled, feeling the easiness of it inside and out. "How are you?"

"I'm fine." She sniffed then rushed on in her high-pitched voice. "But Katie told Jena, and Jena told—"

"Livana." He used his warning tone, winking at Amber. "Slow down."

Amber bent at the waist in a stretch that put her chest on her thighs and her ass in the air. He leaned with her, mesmerized, as blood rushed to his dick. He dropped the phone.

She gave him an upside down grin, her ponytail swishing over the ground.

He returned the phone to his ear and pulled his shirt over the front of his pants.

"—can't do that," Livana said. "Are you there?"

"Yeah, honey. I dropped the phone. Start over."

"Did you threaten Danny Taylor?"

Oh, that. "I didn't threaten him. I simply enlightened him."

Amber straightened, shaking her head and licking the corner of her curved mouth, the vixen.

"Mom already said I could go to the dance." Livana's voice pierced through the phone, cool and sure and just like Liv's.

By *mom*, she meant Mr. E's widow, Carolyn Eary, her legal guardian who raised her from birth and still provided the roof over her head.

What had started out as Liv introducing him as a family friend was now a unique, and often delicate, arrangement. He'd spent a lot of time with Carolyn in those first few months, feeling her out. When he finally revealed his identity, she was understandably skeptical of his intentions. But he'd proved himself as he'd done with Liv, and a year after he'd met Livana, Carolyn told her whom her biological parents were.

Livana knew nothing of their criminal history, but she did know how to play all three of them to get what she wanted. Carolyn was a fucking pushover. He was a drill sergeant. But Liv was the wild card.

"What did Liv say?"

"She said to ask you."

"I didn't hear you ask."

Even irritated, her sigh was the sweetest damned sound. "Daddy, can I please go to the dance?"

"You're too young."

"I'm twelve!"

He dug a toothpick from his pocket and slid it into his mouth. He was done jogging for the night. Amber was in the midst of another erotic stretch and his focus was shit. "You can go, and I will chaperone."

A long pause. "Ugh. Fine."

Well, that was easy. Maybe she didn't realize he would be at her side the entire evening. "Love you."

"Love you, too."

He pocketed the phone and scanned the park for a spot that would offer the most privacy. When an outcrop of rocks up ahead caught his eye, he gripped Amber's hand and led her to them.

Behind the cover of a huge boulder, he pressed her against the flat surface and kissed her deeply and thoroughly. "Go to the dance with me, Mrs. Quiso."

She answered by returning his kiss and flicking her tongue wildly and aggressively. They'd been married for two years, but every day felt like a honeymoon. He ran his hands up her spandex-clad thighs, cupped the hard muscles of her ass, and caressed the soft curves with his fingers.

Yeah, sex in a public park wasn't the best idea for a guy who wanted to remain under the radar. But as she flexed her hips, tangled her tongue with his, and aroused every nerve-ending in his body, his only thought was *Yes.*

She reached for her shirt and pulled it over her head, her tits tumbling over the cage of her sports bra. Jesus. Whether in shackles and hanging naked from a tree or seconds away from losing her panties in a park, her ability to shock and awe him was infinite.

Curling her arms around his shoulders, she rose up on tiptoes to meet his gaze with bright eyes. "Still want to put a baby inside me? Fifty-percent chance you'll get another girl."

"I'll take anything you give me." He ground the aching ridge of his erection against the *V* of her thighs. "Right now, you're going to give me something wet and tight. Turn around. Arms above your head."

CHECK OUT OTHER BOOKS

BY PAM GODWIN

DELIVER

BENEATH THE BURN

DEAD OF EVE

BREAKAWAY (NEW ADULT ANTHOLOGY)

TAKE THE HEAT (ANTHOLOGY COMING FALL 2014)

To my critique partners—Lindsey R. Loucks, Lindy Winter, Jill Bitner, Cristen Abrams, Aries75, and John Kang—for whipping through this book like Speedy McJesus and turning my watery words into wine. My God, your swift and succinct advice was nothing short of miraculous. I owe you all huge slobbery kisses.

To beta reader Jeanice Monson, for saving little girls in dark parking lots from harebrained writers. Your opinions are canny and thoughtful, and I'm a lucky bitch to have your friendship.

To Author E.M. Abel, for reading my stuff, for your endless encouragement, and for being such a down-to-earth, bad-ass writerly chic. I adore you.

To Author Christina Jean Michaels, for beta reading with an edgy mind and a sharp eye. Your advice had me smiling and sighing, and I might've done a little fist pumping and booty-shaking. Here's to the start of an exciting working relationship and friendship.

To Author Barbara Elsborg, for beta reading with your ever-loving brilliance and quickness. Your wealth of experience and sophistication awes and motivates me. I'm forever your fangirl.

To my proofreader, Lesa Godwin, for being the final and most crucial stamp of approval. YOU are the reason I'm able to sleep tonight. I love you, sis!

To my best friend, Amber, for dealing with me in addition to the much more important burdens you're hauling around. You are the most selfless, dependable, put-together person I know. I'd fall apart without you. So yeah... I love you.

ABOUT THE AUTHOR

New York Times and *USA Today* Bestselling author, Pam Godwin, lives in the Midwest with her husband, their two children, and a foulmouthed parrot. When she ran away, she traveled fourteen countries across five continents, attended three universities, and married the vocalist of her favorite rock band.

Java, tobacco, and dark romance novels are her favorite indulgences, and might be considered more unhealthy than her aversion to sleeping, eating meat, and dolls with blinking eyes.

You can follow her at pamgodwin.com

Made in the USA
San Bernardino, CA
23 August 2014